**James Wolff** grew up in the Middle East and now lives in London. He has worked for the British government for the past ten years. *Beside the Syrian Sea* is his first novel.

"Tautly-drawn tale of espionage in the badlands of Beirut. Wolff brings the thriller bang up to date as a rogue agent takes on Islamic State – as flawed a hero as Alec Leamas in *The Spy Who Came in from the Cold.*"

> DAVID LOYN, former BBC correspondent, foreign policy analyst, and author of *Butcher and Bolt: Two Hundred Years of Foreign Engagement in Afghanistan*

"A compelling story of our times, beautifully written and told with all the authority and authenticity of an insider familiar with the complex and dangerous terrain."

> PETER TAYLOR, investigative journalist and author of *Talking to Terrorists: A Personal Journey from the IRA to Al Qaeda*

"*Beside the Syrian Sea* is a gripping tale of plots and counter plots; of militias, spies, and priests; of love of family and loyalty to cause. James Wolff rivetingly describes the lengths to which a British spy will go to secure the release of his father from ISIS."

> EMMA SKY, British expert on the Middle East, Director Yale Greenberg World Fellows and author of *The Unravelling: High Hopes and Missed Opportunities in Iraq*

"Great characters, convincing detail and a compelling story. All too human MI5 desk jockey, Jonas, is no James Bond but he manages to stay one step ahead of his ex-employers, the CIA, Hezbollah, Isis and the reader right up until the final showdown in the desert."

> CHARLIE HIGSON, actor, comedian, novelist and author of the *Young Bond* series

# BESIDE THE SYRIAN SEA

## James Wolff

**BITTER LEMON PRESS**
**LONDON**

BITTER LEMON PRESS
First published in the United Kingdom in 2018 by
Bitter Lemon Press, 47 Wilmington Square, London WC1X 0ET

www.bitterlemonpress.com

A CIP record for this book is available from the British Library

This is a work of fiction. Names, characters, places, and incidents
are either the product of the author's imagination or are used
fictitiously, and any resemblance to actual persons, living or dead,
businesses, companies, events or locales is entirely coincidental.

Paperback ISBN 978–1–908524–98-0
Hardback ISBN 978-1-912242-13-9
eBook ISBN 978–1–908524–99-7

Typeset by Tetragon
Printed and bound in Great Britain
by TJ International Ltd, Padstow, Cornwall

*For my mother and father, with love and gratitude.*

# PROLOGUE

SECRET

FROM: PK3Y
MSG REF: B97–4/68
SUBJECT: Possible kidnap of British national

STRAP 1 CONTROLLED ITEM. FOIA EXEMPT.

1. Meeting early this morning with a jittery ARTISAN. Headlines below. Full contact report to follow separately, along with draft CX.
2. The Syrian authorities are investigating the disappearance of a British national from his hotel in Damascus yesterday evening. The individual is reported to be Rev. Samuel WORTH, PDOB Edinburgh 4-9-1939, passport 936485118. Initial traces suggest a family connection that will have to be handled with sensitivity.
3. According to ARTISAN, the hotel manager called the police at approx. 2130 when a colleague reported him missing. CCTV wasn't working but the doorman says WORTH left on his own and under no apparent duress at approx. 1800 after asking for directions to a restaurant in the old city. There are no reports of him returning.

4. Eyewitnesses in the restaurant describe him eating alone but leaving with a local man described by the waiter as a beggar. Reported time of departure varies from 1930 to 2045. No consistent description of the beggar. There were three checkpoints in the immediate vicinity and several foot patrols but none reported contact with a foreign national. The only physical evidence is a crumpled tourist map from WORTH's hotel that was found in an alleyway several hundred metres from the restaurant and some stains on the ground that may or may not be blood.

5. The investigation was taken over by Syrian Military Intelligence (SMI) within hours. They have already arrested the waiter, hotel manager and doorman.

6. ARTISAN was quick to explain that since the Ministry of Interior (MoI) has no oversight of SMI his access to the investigation will be severely limited from this point onwards. He has offered to re-establish social contact with colleagues in SMI but this will take time. We have praised ARTISAN for his initiative but requested he sit tight for now. We know you will be coming under pressure for intelligence on WORTH but given likelihood he is already in Raqqa, limited rescue options and ARTISAN's history of getting distracted we strongly suggest he remains focussed on existing MoI tasking.

7. We await your prompt response. Separately pls address shortfall in funds as raised in B97-4/66.

# CHAPTER ONE

Jonas couldn't remember the last time he had felt so ill-prepared. He had never been inside the bar before, and wouldn't have been able to answer basic questions about the layout, exits, cameras and customer profile. He didn't know which group controlled this part of Beirut or how they would react if it all went wrong. His target was probably drunk. From his position he could see the open doorway clearly enough, but the women at the bar inside were impatient for customers, and at least one of them had seen him loitering across the street. Theirs is the oldest profession, he thought – they are the better watchers, their livelihood more honestly linked to their ability to observe and manipulate. Spies are the second oldest and the second best. At least that was how he felt.

He had decided to allow the priest enough time for one drink. The woman in the doorway waved at him and he turned away to light a cigarette. He felt weighed down by grief, by the gentle rain that had soaked into his clothes, by simple tiredness. His dark beard was long and unkempt and the stress of the previous months had left him looking older than his thirty-five years. Somehow he brought his mind back to the task ahead. To tell the priest who he was and what he wanted, to deal with his confusion and anger, to identify what might motivate him to help. Jonas had never done anything like this before. As an analyst it was his job to come to terms with the rogues' gallery of assumptions, vendettas, half-truths and bald lies that constituted the majority of the intelligence that crossed his desk and make it useful – to elevate it to something approaching fact. But he had never been operational, and his temperament had kept him away from much of what went on around him. He remembered an agent handler talking about ways of keeping the door open to a second meeting even if the initial pitch went disastrously. This struck him as fantastical. His plan would either work tonight or it would go wrong: there would be no second chances.

The interior was smaller and darker than he had expected. A poorly stocked bar stretched along the right side; a few tables were pushed up against the opposite wall. The woman who had waved at him took his arm and led him to the bar. She pushed her breast against him.

"You going to buy me drink?"

She had begun her pitch without hesitation. As an aspiring practitioner, Jonas admired her directness. He saw the priest sitting alone further down the bar. He looked sad, somehow, his soft, grey, hunched shape a thickening of the gloom. At the end of the room two women danced with a fat man. The women, swaying on their high heels, knew not to risk too much movement – it looked as though they were slowly trying to escape from a set of elaborate foot restraints.

"You want to go to room?"

He put a twenty-dollar bill on the bar, took his drink and walked down to join the priest.

"Father Tobias, this is a surprise. Do you mind if I join you?"

He heard the wobble in his voice and regretted that he had turned out this way. Tobias turned to see who was speaking to him. The tape holding his glasses together at the bridge glittered weakly. He didn't smile when he saw it was Jonas.

"No one here calls me Father," he said.

"Being a priest must be one of those things it's difficult to put to one side for an evening." Unsure what to do, Jonas took the stool next to him. "It's part of you – like an accent, like a preference for tea rather than coffee."

"Like a criminal record."

His speech was clear and his hand as he reached for the glass was steady. Even when drunk, Jonas had learned, Tobias spoke in the measured, unemotional rhythms of a theologian. The only change was that he slowed down to avoid slurring his words, which had the effect of making his Swiss accent more pronounced. They had first met ten days earlier. Jonas had been trying to follow him for three straight evenings, and when Tobias had taken something from his pocket and dropped a folded envelope Jonas decided to act. He had concluded that on balance there were more downsides than upsides to following a drunkard. They might not be alert but they walked slowly, doubled back on themselves, attracted attention – the unpredictable tradecraft of the alcoholic, as challenging in its own way as that of any Russian spy. Jonas had picked up the envelope, read the contents and caught up with him to hand it back. They had gone for a drink at a nearby bar, where Jonas explained that he was a freelance journalist researching an article on Christian communities in Syria. If the priest had been struck by the coincidence, he hadn't shown it.

They had met several times over the following week. On the last occasion, Tobias had been drunk enough for Jonas to have no difficulty stealing his hotel room key. He hadn't planned to do it, and he certainly had no experience of such things. Risk made him uncomfortable, whether it came in the form of a conversation with a pretty girl or a deviation from the precise route he walked to work each day. But he had heard the key clinking and slipped his hand into Tobias's jacket pocket when he thought it would go unnoticed. Although he knew that the best deceptions were those that the target would never know had occurred, he accepted that in his situation he would have to compensate for his lack of resources somehow, and boldness seemed as good a way as any. Tobias would probably assume that he had lost it while drunk. Jonas felt a brief exhilaration at being liberated from the constraints of corporate risk, of reputational risk. He was on his own and had little to lose.

"Do you mind if I join you for a drink?" he asked.

"You have made a strange choice of bar if you wish to have a drink with another man," said Tobias.

"Or to drink on your own."

"Priests should spend more time in places like this. I am no better than anyone else here. At least these people make no pretence about what they are."

Jonas tried to focus on projecting the combination of authority and warmth he knew would be needed when the conversation moved into more challenging territory. In the dirty mirror above the bar he looked stiff, self-conscious. For some reason he had decided to wear a suit, hoping it might be discreetly redolent of influence, government, long corridors. He couldn't understand how he might have imagined anything so crumpled and ill-fitting would be appropriate – Tobias was looking him over with the first sign of pleasure he had shown since Jonas had arrived. He wondered if this might work in his favour. He hadn't yet worked out how to project warmth, but perhaps the only reasonable response to his dark suit, to his evident discomfort, to his lean, funereal intensity, to the parting that made him look less like someone following the fashion for neat hair than a Victorian gentleman – perhaps the only reasonable response was to smile.

"In fact, this is the best kind of place to drink alone," Tobias was saying. "The women never disturb me – they know what I am – and the men are only interested in the women. As long as the men do not find out my profession. It would make them uncomfortable."

Jonas had never seen him wearing a clerical collar. He wondered how the women in the bar would have identified Tobias as a priest and marvelled again at their ability to read people. Jonas saw a short, fleshy, middle-aged man with thinning grey hair and round tortoiseshell glasses. He saw a collar that was frayed, a habit of blinking emphatically when under pressure. A schoolteacher, perhaps, or a watchmaker – it fit with his heavy Swiss accent and his slow, precise way of speaking, but not with his hands, which were dirty and had begun to tremble. It was clear to Jonas that something was wrong, that this was not going to go the way he had hoped.

"Why don't I invent a different occupation for myself – in case someone asks me what I do?" Tobias said. It sounded as though he said inwent rather than invent. "This is your speciality, inwenting occupations. Perhaps I will also claim that I am a freelance journalist."

It was possible Tobias had simply told them he was a priest, Jonas thought. It was important to be sceptical of professional myths.

"I do not know what is the purpose of all this," Tobias said. He waved his hand to show that he was referring to Jonas's suit as well as his unexpected arrival. "I do not know which department you represent, but please understand that I have no interest in being a pawn in whatever version of the great game the British government is playing these days." He picked up Jonas's glass and placed it further down the bar as though moving a chess piece from one end of the board to the other. Pawn to queen's knight 4, Jonas thought, given the size of the space between them, given the position of the napkin holder and the salt shaker, which he had already decided looked like a bishop in his white robes. "Please, though, before you leave, return my hotel key. They will charge me for it otherwise."

Jonas took it from his pocket and placed it on the bar. He had passed a maid in the hotel corridor when leaving the room. She must have assumed they were friends and asked Tobias if he knew someone matching Jonas's description. It did not matter. He did not regret the situation he was in. He had come into the bar this evening to make his position clear. However this came to pass, he knew that he would have to deal with the priest's anger. And he had learned valuable things from his search of the hotel room. That money would not be a factor, for one. Tobias had turned his hotel room into something resembling a monk's cell. The television had been hidden away in the wardrobe, along with a half-empty bottle of gin whose label had been peeled off, and the paint on the walls was darker where pictures had been taken down. A simple wooden cross hung from a crudely hammered nail. Jonas thought that he might even have slept on the floor each night – the maid stubbornly gathering the blankets and remaking the bed each morning – because of the half-empty water glass and coaster placed carefully on the tiles, and next to it a small pile of books: Goethe, Bonhoeffer, an anthology of war poetry, a pocket New Testament. Those the maid would not touch.

There was more. There were things that Jonas had discerned as possibilities from the room, things that came back to him now as he sat beside the priest at the bar. The importance of the woman in the black-and-white photograph, tucked between the pages of the New Testament. The small vase of flowers on the windowsill, picked from a garden rather than bought from a florist, too fresh for a hotel of that standard and at odds with the masculine sparseness of the room. Had they been left there as a gesture of kindness by the maid? Tobias was a compassionate man. Those he came into contact with each day recognized it. Jonas could make use of this.

"I want to explain," he said. He shifted on the stool and cleared his throat. Shyness is too mild a word for this, he thought, it fails to capture the physicality of panic, like being in a fight with yourself – the hurried breathing, the heat, a desire to run. "I understand that you feel tricked, Tobias. I would feel the same in your position. But the things I've done have been necessary because of the bigger picture. A man with your experience – I know you're able to understand that there are more important things than your entirely reasonable sense of grievance."

Bigger picture, a man with your experience, entirely reasonable sense of grievance: Jonas heard himself capture perfectly the tone of a door-to-door salesman trying to talk a dissatisfied customer out of making a complaint.

"How casually people like you intrude on the privacy of others," said Tobias.

"You remember that I went into your room but you forget that I saw what is in there." He could hear himself speaking but didn't know where this stuff was coming from, or whether it made any sense to Tobias. It barely made any sense to Jonas. He fumbled for the point he was trying to make. "What I mean is that your room is not that of someone who believes in privacy. It's the room of someone used to living in a community where everything is shared. Some people put their faith in objects, in worldly things – things that can be searched. You're not one of those people, Tobias."

"You are very quick to tell others what they should feel." Wery quick, Jonas heard. "I should not feel tricked, I should not feel spied upon. As a priest I should be above such trivial concerns." He blinked repeatedly. "Perhaps you forget where I am and what I am doing."

"What I've learned is that you're not one of those people who walks past someone in need." Use his name, Jonas reminded himself. Number four on the list of ten rapport-building tips distilled from a handful of self-help books he had bought at Heathrow just weeks earlier, along with "Maintain eye contact", "Mirror body language" and "Tilt your head at an angle and smile as you listen". He liked lists. They simplified the business of living. "This isn't about politics, Tobias. This is about saving a life."

"So this has been a selection process, is that what you are saying? I have passed the interview and you are offering me the job? This is good news. Except that I did not apply and I think the job is reprehensible. Why do you look so surprised? What do you expect me to say when you have tricked me like this? Perhaps you forget that for most of us lying is considered a bad thing."

"The lie was necessary, Tobias," Jonas said. "It allowed us to establish who you are, what you are. To establish whether you're the right person to help us with something of huge importance."

"Us?"

"I'm not here on my own."

He hadn't planned to mention anyone else. He wondered if he had gone too far. Tobias turned around to take in the dozen or so other men in the room, seated at tables with women or standing at the bar. Dark patches of sweat showed through his shirt. The fat man was still dancing with two women at the back.

"If you mean him," Tobias said, "it doesn't look like he is doing his job."

"You won't be able to identify them. But they are here. And they'll be with us when we leave. They are here to keep us safe, nothing more."

"Call them off. I want nothing to do with you and your friends and your grubby profession."

"I wonder if our professions are so different," said Jonas. "We both listen to secrets, we both exercise authority. We both feel some embarrassment at what we are, I suspect."

"Please do not compare the Church with whichever squalid part of the secret world you represent."

"Do you want to discuss the reputations of our respective organizations? I'm not sure yours would come out on top."

Jonas felt that he had to be bullish, to shoulder his way quickly through the crowd of objections being placed in his path. There was no time to engage in a discussion of the merits of collaboration. The bartender was casting frequent glances their way and Jonas saw there was a limit to how long he would tolerate two foreign men who ignored the women in order to argue at the bar. He put another twenty-dollar bill down and signalled for more drinks. He blamed himself for having forced a priest drinking gin in a brothel into a conversation about reputation. It was to be expected that Tobias would fear his own character had marked him out as weak. This was an error Jonas should not have made. Even the rawest recruit to counterterrorism understood the disjunction between public display and private life: in one, the insistence on law and the violent denunciation of those who believed otherwise; in the other, prostitutes, drugs, petty crime. There was little to be gained from trying to make someone face up to the inconsistencies in their life, especially if you needed results quickly.

"So we are both as bad as each other," Tobias said. "Please, I do not wish to discuss any of this with you further."

"You don't know what I want yet."

"Oh, I know what you want. Everyone wants the same thing these days: aid workers, politicians, journalists. The real ones and the fake ones. You wish to talk about Syria. You wish to talk about the refugees, the fighting, which roads are closed and which roads are open, what the Syrian people feel, what will happen to Lebanon, but most of all you wish to talk about the terrorist groups."

"I know you've had contact with them," Jonas said.

"You don't know anything."

"I know that you learned Arabic in Aleppo as a young priest, fresh out of seminary, and came back ten years ago, to everyone's surprise. I know that soon after your return you cut ties with the Church in Rome, or they

19

cut ties with you. I know that four months ago you left Syria because of threats made against you by pro-regime militias. I know that you have been involved in three attempts to secure the release of hostages taken by extremist groups and that on two of those occasions you were successful."

"I would have expected your information to be more accurate – or is the British government getting its facts from the newspapers these days? Listen, the greatest danger to me and those I was trying to help came from people who believed that I was working for an organization like yours." There was alarm in his pale, bloodshot eyes. "I do not see your government being part of the solution. I do not see spies playing a positive role in any of this. Nobody trusts you, on either side. You believe you must do everything in secret, but it is inevitable that the results of your work sometimes become public, and then we see mass surveillance, torture, rendition, illegal wars. What else is there beneath the cover?"

"Bonhoeffer worked as an agent of the Abwehr against the Nazis and was aware of —"

"Stop. If I did not know you had searched my room you could perhaps use this argument to some effect."

"My point is that neither of us is operating in a vacuum. There are other people competing in the same space – people who want to do far worse things."

"Worse than Iraq?" Tobias asked. "Worse than Abu Ghraib? Worse than Guantanamo?"

Or worse than Mosaddeq? Jonas wondered. Or Balfour? He had spent long enough studying the Middle East to know how poor the West's record was, and long enough working in intelligence to understand how partial its successes were, how corrosive its impact on lives could be. Jonas suddenly felt very tired. He had little to offer by way of defence. The truth was that he felt deeply shamed by those overseas adventures carried out in the name of national interest. He thought of E. M. Forster's line about being given the choice of betraying his country or betraying his friend and hoping he had the guts to betray his country. What were those national interests Jonas had worked for so long to protect? He wasn't sure any more. When he thought about his country, he thought of those people he loved. He didn't think of its politicians, its oil companies or arms manufacturers. He didn't think of ideology, either. Each day Jonas walked down the Beirut street that Kim Philby had been living on when he defected to the Russians. He had told his wife one evening that he was going out to meet a friend and then telephoned while she was preparing their children's dinner. She had been too busy to take the call. He never returned. She wrote afterwards that for months and months she wished she had taken that call. That was where ideology got you, thought Jonas.

Father Tobias had been quiet for a while. He tapped his watchmaker's fingers steadily against the side of his glass: tick, tock, tick, tock. The barman had lost interest in them and was smoking a cigarette in the open doorway. Outside the rain drummed on the cars; it streamed above the blocked gutters.

"There is nothing left for us to speak of," said Tobias.

At the back of the bar the fat man had stopped dancing and was kissing one of the women while the other one watched.

"I am sorry that we shall not see each other again," he said. "I was beginning to look forward to our chance encounters. You must think I am very naive! Certainly too naive to be of any use to you in your business. I thought, here is someone as lonely as me, someone who is also suffering some kind of loss but does not wish to speak of it, someone who can minister to me just as I minister to him. All right, yes, he wears the same clothes most days and looks as though he does not eat enough, but I am in no position to judge." He emptied his glass. "I was so happy that you chose to pick up that letter and become my friend. Now I understand that you probably read it first."

Jonas was surprised to find that he had underestimated the value of friendship. He had underestimated its impact on Tobias, clearly, but what really surprised him was its impact on himself. He was doing this out of love, or so he had thought. How then could he have turned out to be so indifferent, until this moment, to the affection he had cultivated in Tobias? What was wrong with him that he was willing to destroy this man's life all over again? He saw himself in the mirror above the bar – his dark hair and beard sparkling with rainwater, his features made severe by exhaustion – and wondered how it had come to pass unnoticed that deceit had been worn into him like grooves in a record until all he could play were false notes. It hardly mattered, but he understood finally that he needn't have lied. He might have laid out his case simply and truthfully and asked for help. When had his innocence left him? He remembered as a child seeing a priest wearing running shoes beneath his robes and feeling a sense of loss, just as he had when he learned that what made aeroplanes fly was a clever tangle of wires, that there was no magic involved. The shoes that Tobias wore were thin and wet from the rain. They seemed magical to Jonas in ways that he could not begin to explain.

"I am sorry to send you back to your masters with nothing," said Tobias.

You've got it all wrong, Jonas thought. I'm not doing it for them – I'm doing it for my father. The wind blew through the open door and scattered a pile of coasters. They lay across the bar like the squares of a broken chessboard.

"The woman in the photograph," he said finally, letting the cold come close to him like a skin. "If you help us, we'll get her out."

# CHAPTER TWO

Jonas had grown tired, during the three months that had passed since his father's kidnapping, of people telling him to be patient. He had heard it on a weekly basis from SIS, the Foreign Office and the police, and it was a guaranteed occurrence on those days that he had spoken with his own senior managers. The staff counsellor they had insisted he see had phrased it differently. "It's a waiting game," she had said. He sat stiffly, looking at the floor, the knot of his tie so fierce that it lifted the points of his collar. "You must feel so powerless," she said. He wasn't sure whether he was being consoled or instructed.

It came to him around that time that he was powerless only so long as he allowed himself to be constrained by their rules. He had been subjecting his life, he realized, since the news of his father's kidnapping had come through, to the same fretful risk assessment, the same concerns about reputation, the same obsession with worst-case scenarios that had come to characterize his working life. He had no one to blame for this but himself. It was only now that he had begun to act outside the rules he understood just how much power he had.

Evidence of this was a visit early one Friday morning from a stranger in tennis whites carrying in one hand what he insisted on calling an intelligence update and in the other a cottage pie cooked by his wife. To Jonas, who didn't have an oven, the two were of equal value.

"Gas mark six, forty minutes. Those are your orders. Valerie is worried sick about you, as are we all. Not eating enough, that sort of thing. By the look of you she's on the right track. She'll have a fright when I tell her about this beard you're sporting – boys left to their own devices, I can hear her voice as if she were in the room. I'll have to talk her out of sending a barber round. Between you and me, the pie is a bit stodgy, but it'll put fuel in your tank."

Desmond Naseby introduced himself as a visiting SIS officer who had dropped in to Beirut to see a few old friends, brush up on his Arabic, take the temperature of the place. They sat in the living room of Jonas's small, sparsely furnished flat, ten minutes' walk from the sea. Naseby moved a chessboard to one side to make space for the cottage pie on the low table between them and then paused, as though he had spotted a clue to the identity of the other player among the pieces. He looked so excited that Jonas didn't have the heart to tell him it was a thirteen-year-old Bobby Fischer. Naseby had somehow punched a hole with his thumb through the silver foil and he licked his finger clean while looking carefully around him, as if trying to commit to memory the layout of the room. He had already wandered in and out of the bedroom and kitchen, explaining that he had a niece thinking of coming out to study whom he would need to advise on accommodation, rents, that sort of thing. It seemed odd to Jonas that a man so interested in kitchens that he opened all the cupboards would fail to notice that there was no oven.

"She's thinking of doing something at the American University here," he said. "It's a pity that the language school in the mountains where I learned my Arabic closed decades ago. Place called Shimlan, but everyone used to call it the spy school. Heard of it? George Blake was the most celebrated alumnus. Broke out of Wormwood Scrubs in 1966 and fled to Moscow. That's where they all end up. Even this Snowden chap, funnily enough. Sed quis custodiet ipsos custodes and all that."

It was hard to tell Naseby's age. Jonas knew that the school in Shimlan had closed in 1978, meaning that Naseby must be at least in his early sixties, but his plump face and long sweep of red hair made him appear younger. The sun poured through the windows and Naseby's tennis whites glowed as though stitched from light.

"Thought I'd pop by on a whim, introduce myself. I've got a game just around the corner in half an hour, so I won't stay long." Jonas didn't ask how Naseby had come by his address. "Probably worth us starting with first principles, make sure we're both on the same page. We're devastated about your father. I can't begin to imagine how difficult this has been for you. There will be some people who ask whether it was wise for a British civilian with no training to go within a million miles of Syria, humanitarian mission or not, but I'm not one of them. People like your father make the world go round, far as I'm concerned."

Despite sporting a pair of bare legs, Naseby's manner was businesslike, and Jonas, dressed in a pair of pyjamas worn through at the elbows and missing three buttons, felt that he was on the back foot. He ran a hand through his beard to see whether any food had settled there and found a piece of eggshell from breakfast the day before. "You'll be keen to see the latest intelligence update," Naseby said, handing a file to Jonas. "There's a huge amount of work going on behind the scenes, and I've persuaded London to direct even more resources this way. Quite a coup, by the by. This one is different, Jonas. We all understand that. You're one of the team."

Jonas flicked through the papers. He had a good memory and processed information quickly; facts clung to him, whether he needed them or not. He could still recall without difficulty the number plate of every car his parents had driven, the names and dates of tenure of the eighteen permanent British representatives to the United Nations, the code names and file numbers of many of the terrorist suspects, numbering in the hundreds, whose files had crossed his desk. But he had to look twice through the papers Naseby had given him because there was nothing there his memory could take hold of, certainly no classified information, just a typed summary of recent press articles, open-source satellite imagery of northern Syria and some stills of the kidnappers taken from an old YouTube clip. He had expected nothing more, but couldn't help smiling when he saw that Naseby had even included a weather forecast for the next ten days.

"Come now, you understand that I can't bring you the kitchen sink," Naseby said. "Telephone numbers, IP addresses, sigint – I know what you're after. The vetting people in your office have put you on some sort of gardening leave arrangement, as I understand it, which means that your security clearance is a bit up in the air. My hands are tied. The long and short of it, however, is that there's been some real progress in recent weeks. We believe your father is being held in the Raqqa area by the same group but that certain power shifts within the extremist landscape have changed the mood music significantly. The cognoscenti in Whitehall are very confident of a breakthrough in the next few weeks."

"What kind of breakthrough?" asked Jonas.

"That the people holding your father will come under the control of more moderate forces within the broader opposition and be persuaded to release their hostages. There are plenty of people out there speaking with a more sensible voice."

"Without any ransom being paid," Jonas said.

"You know the British government's policy on that as well as I do. It's just not going to happen."

"So they would release him for what – good PR?"

"This is a different kind of conflict, Jonas. These nutjobs are all over the internet. Did you know that the Shabaab have a Twitter account? Christ, can you imagine the mujahideen running round Afghanistan in the 1980s stopping to update their Facebook status? But this global jihad stuff has always been about PR. 9/11 was the biggest PR stunt ever. There is no way that extremists – in the numbers they are now – are going to defeat the West militarily. The only hope they have is to recruit, recruit, recruit, and they do that in the same way that the British army does it, by making slick videos aimed at boys who don't know what else to do. Be the best you can be: kill the kuffar, but make sure it looks good on film. I don't know why I'm telling you any of this – you're supposed to be the bloody expert. Funny thing is, recruitment in my day was the tap on the shoulder. Everybody ridicules it as old hat, but it's the same system the jihadis use. Tazkiya, they call it. Referencing. You only get in if someone vouches for you. With a bit of luck that's the only thing we've got in common with those chaps who've taken your old man."

As he spoke, Naseby nudged at a dead cockroach on the floor with the toe of his tennis shoe. Jonas knew how the cockroach felt. He had no aptitude for conflict, but understood that he would have to push back, for appearances' sake. He needed Desmond Naseby for his plan to work. It was important that the report sent back to London – he was under no illusion that Naseby had passed by "on a whim" – did not suggest that Jonas was under control and no cause for further concern. If he had known Naseby was going to pass by he would have prepared the flat. An empty bottle of whisky would have done some of the work, or vodka, even better, with more than one glass. As things stood, however, he was going to have to raise the temperature if he hoped to leave a dent in Naseby's self-satisfied veneer. The problem was that he found it difficult to fault anyone's position in this matter. He could see the logic in the British government's policy of not paying ransoms, and more than anything he envied Naseby that blithe confidence which allowed him to assure a person in Jonas's position that he was doing his utmost while on his way to a tennis match. He even felt some admiration for the kidnappers, young men so committed to their beliefs that they had left home and travelled to a foreign country where they might die. At times he felt more than admiration for them. He felt kinship, as someone also pursued by his own government, as someone also likely to die in a foreign country.

Jonas's father had been part of a church delegation visiting Syria to offer support to Christian communities being targeted – their churches demolished, their leaders killed, their members forcibly converted to Islam – by ISIS and the other extremist groups that together controlled most of northern Syria. The Syrian government had welcomed the idea, which presented an opportunity to highlight the barbaric nature of elements within the opposition, and the British Foreign Office had reluctantly approved – or agreed not to oppose – the visit on condition the group did not travel beyond Damascus or allow itself to be manoeuvred into making public statements in support of the regime. The schedule had been the subject of protracted negotiations. The final version included visits to one church of each of the main denominations, a tour of the Umayyad Mosque, a meeting with the minister for religious endowment and a public statement against attacks on Christians made alongside a handful of pro-regime Islamic clerics.

Jonas often thought about the hour he had spent with his father the day before he flew to Damascus. In the six months since he had last been home, his father had celebrated his seventy-fifth birthday. Each time Jonas saw him he seemed to have aged. He was sure that hadn't been the case when he was in his sixties. Everything is supposed to slow down when you get to that age, he thought, except, it turns out, ageing itself, which speeds up, as though spotting the finish line. On that day he had grown impatient with his father's slow pace of packing. He liked to refer to the list he had drawn up as a young man and kept taped to the inside of his diary. Shaving kit, wash bag, comb, radio. Jonas felt obliged to dispense second-hand security advice as he sat and watched his father pack. Don't allow yourself to be separated from the rest of the group or your minders. Hang the "do not disturb" sign in Arabic rather than English so people passing your room don't realize there is a foreigner staying there. Make sure you have walked the route to the nearest stairwell. Jonas told him about a colleague, somewhere in Africa, who had evaded a group of gunmen searching his hotel by making up the room so that it looked unoccupied and hiding in the wardrobe. His father placed a pencil tick beside each item as it went into his old brown suitcase: pyjamas, underpants, vests, handkerchiefs. They argued about something unimportant, as they always did, and Jonas left early.

Don't allow yourself to be separated from the rest of the group. Jonas had in mind when he said this that someone might invite his father to a meeting on his own or try to get him into a different vehicle. He certainly didn't imagine that his father would come down from his hotel room one evening wearing blue trousers and a white, short-sleeved shirt, ask the concierge to mark a good local restaurant on a street map and set off towards the old city on foot. It had proved difficult to establish the events of the evening beyond that. Intelligence channels had yielded nothing: there was no functioning liaison relationship with the Syrians. He only knew what his father had been wearing that day because his suitcase had been returned to the UK via the embassy. Jonas had gone through its contents, checking them off against the list taped to the inside of the diary. Suspicion was voiced in some quarters that the Syrian government had allowed it to happen, or even that they had facilitated it in some way, to elicit international condemnation of the more extreme opposition groups. Good PR, Naseby would have said. Jonas didn't know if this was true. In any case, it would have been pointless to blame the Syrian government. He had tried to blame his father for being reckless, but found that he couldn't do that either. He could only feel admiration for the spirit of adventure, undiminished by age, that had led a father to ignore a son's advice, leave the confines of his hotel and wander out into a warm Damascus evening. He wasn't seen for seven days after that. Then one morning he appeared in a grainy online photograph wearing a blindfold and with his hands tied behind his back. They had dressed him in an orange jumpsuit that hung piti-fully off his stooped, thin frame. He looked older than ever, Jonas thought.

A demand for ten million dollars was made within a week. In the statement posted on YouTube, the kidnappers described Jonas's father as an official representative of the Church in the UK and claimed he had been in Damascus to offer its support for the Assad regime. In justifying the sum, they said that the Church had billions of pounds invested in hedge funds, oil companies and UK government bonds, making it complicit in atrocities carried out against Muslims around the world. "Its leader lives in a palace," said their spokesman in a London accent.

Most species alter very little over the course of their history except for rare periods of rapid and significant evolutionary change – a process called punctuated equilibrium. Jonas felt this term could be applied equally well to his personal and professional decline. He sat calmly through at least a dozen meetings on the operational strategy, meetings he had only been invited to attend as a courtesy, before, in the same week, drinking six pints of beer and throwing up in a Hyde Park flower bed, smoking his first cigarette, forgetting to get off at his Tube stop on three separate occasions and refusing to leave the director general's outer office until he had been allowed to present him with a list of fourteen missed opportunities and strategic errors. In his ordered world it was what passed for extreme behaviour.

He was struck for the first time by how much time and energy a large organization could use up maintaining itself, informing itself, having arguments with itself, ensuring its different parts were joined up, as though his father's disappearance was a vast dot-to-dot that could be solved by connecting every conceivable part of the intelligence world by email, telegram or secure telephone. He did not exempt himself from this judgement. He had played his part, over the course of eight years and almost six hundred cautiously worded reports, in spinning the wheels of the intelligence cycle, like one of those exercise bikes that goes nowhere. It was difficult to put a finger on any one thing he had done to make a difference. Outcomes, they called them these days. He had never recruited a disillusioned terrorist, he had never planted an eavesdropping device in a Belfast tenement. What had he done, then, on any given day? Printed armfuls of raw intelligence, mostly, in the form of liaison reports, agent debriefs, intercepted communications, satellite imagery and surveillance logs, turned his back on the unimaginable chaos of an open-plan office and retreated to a tiny room off the back stairwell where the cleaners stored their carts at the end of a working day. He would dust off the chair, turn it to face the reinforced window and read at his own pace, without the distraction of other people and the way they made him feel. He was away from his desk so much that he would have got a reputation for being lazy if he hadn't been able to recall at will file references, dates, names, addresses and telephone numbers, if he hadn't been able to see those connections that other people missed between a website visited six months ago and an item of clothing worn by an unidentified male pictured in a CCTV still. Instead he got a reputation for being either aloof or shy, depending on who you asked, for refusing invitations to the pub, for stammering when asked to speak before an audience of more than five people, for wearing suits and ties when others wore jeans. Unlike now, he thought, when nothing fit him properly any more, when he selected his outfit each morning from a dirty pile of clothes in the corner of the bedroom.

And then, over the course of a few days and within a week of his thirty-fifth birthday, Jonas's career effectively came to an end. On the Monday he approached the Church of England's director of security on the street and offered to arrange for the clandestine payment of the ransom without the knowledge of the British government, and on the Tuesday he was called before MI5's director of personnel and told that a situation could not be tolerated in which an employee was acting in direct contravention of government policy. He was not dismissed; he had been a loyal employee for eight years, and everyone he worked with felt genuine sympathy for his situation. Unpaid Special Leave, they called it.

Jonas left the office for the last time carrying a few personal possessions in an old briefcase. He wandered around with no idea where he was until darkness fell. Through the dirty glass of the telephone box he could still see the Thames, and beyond it his old office, as he dialled from memory the eight Syrian mobile numbers used by the kidnappers in recent weeks. None of them were still in use. He would have offered them anything to get his father back, he would have offered them all the money in the world.

There were reasons, certainly, for what Jonas had by that point already done, for what he would go on to do.

That he couldn't bear to see his mother suffer so terribly, that he wanted one last chance to make things right with his father. The Behavioural Science Unit consulted widely among academics and practitioners and concluded, months after it was all over, that Jonas had been suffering from PTSD, noting "the persistent and profound effect of violent imagery, coupled with complex and unexplored feelings of grief and anger, upon an individual lacking a strong and supportive social network and character-ized by avoidant personality disorder". Jonas himself felt differently, not that he ever read the unit's report. Rational by nature and trained to attach importance to facts, he experienced the change within himself as a wildfire, as a puzzle with no edges, as a cracked plate, as an army of tiny flowers disrupting the placid streets of England.

Naseby was still talking.

"Frankly, Jonas, no one in HQ understands why you're here. I get it, though. You might have been writing intel-ligence assessments for Whitehall for the last however many years, but beneath that placid surface beats the heart of a field man, an operator – like me. You can't stand to be cooped up. Smell of the sea, bustle of the bazaars."

"Thwack of the tennis racket," said Jonas.

"Why not Turkey, though, eh? That's what I can't work out. Turkey's where the freelance security chaps are based, where the jihadis come and go. But you've chosen to come here because you like hummus."

"I'm here as a private citizen. I'm not entitled to your secrets, you're not entitled to mine."

Naseby looked unperturbed, as though this was all in a day's work. Jonas had to do more. He threw the file into the air and watched the papers come loose mid-flight and settle on the floor, on the cottage pie, on the chessboard, surrendering the king in the process. He had never done anything so aggressive before. He felt mildly heroic. There's another way of being, he suddenly realized; things can be different. "I'd be happy to look up the weather forecast for you, though, if that would help," he added.

The cockroach came to life and scurried away from Naseby's shoe. He looked around him at the scattered papers, sighed and said, "Look, Jonas, no need to be a prick about it. I'll be frank with you. There are two issues. Firstly, on the human level, whether you like it or not, people are worried about you. This isn't London. Plenty of fish swimming in this sea and some of them have teeth. Secondly, everyone's in a state because of that Snowden chap. It's opened our eyes to how much damage one person can do with a USB stick. The only good thing to come out of it is that we've been able to take the moral high ground with the Americans for once. We don't want to have to tell them about some cock-up of our own, do we now? They want reassurance back in London that we're not looking at something similar here. You know, Snowden gets pissed off, runs to Hong Kong; you get pissed off, run to Beirut. You haven't got a couple of *Guardian* journalists hidden away somewhere, have you?"

"Is that what you were looking for in the kitchen cupboards?" Jonas asked.

Naseby looked out the window. His approach was symptomatic of the confusion in certain parts of government as to how the issue of Jonas should be addressed. They would see his travel to Beirut as a disciplinary issue, certainly. They would expect him – still technically a Crown Servant – to obey orders and stop causing a fuss. But they would also be worried enough about his motives to see him as a target for intelligence collection. It was their job to imagine the worst. They would be trying to measure the scale of the damage that could be done by one person with the right access, and arguing amongst themselves whether that person might be Jonas. Cottage pie and a telling-off: they had decided to throw it all at Jonas and see what landed.

"For your own sake," Naseby said, "please do not underestimate the seriousness of this matter or the consequences that may follow. Let me spell it out for you. If you are here to exact revenge on the British government for refusing to pay your father's ransom, be aware that a zero-tolerance approach to such behaviour has been authorized back in London. If you are here to try to get your father released through some unorthodox back-channel, be aware that you may obstruct other things going on and unwittingly make the situation worse. You have neither the training nor the experience for this. The best thing you can do, Jonas? Go back to London and exercise a little patience."

The cockroach skittered across the silver foil covering the cottage pie and dropped through the hole in its corner. Neither of them moved.

"I appreciate you coming round here to spell things out for me," Jonas said, forcing himself to look Naseby in the eye. "But I'm not going anywhere. I'll be here until my father is released, or until you come up with a better strategy than waiting for the kidnappers to deradicalize themselves or for my father to die, whichever comes first. I know that you are worried about my loyalty. I don't know what to say that might put your mind at ease. I'm not entirely sure your mind should be at ease, to be honest. All I can say for certain is that I'm here out of loyalty to my father. Loyalty to a country feels like one of those old myths used to control people that we're slowly growing out of, like the class system."

"What are you going to do?"

"I'm going to get him out."

"They must pay well in your outfit if you've got ten million dollars squirrelled away."

"There are other ways."

"Other than paying the ransom? What – blow up an airliner for them? Knock off the British ambassador? Or are you planning to sell secrets to the Russians for a spot of cash? You're living in a fantasy world, Jonas. Do you really think we're going to stand by and let that happen? Have you completely lost your mind?"

Naseby might have been surprised at how frequently Jonas considered this question. He thought about asking Naseby for his views on the subject; he would have appreciated being able to talk it over with someone. The loss of appetite, the insomnia, the sudden tears – none of it felt normal. The last thing Jonas had said to his father before he left without saying goodbye was that he should avoid at all costs telling anyone in Syria that his son worked for the British government. It troubled him more than he could express that the last words he had exchanged with his father had been selfish ones. He wondered whether the interrogations had been more arduous because he felt obliged to keep his son's secret, whether they had beaten him to get at the truth after he stumbled over an answer. In the most recent video released by the kidnappers his father had been made to read aloud a statement condemning the British government. There were bruises on his face and he held his arm at an awkward angle. His hair was neat, though; Jonas had noticed that a comb was not among the items returned by the Syrian authorities.

"You must be keeping your tennis partner waiting," he said.

Jonas smoked a cigarette on the balcony and watched Naseby stride down the road, throwing his keys into the air and catching them. There were empty parking places across from the building but Naseby had left his car around the corner. No need to expose your car unnecessarily to the enemy. By the time he was finishing his cigarette, though, Jonas saw Naseby's red hair behind the wheel of a nondescript Audi without diplomatic plates that sped past his building. Undone by the one-way system, thought Jonas, and he waved.

# CHAPTER THREE

## 1

Jonas wasn't sure what technical resources SIS would be able to produce at short notice in Beirut, but he wasn't taking any chances. It was only two days since Desmond Naseby had passed by to take a first look at him. Jonas was certain that he wouldn't have been authorized to borrow any Lebanese surveillance teams, because of the political sensitivities involved in declaring to a Middle Eastern government – in particular one whose cabinet included members of Hezbollah – that a British intelligence officer was suspected of disobeying orders, and Naseby himself had suggested that the Americans hadn't yet been briefed. He would therefore have had to argue the importance of the case with London and wait for a team to arrive from the UK.

It was possible that anyone sent out might also be tasked to mount a covert search of his flat. He went through all his possessions for the third time to check he was not leaving anything behind that would be of genuine use to them. He had bought a USB stick and two mobile phones, and he put the empty packages in the rubbish bin, where he knew they would look, before pouring the uneaten cottage pie over the top so they were partially covered. The last thing he wanted was for it to appear they had been placed there deliberately.

Within an hour of leaving his flat Jonas had seen two people behaving in a manner consistent with surveillance – or rather, given that he had never received any tradecraft training, in a manner consistent with what he imagined to be surveillance. It worked in his favour that very few tourists came to Beirut, and he already knew by sight the handful of westerners living in the same part of the city as him. He couldn't be sure, though, and it would take him most of the day – time he didn't have – to lead them around for long enough to confirm his suspicions. But he had seen a fair-haired man wearing linen trousers and a blue jacket in a bookshop and then from the upper level of a shopping centre a taxi-ride away, and a middle-aged Indian woman had hesitated, briefly but self-consciously, after turning a corner to find Jonas buying cigarettes from a kiosk directly in front of her. There may have been others.

As much as Naseby may have been concerned enough to order a surveillance team on to the streets, Jonas knew it would take more than a mildly alarmed telegram to London to generate the level of interest he required. It was always possible that Naseby was regarded as an idiot, his judgement questionable. He certainly hadn't climbed very high to be ending his career as a roaming case officer, if that was what he was, rather than as a head of station in some European capital. His superiors in London would be weighing the situation up against other, genuine regional crises. Jonas had to ensure they possessed enough evidence to conclude that he posed a serious threat. And not just any kind of evidence. Jonas knew two things: that spies value information they have stolen more highly than that which they have been given, and that they like nothing more than the feeling that they are stealthily acquiring rare fragments that will add up not to a complete picture, for that would be vulgar, but enough of a picture to get at the truth of things. He would let Naseby steal a fragment for his masters.

Jonas wondered what account they would later give of his movements that day. They would have seen him go to an internet cafe, choose a terminal in the corner that couldn't be overlooked, insert a USB stick, make a call on a mobile phone – not the one they knew about already, it was later confirmed – and print about a dozen pages of closely-typed text. No one managed to get close enough to identify the subject matter. He was noticeably more on edge after leaving the internet cafe, they would agree: his pace was quicker, he made crude and unsuccessful attempts to catch out surveillance, he smoked more than usual. He held the papers rolled up so tightly in his fist that they crumpled. The team almost lost him when he stepped into the street and started waving for a taxi, but the first one that stopped wouldn't take him where he wanted so he had to look for another one, which gave them time to call their vehicles forward. He was eventually dropped off outside a nondescript office block in the central district of Solidere. By the time he emerged, seventeen minutes later, they had matched the address to that of Al Jazeera's Beirut office. Jonas was no longer carrying the rolled-up papers, they would observe.

## 2

"I wish to be clear from the start."

Father Tobias sat on the edge of his hotel bed. He was wearing a grey clerical shirt and black trousers with a large grease stain on one leg; his feet were bare and pale. The room was lit by a single desk lamp. The television sat by the wardrobe, its confusion of wires like an inky spill across the tiled floor. His vehemence as he spoke made the mattress squeak.

"I will not lie to anyone for you. I will not conceal a single detail of our agreement from the kidnappers."

Jonas didn't know how much Tobias had drunk, but it was enough that he had slowed his speech to the point that each word seemed uncoupled from those around it.

Tobias was breathing audibly through his nose. "I will not provide any personal assurances that your motives are sincere. When this is all over I will not answer questions about how many of them there were, what did they look like, which weapons did they carry. You should not consider for one minute that I work for you. Is this clear?"

"Perfectly."

"I will not participate in any negotiations."

"I don't expect you to."

"None of your people will follow me into Syria."

"Agreed."

"You will not ask me to do anything else once this is finished. You will not…"

Tobias appeared to forget what he was saying. He took off his tortoiseshell glasses and cleaned them on the corner of his shirt. When he put them back on there were dirty smudges across the lenses and they had buckled across the bridge, where tape held them together.

"Your responsibility to me ends once you have delivered the message," said Jonas. "Are you clear what it is? For your own safety, you shouldn't write it down."

Tobias counted off the points on his fingers. "That you come from a part of the British government that wishes to pay the ransom of one of the hostages they are holding. That in light of the British government's public policy of not paying ransoms, you wish the negotiations to be conducted in secrecy." Sweat was slowly staining his grey shirt under his arms and where it was tight across his belly. He burped softly. "That other representatives of the British government the kidnappers may be speaking to will not be aware of the existence of this message. That you are using me as an envoy to open a completely new channel of communication with the kidnappers that is not known to other people. That they should under no circumstances discuss this message or their negotiations with you with anyone and that if they do it will put at risk the payment of a ransom." He had used all the fingers of his left hand to count the points as he said them and now he stared at his right hand, trying to remember if there was something else. He blinked several times in quick succession. "You are the sole negotiator for the government and this is how they should contact you." Tobias fumbled for the plain business card on which Jonas had written an email address. "Now it is your turn," he said. "Tell me what you are going to do."

"You'll tell Maryam to cross the border as a refugee and make her way to Beirut. Six months ago we would have had to send the SAS in to pick her up, but these days there's a pretty constant stream of refugees. Believe me, Tobias, hiding in a crowd will be a much safer way for her to travel than in the back of a Chinook. There's a thousand US dollars in that envelope in case she needs to bribe anyone. Any additional sums she has to pay along the way we will reimburse. Once here she will contact me on this mobile number – not through the embassy. This is very important. Tobias? Are you listening? I will be arranging her visa behind the scenes and it will only complicate matters if the consular staff see her asking for me. The visa will take a few days, depending on what kind of travel documents she has with her. Then she is free to leave. The British government will cover all travel costs and living expenses for her first six months in the UK."

Tobias looked at Jonas's hands, he looked at his pockets. "You are not carrying a phone. If she must not go to the embassy it is important that she is able to contact you without difficulty when she arrives. Why do you not have a phone? What if your team wishes to contact you?"

"They'll find a way." Jonas had pushed the mobile he had used in the internet cafe down the back of a taxi seat. "Don't worry about phones. We know what we're doing." It had come as a surprise how easy it was to deflect questions by referring to a non-existent expertise. "I'll make sure I'm available on that number when she calls."

Tobias closed his eyes for a moment and swayed a little. "Did I tell you her name is Maryam?" he asked.

"Yes."

"Please take good care of her. She is…" He started to cry. "She is very important to me. I only found her… it came as a surprise, you don't expect, an old man like me…I don't deserve —"

"Tobias? You need to focus. Is there anything else you think we should know?"

He shook his head. "You keep on saying you've done this before. Tell me what *you* want to know."

There were dozens of questions Jonas would have expected to ask if any of it had been real, questions about routes and cover stories and timescales. He considered asking them to ensure that everything appeared genuine. Too few questions might suggest he had no intention of keeping his side of the agreement, that he had no practical arrangements to make in preparation for Maryam's arrival, whereas too many questions – or simply a single wrong question – might create doubt in Tobias's mind. Jonas decided to stay quiet. It wasn't only the doubt in Tobias's mind that worried him. He was himself already far from sure that what he was doing was in any way defensible, and he was frightened of new information that might confuse the matter further. He had made his lists and calculations, he had piled the scales high with pos-sibilities and probabilities – that his father would almost certainly die if he remained in captivity, that Tobias would be in harm's way but had survived previous contact with extremist groups, that Maryam might suffer distress when she learned that there was no visa waiting for her – and he felt morally exposed. How should he measure her distress? What value should he place on her loss of faith in Tobias? The moral order seemed to Jonas enormously complex, its inner workings calibrated like a watch to produce a single truth, a correct answer, but he had no idea what it might be. He wondered if Tobias knew.

Certainly nothing in his professional life had prepared him to make such a fine judgement. He was more accustomed to assessing data than weighing up right and wrong, terms which had in any case been replaced by the more practical and flexible categories of necessity and proportionality. He had done things without first examining his conscience because he had accepted at face value the morality of the organization he had joined, or because he had believed it was in the best interests of his country. Now he was planning to set aside his conscience in the interests of his family. It occurred to Jonas that when this was over he would have used up just about every possible defence for doing the wrong thing.

Tobias dried his eyes on the corner of his shirt. He walked to the wardrobe, almost tripping on the tangle of wires, and gathered a few items of clothing. He folded a shirt on the bed before placing it in a small holdall.

"Nothing about this plan of yours will be straightforward," he said. "Crossing the border into Syria without being arrested, finding the right group, finding the right people in the right group. Persuading Maryam to leave her mother. She walks with a stick; other than a couple of neighbours she's only got Maryam. Are you really certain you can't help her mother leave too? I know, I know – she will slow everyone down, the danger is too great. But I don't know how I can persuade Maryam to go without her."

"You have a difficult task ahead of you, I can see that," said Jonas. "Do you want to talk through what you could say to her?"

"Let me worry about that. In any case, we should not imagine for a moment that my situation is more difficult than that of the hostage. It is the British one you wish to have released, is that right? Isn't he a priest too? I remember there is a connection to the Church." He stopped to take a drink from a glass on the bedside table. His hands were shaking. The bottle it came from had been placed out of sight. "It is reasonable to request that the kidnappers prove the hostage is still alive. If they allow me to see him, do you wish me to give him a message? It may be some reassurance if he learns his government is trying to have him released."

Jonas wondered if this was an opportunity he should take. Even if Tobias made it to Syria, even if he found the right people to speak with, even if they believed his message and made contact with Jonas...What message should he pass? Tell him I am sorry. Tell him I am doing my best. He couldn't think straight. Outside he could hear the hum of the hotel generator, the squeal of traffic, city birds. Tobias moved slowly through the dusk, gathering his clothes. "Jonas?" he said after a while. "Are you all right?"

"He likes to play chess."

"You must learn the most curious things about a person in your job. But I doubt a game of chess will be possible under the circumstances."

"Then pray with him. That will bring him some comfort."

"You are a man of surprises. Do you come from a religious family? You don't have to answer – I can see that you guard your privacy. No doubt this is a necessary measure in your kind of work. Certainly I will offer to pray with him. I have some experience of what he may be going through. The last time I attempted this, on that occasion I was trying to negotiate the release of a Syrian journalist, I was taken by one of the groups and kept in a cell for ten days. They were using the town's former police station to hold Islamic courts. There were hooks in the walls, there was blood on the floor that couldn't be washed. A terrible place. Not as terrible as the belly of a whale, Jonah, but not so far away."

After a short while, Tobias had finished his packing. The gloom in the room had deepened. There was a knock at the door.

"Are you expecting anyone?" asked Jonas in a quiet voice.

"I don't know anyone in Beirut other than you."

"Cleaner? Room service?"

"She has already been. I don't think they do room service here."

There was another knock, louder this time.

"It's probably someone from reception."

Tobias crossed the room and looked through the peep-hole. Jonas moved so that he was out of sight. When the door opened, the voice he heard was American.

"I'm looking for a friend of mine. Fellow in reception said he couldn't be sure but thought this might be a place to look. I've tried 163, 194, 320, 351 and 404. I wasn't expecting there to be so many foreigners in such a dive, no offence meant. Now I'm at your door."

An East Coast accent, Jonas thought. Possibly Boston. Mid-forties. From the way that Tobias was standing it looked as though the American wasn't much taller than him.

"There is no one here," Tobias said.

"There is no one here." He said it as though he was quoting Tobias, except that he had a fast, urban, nasal way of speaking. "Didn't say there was. Said I was look-ing for a friend of mine. Sure I heard a couple voices, though, and it does say room 480 on my piece of paper. This is 480, isn't it?"

"It is probably just the television."

"TV's not on, though, is it?"

"I have turned it off."

"Anything interesting on? You look like the brainy type to me. You watching a quiz show or something like that? It might just be your foreign accent makes you sound clever. Where is it from?"

"I'm Swiss."

"I'm Harvey. Pleased to make your acquaintance. What's your name?"

"Tobias."

"Tobias from Switzerland. Come on, shake my hand – I won't bite. Say, now that we're talking, can I come in for a second, catch my breath?" He didn't sound remotely tired. "Don't know how you can do all those stairs every day. I feel as though I've climbed a mountain."

Jonas was standing by the wardrobe, pressed against the wall, his heart racing. If the American took even one step into the room he would be able to see everything. Jonas wondered if he could hide in the wardrobe without making a noise in the process. He tried to think through what was happening. How had the Americans heard about him? Did Naseby know they were here? He had been so sure that he had lost the surveillance team earlier, that hurrying out of the back entrance of the cafe and changing taxis three times on his way to the hotel had been enough. This would teach him to underestimate their capabilities.

"This is not a very convenient time, I am sorry," Tobias said. "I am in the middle of packing."

"Not wery conwenient, huh? Are you going somewhere nice?"

"Well, I…not really."

"What is it, one of those last-minute deals, don't know where you're going till you get to the airport?"

"I am very sorry but I have so many things to do. Will you please —"

"Your shy friend, the one hiding in your room, is he going on holiday with you?"

"I told you, there is no one here."

"You told me that already. Literally first words out your mouth. Hey, Tobias, I'm just kidding you. And killing a little time. I've been humping up and down these corridors looking for my friend and you're the first person willing to have a conversation with me. You're an unusually patient man. Not many people would still be talking to a rude fellow like me just turns up at their door. It's almost as though you're hanging round to make sure I believe you."

"I hope you find your friend," Tobias said. He began to close the door but the American must have stepped forward because suddenly Jonas could see the tip of his shoe, holding the door open by force. Tobias stepped backwards and almost stumbled. He had begun to breathe quickly. The light from the corridor made his face glisten.

"Don't you want to know who I'm looking for?" asked Harvey. "Just in case you see him at some point? Don't you want to know if it's your neighbour or the funny-looking man who sits across from you at breakfast? I was in your shoes I'd be a little bit curious. Let me describe him for you so that if you see him you can tell him about our conversation. He looks like – how should I put this? If you saw him, you might think he was a junior profes-sor down on his luck. He's got that fusty, academic thing going on. A head too filled with ideas to bother about eating. Buys his clothes from the thrift store. People who should know better tell me he'll think through everything a dozen ways before acting, that he's a cold fish, that he's milquetoast. But I saw him earlier today, Tobias, and I'm not so sure. He looked to me like if he was having a bad day you might cross the road if you saw him coming. Looks like he has a mean streak. It's always the skinny guys who fight the meanest, right? Okay, okay, one last question,

Tobias from Switzerland who is in a rush to get back to his packing. Can you recommend a good restaurant in this shitty neighbourhood for when I track him down? I want to sit down and talk, resolve our differences, break bread together. Perhaps you can tell him to meet me there – if you happen to see him, that is."

"Please, remove your foot. I am sure the staff at reception can help you."

"Maybe if I tell you what he likes to eat, Tobias. British food. You like British food? Pie and gravy, fish and chips, little dainty cucumber sandwiches? You strike me as being more of a drinker than an eater, Tobias. Your eyes – they're a little glassy. Have I interrupted a going-away party? No chance I could come in for a tipple? Can't have you drinking on your own, if in fact that's what you're doing. If my friend was in there keeping you company he'd be drinking with his pinky finger stuck in the air. Don't look so surprised, Tobias – that's what the British do. Between you and me, I might just snap it off when I see him, the amount of trouble that cunt has caused me today. He's had me running all over town. Don't get me wrong – we'll be friends again before long. It's just a little finger. That's all I want at this stage. Friends sometimes need to get angry with each other and have a fight, roll around in the dirt, and then they're friends again. Don't you agree, Tobias? He hasn't done anything too bad yet, far as I know. Clock's ticking, though."

Harvey the American whistled as he walked off down the corridor. Tobias closed the door. His shirt was soaked through with sweat.

"Your world is every bit as unpleasant as I imagined."

"I'm sorry you had to go through that," Jonas said. He didn't know how to explain what had just happened. "The Americans…the Americans get angry when we conduct operations without them and take any opportunity to cause problems. It's a political thing. Someone must have seen me coming into the hotel and called him. He was fishing – you did very well."

"You mean I lied very well. This is high praise. You are the experts, as you keep on telling me." He was breathing heavily. "Only an hour ago I was saying that I would not lie for you. It is not difficult to see that you have chosen me because of my weakness."

Together they took the pictures Tobias had stored in the wardrobe, wiped them clean of dust and tried to match them against the patches of darker paint, unbleached by sunlight, where they had previously hung. Tobias took down the wooden cross and packed it away in his small bag. He pulled out the nail and did what he could with his hands to sweep up the plaster that fell to the floor, but he found it hard to balance and began to breathe heavily. "I don't want to leave a mess," he said quietly to himself. He went to the bed and sat with his head in his hands for a while and then he lay down and fell asleep. Jonas left the hotel soon afterwards. He didn't see anyone waiting for him. It was three days before he had the first message from Tobias saying that he was in Syria.

# CHAPTER FOUR

## 1

Jonas smoked a cigarette in the doorway of the internet cafe and watched the rain. His dark hair lay cold and damp against his head but his clothes were kept dry by the blue plastic raincoat he had found that morning at the back of a kitchen cupboard he had never thought to look in before, along with a child's shoe and two blank cassette tapes. The coat was torn in places, decorated with tiny gold stars and several sizes too large for him, but it was better than nothing.

He was frightened. It seemed to him that there was no edge to his thoughts, that the city shared his state of restless alarm. Above him wires that hummed with secret information were slung between rooftops like a fine net that held everything down. He understood why the car horns were so insistent. What he didn't understand was why the small, angry Chinese man in sodden tennis shoes was using the payphone across the street when he carried what looked like a mobile in his pocket. Jonas had heard stories about investigative targets becoming so paranoid that they accosted passers-by, thinking them to be surveillance officers, and he had seen letters from members of the public who believed themselves to be under investigation, complaining about the clicking noise on their telephone line or post that had gone missing. It surprised him, though, that he had been on the outside for a matter of weeks and already he was proving susceptible to the same kind of irrational, runaway anxiety, however quickly he might dismiss it. That they had stitched tracking beacons into his clothing, that they were using satellites to watch his every step, that they had found a way to stop him sleeping at night. He needed to make a phone call.

Getting Tobias to accept the need for tradecraft had been a challenge. Jonas had tried to persuade him that at the very least they would have to disguise the nature of their emails and phone calls. Pleased to have a task he could think his way through, he had devised a system according to which he would communicate as though he were a fellow priest making general enquiries about how Tobias was getting on. In his replies, Jonas had suggested, Tobias should refer to the "church council" instead of the kidnappers, "church funds" instead of ransom, "icon" instead of hostage, and so on. He wrote out a list for Tobias to memorize. It was probably longer than it needed to be: number sixteen stipulated that "Monday" should be used in place of "Tuesday", "Tuesday" in place of "Wednesday", and so on. By the end the whole thing seemed hugely complicated and faintly absurd even to Jonas; he wasn't surprised it was difficult to get Tobias to take it seriously, especially after a few drinks.

"I like the idea of making the church council a substitute for terrorists," he had said, looking down the list. "It tells me you have had some experience of church councils.

The last time I went before one – well, it is sufficient to say that I walked into the room a priest and I walked out of the room a former priest, at least in their eyes. They were very hard with me. There were people in there with no understanding of human weakness. Less than an hour to reach their decision, one from Rome and the other from Columbia, or was it Peru, two fat bishops hurrying to attend their lunch appointment. All because of that tiny little thing on 15 May 1985, or maybe it was August the year before that really upset them, it all depends on your point of view. I tried to keep it from them but it's hard to hide something like that. I tried to say it was a mistake but they could see I didn't mean it. Still, it took them twenty years to get round to —"

"Tobias? We need to focus. If you don't think the code works, suggest something else," Jonas said. "You're the one who will have to defend it. But we won't be able to speak over an open line without using some form of cover."

"You even look as though you might be a priest. It is this Old Testament beard of yours," he said, reaching out a hand to smooth Jonas's cheek. "These simple clothes you wear. You know that colour is not a sin?"

"Please, Tobias. This might seem silly now, but it'll be very important once you're inside Syria."

"Perhaps it will be better to promote you to bishop. In case you need to give me instructions. How proficient is your Latin?"

In the end the wording he had used in his email could not have been more plain, or more alarming: "I have arrived. Please call me. It is urgent."

Jonas had to find a payphone far enough away from the internet cafe that his call would not be linked to Tobias's email. The last thing he could do was allow anyone to follow him. He knew that he had come close to ruining everything by leading the American, Harvey, to Tobias's hotel, a mistake he couldn't afford to repeat under any circumstances.

The problem was that when it came to surveillance he didn't know what he was doing. The Americans would have resources he wasn't aware of, they would use techniques honed over the years to allow them to follow highly skilled Russian and Chinese spies around Western capitals. What chance did he have? How could he ever be sure he was alone? The answer came to him late one night as he tried to sleep. They weren't in a Western capital. They were in a city largely without CCTV, a city where few streets had clearly marked names. They were in a city that still bore the scars of a fifteen-year civil war, a city still divided along confessional lines, a city large swathes of which were controlled by Hezbollah. He would make that work in his favour.

The only way to lose surveillance, he decided, was to lead them towards an area in which they were unable to operate. Such an area was the Hezbollah stronghold of Dahieh – a district avoided by foreigners, where heavily armed checkpoints could appear at a moment's notice, where people daubed anti-Western slogans on walls, where the peculiar driving style required by surveillance would be noticed by a local population targeted by numerous ISIS car bombs. Surveillance teams are subject to risk assessments, he thought, just like everyone else in government. The only drawback was that for his plan to work he would have to go to Dahieh himself.

Jonas tried to dampen his paranoia by thinking logically about what surveillance would look like. He drew up a list in his head as he walked. 1. A man or a woman, on foot or in a vehicle. 2. Aged somewhere between twenty-five and forty-five, assuming that the older they got the more likely they were to be promoted off the streets into a managerial position. 3. Possibly on mopeds or motorbikes or even bicycles. 4. Some with military backgrounds, visible in a certain kind of physicality but also in a thoroughness of preparation: they would have good shoes, waterproofs, a bag with water and food. Anyone in flip-flops or sandals could be discounted. 5. A few Mediterranean-looking but the majority western Europeans. 6. Phones bought clean for this operation and therefore cheap; no one would authorize the purchase of twenty smartphones for a single job. Without smartphones they would be reliant on paper maps, they would be looking around for street signs. 7. No more than a dozen individuals, and the utility of each team member would decrease each time they got close enough that he saw their face. In other words, Jonas thought, they couldn't do this forever. They could be beaten.

Walking through the backstreets, taking every turning that took him towards Dahieh, he soon lost track of time, watching to see who came with him. The rain was keeping most people off the streets and he saw no sign of Hezbollah other than their distinctive yellow flag on a handful of lamp posts. It wasn't long before he didn't know where he was. Once or twice someone followed him round two corners in succession and he would slow down, or speed up, or cross the road to get a good look at them; he must have stopped to retie his shoelaces a dozen times. No one stayed with him for long. He found it was more difficult than he had expected to spot unusual behaviour. Either everyone was acting suspiciously or no one was – he couldn't be sure. He felt foolish and might have concluded that spying was a fundamentally unserious pursuit if only he hadn't needed to speak with Tobias so urgently. With its hide-and-seek and make-believe, its puzzles and code words, its insistence on the sanctity of secrets, spying seemed to belong to the realm of childhood. He remembered reading of Kim Philby that what had allowed him to retain through adulthood the undergraduate ideology that led him to betray his country was the simplistic, closed and unreal world of espionage itself. There were good guys and bad guys, and everyone knew who they were. Philby would have done a better job of anti-surveillance than he was managing, Jonas thought. All those meetings with his Russian handlers in London parks. Chalk marks on benches, bread for the ducks. The loose brick in the graveyard. God watched you all the time but you could never see him. In the dark you whispered prayers to him like secrets. The rain came down and he pressed on, looking for surveillance, looking for a payphone, looking for his dad.

# 2

Jonas had no idea where he was. It was getting dark and the rain was falling heavily. It had been two hours since he had read the email, nine hours since it had been sent, three days since Tobias had left Beirut. The email had come from a Lebanese IP address, but that didn't mean anything: the infrastructure in Syria had been so degraded by the war that people there regularly dialled in to Lebanese providers. Had Tobias run into some kind of practical problem? He had said he would stay with friends along the way but had refused to give any details or accept any money for himself, claiming that since he had no intention of bribing anyone his expenses would be minimal; Jonas couldn't imagine him changing his mind on that. He couldn't imagine either what sort of help Tobias would think he could provide from Beirut, even with the array of resources he undoubtedly assumed Jonas had at his disposal. Tobias knew better than anyone that the challenge he faced was to persuade the right people that the message he carried was genuine – it was not a logistical matter, it would not require great feats of endurance. It was only fifty-two miles to Damascus, one hundred and eighty-six miles to Aleppo, two hundred and forty-four miles to Raqqa. If Jonas kept on walking he would be there in three days.

The street he was on was narrow and steep and the wind flung the rain against the tall, grey buildings. High above him he could see someone securing their shutters against the storm. He was startled by the shout that came at him from an open doorway.

"My friend! My friend!" He whistled to help Jonas locate him. "Where you are going?"

Jonas looked around. The man waving at him was young, muscular, in his early twenties, dressed in camouflage trousers and a tight red T-shirt. His dark hair was slicked back.

"You are lost? I gonna help you, my friend," he said, beckoning Jonas towards him. "Where you are from?"

"England."

"What you do here?"

"Just a tourist."

They were standing in the doorway. Rain had filled the slack awning above them so that it hung dark and plump, as though a body had been hidden there. Water spilled over the edges and clattered to the pavement.

"No, what you do *here*?" He pointed at the street. He wore rings on both hands. "What you do in this place?"

Jonas had expected something like this. In fact, he had hoped for it, since it suggested he had walked far enough into a Hezbollah area to compromise any surveillance behind him. Nonetheless he felt his breath coming fast. All he had to do was stay calm, make his excuses and leave. He tried to smile.

"Nothing. Just walking around."

"Why you are walking in the rain? Nobody other he is walking in the rain."

"Nobody?" This might be his chance to confirm he hadn't been followed. "You haven't seen any other foreigners here today?"

The young man laughed. "No foreigners they gonna come here, my friend."

"No strangers, no outsiders?"

"You know why?"

"Why what?"

"No foreigner he is gonna come here. To this place. Because they will be scared."

He was in the clear; he could call Tobias. The open doorway behind the man was dark. Jonas could make out a flight of stone steps, a torn political poster, a swaying light bulb.

"I'm really sorry," he said. "I didn't realize where I was. Thank you for the offer of help, though."

"Passport, passport."

"What?"

"Give me passport."

"Why do you need my passport?"

The young man stepped out and spat into the street. He whistled loudly, turned and stood close enough that there was no easy way for Jonas to leave the doorway.

"You are walking like this." He wiggled his hand like a snake in front of Jonas's face. "You are not looking at the things like a tourist he is gonna look. You are walking very quick like there is a problem somewhere. You are not a tourist."

Two other men were walking up the street towards them in the rain. One of them carried a radio in his hand.

"All right, I'll leave the way I came," Jonas said quickly. "I didn't mean to upset anyone." He tried to edge to one side as he spoke but the young man pushed him backwards and he slipped on the wet floor so that his head banged against the sharp edge of the metal door. The man was lifting his hands as though to placate or reassure or threaten – he couldn't be sure. Later on he realized that he should have remained calm and handed over his passport and told them a story about how he was a pro-Palestinian activist from the UK who wanted to see at first-hand the neighbourhood so viciously bombed by Israel in 2006. But instead he decided that he had to get away before the other men arrived. It was the wrong decision. He pushed hard against the door to gather momentum and with his head down drove outwards to force his way on to the street. He heard a cracking noise and felt a smear of something sticky near his eye that might have been the man's blood or his hair gel. Then the other two men were suddenly next to him and there was something professional about the way they restrained him without causing any harm. But the young man, his mouth wet and lurid with blood, wasn't going to let it go, and he stepped round and swung a punch while Jonas's arms were pinned at his side. And the last thing Jonas remembered was the torn poster and the light bulb swaying wildly above him, as though trying to tear itself free from the ceiling.

**3**

"When you have calmed down you will understand that you overreacted out there."

This seemed to Jonas a harsh assessment, given that he had just been knocked out. A cut had opened above his left eye. He was seated on a wooden chair in what looked like a cellar. Water was dripping somewhere nearby. The throbbing in his head made it difficult to focus on anything but he could see his wallet, passport and keys clearly enough on the table in front of him.

"Do you know why the people here are nervous? Do you understand why the boy wanted to see your passport?"

The man angled a lamp to point directly at Jonas. He was wearing a grey shirt and a black knitted tie and sitting in a wheelchair; he pushed himself out from behind the table so that they were next to each other. With a piece of cotton wool he began to dab gently at the blood on Jonas's face. "My name is Raza," he said. "Don't look so frightened. The last thing we want is for you to go home and tell everyone that this is what Lebanon is like."

"I thought I was being mugged," said Jonas. "Or kidnapped."

Raza was in his sixties, thin and upright, with bright unblinking eyes, grey hair and a neatly trimmed beard. His legs were covered with a pink blanket. There were slight traces of a French accent in the way he spoke English.

"Permit me to explain the situation," he said. Jonas could see scarring on his neck that began under his beard and continued beneath the shirt collar. "On one side we have Daesh. They pack vehicles with explosives and drive them into our most crowded squares on market day in order to kill as many Shia as possible. Everyone knows they have numerous European fighters among their ranks. Now, I would be surprised if you were one of them, but please understand that this may be what our young friend outside was thinking. Consider your behaviour, consider your appearance. He did not have the advantage of studying you up close and seeing that you may have grown your beard long, as many Western fighters in Syria do, but you have neglected to shave your moustache in accordance with the Sunnah." He pressed the cotton wool against Jonas's bloody eye. Warm pink water made a tapping noise against the oversized plastic raincoat. "On the other side we have Israel. They bombed this neighbourhood in 2006 and it is a certainty that they will bomb it again at some point. They know where the people they wish to kill are living and which buildings are used by whom because they send spies here to collect the kind of detailed information their satellites cannot see and to leave markers that are visible only to their fighter jets. Alternatively, if fighter jets are not appropriate, they will send someone to place a bomb in the headrest of a car seat or strangle a person with a towel in his hotel room." He took a pair of tweezers and picked a piece of grit out of the open cut. "So you will understand that we are a nervous neighbourhood. We are curious when strangers come to visit. We like them to ring the doorbell and introduce themselves first."

"They used stolen British passports for that operation," Jonas said. It seemed a good idea to show that he wasn't on Israel's side. "There was a row. We expelled some of their diplomats."

They were both quiet for a minute. There was mint and garlic on Raza's breath. Jonas could feel warm water running down his face.

"We?"

"I'm British."

"Ah, this is what you meant. I thought…no, never mind. You will need stitches."

Jonas felt alarmed by the gentle pressure already being exerted on his thin cover story, and before any real questions had been asked of it. He knew that he was no match for a skilled interrogator, just as he had been no match for a professional surveillance team. People these days talked about comfort zones. His comfort zone was a tiny room off the back stairwell where the cleaners stored their carts at the end of a working day. His comfort zone was a studio apartment, a neatly organized bookshelf, the same meal every night. Why had he imagined he would be able to handle the real world? He didn't even play chess against real people. He couldn't even handle an open-plan office.

"I've got to go," Jonas said weakly.

"It's important that the cut is properly cleaned. I will have to insist, as would any responsible doctor. After all, it was our fault. It won't take long. Please make yourself comfortable. Would you like to take your coat off? No? It looks a little like an American flag, your coat, all these tiny gold stars. Like you have wrapped yourself in a flag. Would you describe yourself as a patriot?"

A drop of water fell from Jonas's chin, ran down the smooth slope of the raincoat and disappeared into a tear in the plastic just above his left elbow. He closed his eyes in the hope it would shut down any conversation. For a while the only noise was the sound of Raza's steady breathing. Jonas set about countering a Spanish Opening, but after only eight moves found himself imagining that he was playing against his father. Before long his defences were in disarray and both his rooks were vulnerable. He had been a strict father, an Old Testament father, more judgement than love, or so it had appeared to the dark-eyed little boy who filled his storehouse with grievances that were a sort of wealth, like things that could be hoarded and weighed and treasured. Forgiveness would have felt like poverty. By the time his father began to soften, it was too late. Jonas was bruised, wary of other people and the unmanageable demands of friendship, not to mention love. Now that it was no longer possible, he wanted nothing so much as to talk with his father. In the instant he had heard of the kidnapping their bitter history of disagreement – about politics, about the Bible, about chess – had been revealed as an illusion, as an unforgivable trick he had played upon himself. He wanted to tell his father that he was good at his job, that he was trying to make friends. He wanted to tell him how working in intelligence had changed his attitude to the Bible, that he finally understood how messiness is what makes something true because if four Russian defectors gave identical accounts of something they would never be believed. He wanted to ask him how everyone else seemed to know how to live but it was still such a mystery to him.

"This cut is deeper than it appears," said Raza.

In an odd way, Jonas suddenly realized, it was the fact that their relationship had been so difficult that had led him down this path, that was driving him to find some way, any way, to get his father released. A good relationship, he imagined, might have felt complete; he would have been able to let his father go knowing he had said everything he wanted to say.

"Do you have health insurance?" asked Raza.

Jonas was determined not to be drawn into conversation. He screwed his eyes tight, as though in pain. He thought about his mother, on her own back in England, about the phone calls and emails in which he had told her he was still overseas with work but hoped to return soon. He listed significant dates in the history of Lebanon: 22 November 1943, 16–18 September 1982, 14 February 2005. He thought through what he knew of Hezbollah: the kidnapping of Western hostages between 1982 and 1992, the Marine barracks bombing of 1983 that killed two hundred and forty-one Americans and fifty-eight French, the network of international drug traffickers and money launderers that funded their activities.

He remembered a trip to Berlin several years earlier at the invitation of German intelligence. The traditional formalities of a liaison visit had been observed: the awkward dinner, the visit to a tourist attraction – in this case Checkpoint Charlie – and the pre-Snowden noises about greater openness and joint working. No need for aliases in Western Europe any more, everyone in London agreed. He was there to observe the debrief by the BND of a German national who had disappeared early one morning from the street outside his Beirut apartment only to reappear two days later. The German authorities were considering advising their citizens to leave Lebanon but had decided to consult with their European partners before taking what would be in diplomatic terms a drastic measure.

The man described having been pulled into a car, a dark blue Mercedes estate smelling of thyme and coffee and with more than the usual number of aerials and a number plate that started with either a three or an eight, and made to lie on the floor with a rolled-up carpet on top of him while being driven at a sedate pace for between forty-five and fifty-five minutes. He was shown a handgun but at no stage was it pointed directly at him. A pillow was provided for his head. They put him in a basement – air-conditioned, well-lit, clean, with a proper bed and fresh sheets in a side room for when he grew tired. The room was seven paces wide and twelve and a half paces long. It had no windows and the door was metal. There was always a fresh bottle of water on the table and they gave him a choice of pizza, sushi or mixed grill at every meal time except breakfast, when they brought him eggs, cheese and fresh bread, whether he wanted it or not.

They kept on returning, in their patient questioning, to a particular day three weeks earlier. The tall, thin one with a reedy voice and acne scars on his face and neck would ask him in formal, heavily accented German to describe the day, a Tuesday, starting from the moment his alarm went off, and the older one in brown cordu-roy trousers who smoked unfiltered cigarettes and liked to pace about would shake his head each time he got past five o'clock in his narrative without having admit-ted to whatever it was they were looking for. It was not until the second day, the eighth or ninth retelling and the first use of violence – in this case the brief applica-tion of a lit cigarette to a patch of skin just above the elbow – that he mentioned a phone call he had made in the middle of the afternoon, immediately after his wife had left the house with the children, to a young French woman he had slept with twice while on a diving holiday in Sinai the previous month. This triggered a round of extremely detailed questions about the affair – almost as though, he complained, they didn't really believe the woman actually existed. What district of Marseilles was she from? Did the yoga studio she worked at have a website? Would he be so kind as to describe their lovemaking? He was returned to his Beirut apartment that evening in the same gentle manner, a tube of antiseptic cream in his pocket, completely in the dark about what had happened.

The likely cause of the incident was apparent to Jonas, once he had been permitted to ask two clarifying ques-tions of the German. In his written report he highlighted several pertinent factors. The first was an Iranian delivery the CIA had watched several months earlier being moved through eastern Turkey, down to the coast and on to a ship that stopped for a matter of hours in Beirut before continuing to North Africa. The second was humint from a source related by marriage to a programmer in Hezbollah's technical section suggesting that around the same time the group took receipt of Iranian equipment that would allow it to capture communications data in bulk and search it for (among other things) handsets or SIM cards that were only in contact with one other phone, or that were only used for short periods of time before being switched off again. The third was that a large number of travellers crossed from Sinai into Israel. What seemed most likely, Jonas suggested, once the German had confirmed that he had used a dedicated, unregistered mobile to contact the young woman and that she had spent at least a weekend or two at some point in the Israeli resort of Eilat, was that she had inadvertently given her lover – in communications data, at least – the profile of someone secretly in contact with an Israeli, which is to say an Israeli spy.

"Do you have health insurance?" Raza asked again.

Jonas didn't know what to say. Did Raza want to be paid for his services? If that was all it would take to get away from him he would happily pay any sum. It seemed like an odd question, but Jonas had no experience of such things. A typical tourist would certainly have insurance, given Lebanon's reputation, but the last thing he wanted was to be caught out in a lie. This was one of the few things he thought he knew about interrogations, that you should stick to the truth wherever possible.

Raza pressed the tweezers hard into the cut above Jonas's eye until he pulled backwards and cried out.

"My apologies," said Raza. "I am a little out of practice. But it seems I have got your attention. I was only going to point out that your insurance is probably invalid since the accident occurred in a part of Beirut the British government advises its citizens to avoid," he said. "Do not worry, however – I can put the stitches in myself, if you will allow me."

"Are you a doctor?" Jonas asked.

"Enough of one to do some simple stitching."

"I'm not feeling very well – I think I should go."

Raza took a gentle hold of Jonas's wrist and felt for his pulse. "I will be the judge of that. The truth is that you may be too unwell. Tell me, how long have you been in Beirut?"

He has your passport, Jonas thought – he already knows the answer. He tried to control his breathing. "A few weeks."

"That is a long visit for a tourist, no? You must have been to every museum in the country several times over."

"I'm thinking of staying out here to learn Arabic. Maybe get a part-time job teaching English. It's all a bit up in the air, to be honest."

"You have enough money to stay here indefinitely?"

"Probably not. I'm playing it by ear, to be honest." He wondered whether repeating "to be honest" underlined his truthfulness or flagged him as a liar. He decided not to risk saying it a third time.

"What is your occupation?"

"I work in a bookshop."

"Do you have any friends here?"

"Not really."

"Not really?"

"Just the odd person I've met. No one I would call a friend."

"Have you had any contact with the British embassy?"

"No."

"Have you met any diplomats, even in a social setting?"

"No, why would —"

"What brought you to this area today?"

"I wasn't lying when I told the man outside that I was just going for a walk – I had no idea where I was. But I completely understand that people here are nervous of strangers, and I'm sorry for any problems I've caused. You have been very kind to me."

"Not at all. It will only take another few minutes to put the stitches in."

"Listen, thank you for the offer, but I really should go." Jonas pulled his hand away and stood up. The cellar walls came close and then retreated. He felt dizzy and had to lean on the chair for a moment while his head cleared.

"At the very least let me call you a taxi," Raza said. "Which hotel are you staying in?"

Jonas was about to name a big hotel in the centre of town when he caught sight of his keys on the table. He put them into his pocket along with his wallet and passport. They didn't look like hotel keys – there was no room number, no logo.

"I've rented an apartment."

"An apartment? And you are a tourist? How unusual. This is quite a commitment for someone so unsure of their plans."

Jonas took an unsteady step towards the door and pulled at the handle. It was locked.

"I have no objection to you leaving," Raza said quietly from his wheelchair. "But you will do me the courtesy of listening to what I have to say first. I would like it very much if you called me on this number within the next forty-eight hours." He wrote on a piece of paper and pushed it across the table. "I think that we could have a fruitful conversation on several topics. What do you say? And before you tell me that you don't have a phone, Mr Jonas, or some other kind of nonsense, please be aware that I found receipts for two of them while I was looking through your wallet." He rolled his wheelchair around the table. "You must understand that this is not your playground. You are not free to do whatever you wish. There are consequences – you have experienced this yourself today. But there may also be rewards."

It came to Jonas all of a sudden that there was an advantage to the situation he was in. There were disadvantages, certainly, chiefly that he was finding it difficult enough to deal with the attentions of British and American intelligence without introducing a group like Hezbollah that had an entirely different agenda, that was able to operate outside any legal framework, that had hundreds of people on the ground. But he also knew that Naseby would see Jonas's phone making contact with a new Lebanese number and quickly reach the conclusion, based on locational data and voice analysis, that he had established contact with a member of Hezbollah. This, he knew, would alarm London and Washington – and he needed to keep increasing their sense of alarm if his plan was to have any chance of working.

Jonas picked up the piece of paper. "I'll call you," he said.

Outside it was still raining. It had been four hours since he had read the email, eleven hours since it had been sent.

# CHAPTER FIVE

**1**

Jonas had a keen sense that he would need to do better. This was true of his ability to detect and evade surveillance, to withstand questioning, to persuade others to do what he wanted. In getting this far he had relied heavily on luck and Father Tobias's native kindness, but as things progressed he knew he would be subject to a pressure that was more intelligent, more calibrated, more sustained that anything he had experienced so far. To succeed he would have to stop making mistakes.

For any change to take hold, though, to the extent that it could not be dislodged at the surface by mere circumstance, it could not be limited to behaviour, it must be deep-rooted, it must require a change in character. He would not just need to *do* better: he would need to *be* better. He would have doubted that real change was even possible had he not seen his own character fall apart so quickly in the weeks after his father's disappearance. It had turned out that for his character to be a discernible thing, a thing that could be described as this or that, it needed to be propped up by other things: a job, people, daily routine. In isolation there was nothing other than a random assortment of traits, like items forgotten in the bottom of a drawer: a fondness for peanut butter, the ability to sing entire hymns from memory, the habit, only recently discovered, of being most prone to tears just as he was falling asleep.

That only religious examples of meaningful and dramatic change came to his mind suggested it would be a difficult process. The thief on the cross, Jonah before and after the whale. Did anyone take such stories seriously? Was an experience like that of St Paul on the road to Damascus really possible? Surely the modern equivalent was the experience of those young men who had kidnapped his father, and it was called radicalization. He knew *that* was a real thing; he had spent eight years studying the evidence. Perhaps that should be his goal, he thought. Perhaps to match them he needed to go through what they had gone through: a cleansing, a sharpening, a shift away from the centre towards the margins. Perhaps he needed to get extreme.

Through the sheets of rain he saw a telephone.


## 2


"I don't believe a word you have told me."

Jonas was standing by the side of a busy road, his face turned away from the oncoming traffic. The plaster Raza had given him for his eye had been dislodged by the rain and he was trying to staunch the flow of blood with the sleeve of his plastic raincoat.

"Why is it always you, Jonas, why is it only you?" The line crackled and settled. "…stopped at an airport there were always two people. Why have I never met one of your team? Why does nobody ever phone you? Why do you never send a message to…" Another crackle, longer this time. "…never talk about your colleagues? Why is it that when the hotel maid tells me that someone has broken into my room she describes a man with dark hair and a beard? He looks like a gravedigger, she said. This one man does all the surveillance, he does all the breaking into hotel rooms, he does all the talking. He can obtain visas without any difficulty but under no circumstances must he be contacted through the embassy."

Jonas didn't know what to say. "This is standard field protocol," he said. He had never heard anyone speak like that but wondered whether the problem was that he hadn't been cinematic enough. "A covert operative in hostile territory is trained to carry out a wide range of tasks." Should he keep going? "It's in section 4, subsection B2 of the field manual under the heading —"

"What are you talking about?" said Tobias.

"I'll tell you anything you want to know about my team." At the other end Tobias was quiet. "Hello? Can you hear me?" Jonas cupped his spare hand around the telephone to ensure he would be heard above the roar of traffic. He had to do something quickly in case the line was cut. "Jack is my right-hand man," he shouted. "He's been organizing logistics behind the scenes – the vehicles, the encrypted phones, the hotel rooms. Can you hear me? He's only been with us for the past year but he's got a great career ahead of him. A very solid operator. Mahmoud and Hilary have been working all hours on surveillance duties." Mahmoud and Hilary? His only hope was that the phone line would make parts of this incomprehensible. Now that he had started down this path he had to keep going. How could he make these people sound real? Give Jack a shock of unruly red hair, Hilary a glass eye? "Mahmoud was there in the bar that night when I told you what this was all about, Tobias. He's a local guy, medium height, stocky. You might remember him – he was talking to a woman with peroxide-blonde hair." Was it conceivable that anyone would actually name and describe an entire covert team over an international phone line? "Then there's Luke. He's always asking to meet you, always asking how you are, if you're getting enough rest."

Silence, crackle, silence. Jonas was out of ideas. "Hello?" he asked.

"Hello?" said Tobias eventually. "Hello? Jonas, are you there?"

"I can hear you. Can you hear me?"

"…me this. The last time I…my hotel room, you didn't have a phone with you. Do you remember? You said that if anyone from your team needed to contact you they would find a way. But when the American knocked at the door you didn't even consider the possibility that it might be one of your team. You didn't even consider it, Jonas! What if there was a problem, what if…danger? You just said it would be room service and hid in the wardrobe."

Jonas scrambled for an answer. That he had told his team to walk in without knocking? That he had set up some other, more circumspect system for delivering messages – someone whistling in the corridor, say, or a pebble against the window? "They would have knocked in a different way," he said. "Three taps, a pause, another two taps."

It was not as though he had failed to prepare. He had written out answers to questions Tobias might ask him about risk, about the life Maryam could expect in the UK, about recent air bombardments. He had written out a moral justification of bribery alongside the details of one of the few money-transfer bureaus still operating in Aleppo in case he needed to send funds. He had written out details of persuasion techniques he had found in one of the self-help books – "ask for a small favour before you ask for a big one", "frame your objective using positive language", "use fluidity to negate the perception that you lack confidence" – and practised motivational speeches in the bathroom mirror. He had thought he was prepared for the call, but he was completely unprepared for what he was being asked.

"I don't believe you," he heard. "I just don't believe you any more, Jonas. I'm afraid this will be the last time —"

"Are you ready for the plain truth?" Jonas said quickly. Two teenage boys walked past him, wide-eyed at the sight of the blood smeared down one side of his face. He stared back and they quickly looked away. "You don't know what you're talking about. You have no idea how this sort of thing works – no one on the outside does. You've been stopped a couple of times at an airport and all of a sudden you're able to spot patterns, you know what looks right and what doesn't. Do you know why we don't let you see other people? Because you're an alcoholic, and alcoholics behave in unpredictable ways. Because when you're tortured by Daesh you won't be able to describe anyone other than me. Because it confuses people in your position when they meet too many people in my position – it dilutes the impact, any personal affection you feel is divided between two people, it's easier for you to walk away. We make this sort of calculation. But the fact that we are calculating about it only means that we think it is important, that we want to get it right. Nothing I've said should change what we are doing together, which is trying to save a life. Now tell me where you are."

The rain had stopped. Jonas felt drained of energy, of words, of blood. He had nothing left to offer. He wondered if part of him wanted Tobias to give up and come back to Beirut, if the guilt he was feeling for sending such a good man into a place like Syria had weakened his resolve to get his father back at all costs. It was difficult to know why else he might have suggested Tobias would be tortured, why he had called him an alcoholic. It was as though he was trying to loosen the threads of obligation that bound the priest to his task.

"Hello? Hello?" he said. Maybe this was the end. He was surprised it had worked this far. Perhaps it had been too much to claim that he was working on behalf of a government, that he was competent and trained, that he was not on his own. He should have known he would never have been able to disguise that. When he looked in the mirror he could see it himself. It was not loneliness that was visible so much as an air of neglect, as though love left a mark on people and he had been passed by.

"…outside Aleppo," he suddenly heard Tobias say. "It is worse than I could have imagined…armed children on the streets, stray dogs everywhere, human and animal waste, every building you can see is… Nobody has enough food. If neighbours have a dispute they resolve it with… tell an armed group that the other is not devout and he will be put in prison. Kidnappings for money happen every day."

"Tell me about the church council." He felt light-headed and leaned on the payphone to stay upright. "Have you been able to make contact with the church council?"

"The what? Oh, yes… The problem is that everybody changes their phones at least once a week because of the flying things. I don't know what I should call them. Angels?"

Better than nothing, thought Jonas.

"I have spoken to several people," Tobias was saying. "…contact with the group that has the British…er…thing. The news I have had until now is not positive. Nothing is certain, but several people told me that he is very ill and will not recover without… One person told me that he has died. I don't know whether this affects your calcula-tions. Do you want me to continue?"

Jonas pushed his forehead against the payphone. He rolled his head to the side and pressed hard until the edge of the metal hooked into the torn skin above his eye. The pain was a distraction from thoughts of his father.

He started to bleed again. "Calculations" focused him on the need to remain professional. This was the kind of intelligence to hold at arm's length: uncorroborated, single source, pure rumint. He felt his father slowly slipping away, like a boat from its moorings.

"We'll just have to work more quickly," he said. "What else have you heard?"

"Security is very tight. He is moved every few days. He has not had any contact with other hostages. One person said he was in Raqqa, another told me he has been in Mosul since the beginning. I don't think this will be of much use to you."

"Tell me everything."

"They are going to broadcast another video of him in the next few days to increase the pressure on your government. He has refused to be filmed making political statements, and this has had consequences."

For weeks Jonas had been reading reports that another video was going to be released soon. He followed social media closely; it was the only source of intelligence he still had access to, the only source the government could not turn off. Each day he read the tweets and postings of dozens of foreign fighters in Syria and watched videos released on the Al Furqan YouTube channel. His notebook was filled with details of individuals and their accounts. What was said was mostly propaganda and gossip, but so was much of the raw, unassessed intelligence that came into Thames House or Vauxhall Cross. He applied himself to it diligently. At night in his apartment he grew a vast spider diagram that sprawled across dozens of pieces of paper on his bedroom wall. He looked for individuals who had inadvertently revealed their location and tried to link them to his top-tier targets, he examined postings for changes in language or tone that might reflect a recent move or promotion, he studied fighters who had been silent for long periods of time only to reappear noisily, suggesting they had been deployed on some kind of sensitive duty, like protecting senior leaders or transporting hostages.

This was how he spent much of his time. More often than not, with all those images on his bedroom wall, he would dream of his father, of desert landscapes and crusader castles, of rescue attempts that were unsuccessful because of some minor failing on his part, such as a key he couldn't turn in a lock or a form he had filled out incorrectly. Jonas knew it wasn't good for him. He had lost any softness in his body, despite his best efforts to maintain the semblance of a healthy routine: regular meals, plenty of fresh air, exercise. The stress must consume its own share of calories, he thought, like a virus inside a computer, drawing down the battery in secret. His reflection in shop windows had become that of a stranger. It was not simply the beard but the gauntness in his face, the blankness of his expression. The hunched posture of an office worker had been replaced by a new alertness, as though the kidnappers might appear before him at any moment. He tried to fill his mind with other facts to counterbalance his obsession with them. That his nightly walk along the Corniche – from the St George Hotel at one end, past the lighthouse and Pigeon Rock to the beach at Ramlet al Bayda at the other end – took him anywhere between sixty-two and seventy-two minutes. That he had to climb forty-one steps to reach his apartment. That he couldn't eat more than seventy grams of rice in one sitting, that it took fourteen minutes to cook.

"How are you holding up, Tobias?" he asked. The blood was pouring from the cut above his eye. It was cold and sticky in his beard. "I don't want to interfere in your private business" – he heard distant laughter – "but we can talk about things like your health if you want. I can't imagine it's very easy for you to be coping with that alongside everything else I've asked you to do."

Tobias hesitated before answering. "I am dealing with it, Jonas," he said. Another pause. "I went to see a doctor shortly...here."

Another crackle. He waited for it to pass. "Was it useful?"

"They had run out of medication. She gave me a leaflet."

"Did it have any helpful advice?"

"In its own way."

"What does it say?"

"Jonas, we do not need to —"

"We can discuss this. How you're feeling is important."

"Oh, reduce the amount you drink slowly rather than... Let the people around you know that you are planning to cut down. Things like this."

"Sounds like good advice."

"Avoid stressful situations."

Jonas slumped to the ground and watched blood drip from his head on to the dark-blue plastic raincoat with the tiny gold stars. Light-headed didn't begin to describe it. Was it a ladies' coat? He searched tirelessly for a label. 100% nylon, Made in China, 40 degrees.

"Are you still there?" asked Tobias.

"I owe you a great deal." It must have looked as though he was a victim in the middle of his own crime scene. "Much more than you are aware of, and much, much more than I can explain right at this moment." He closed his eyes. Something akin to sleep approached him but he fought to keep it at bay. "I may not have made this clear enough before now, Tobias, but you really mustn't put yourself in any more danger than you have already. You've made contact with various people – that's more than enough. It's more than I expected, if I'm honest with you. The last thing you should do is meet anyone connected to the kidnappers face-to-face. I mean the church council. Is that clear, Tobias? We've got to think about your safety too. In fact, maybe it's time to come back. You've done a great job, but let's call it a day. When you get back here we can sit down together and talk this through. We've got a lot to talk about, you and me. You deserve to know the full picture after all you've done. Some of what I'll tell you might come as a surprise, although you've already guessed half of it. Does it sound as though I'm making a confession? Tobias? Can you hear me? Hello? Hello?"

# 3

It was dark outside as he climbed the forty-one steps to his apartment. Inside everything was exactly as he had left it, except that a mobile phone he didn't recognize had been placed at the centre of the living-room table. When it rang he didn't know what to do. He looked at it for a while until it stopped ringing. Then it started again. He picked it up.

"Almost midnight, Jonas: this is your wake-up call. Time to stop fucking around." That same urban, nasal voice, hurrying through the words. "It falls to me as an American to point out the pitfalls of this free-market, capitalist project you got going on, trying to find the customer who'll pay the highest price for the information you're selling. That's what you're doing, right? You've tried Al Jazeera, now you go missing in Hezbollah-land. Before you do something you can't take back there's a few things you need to know about the practicalities of being a traitor. I'm a bit old-fashioned, I prefer the word 'traitor' even though I know everyone likes to say 'whistle-blower' these days. 'Whistle-blower' is a funny word, don't you think, Jonas? Sounds like there's a fire in the barn, like a fat kid's flailing in the grown-up end of the swimming pool. Doesn't sound like some geek's copying terabytes of stolen data on to a USB. And they say that governments manipulate language. Anyway, back to my point, which is, number one, that you basically got two options in terms of how things play out for you: prison or exile. Or things go bad in a different way and you end up living in the broom closet down the hall from the visa office in some third-rate embassy, eating refried beans for the rest of your days, which is really a combination of the two. Nobody is going to take what you're thinking of doing lying down, Jonas, kidnapped father or not. You continue down this path and you either get locked up for a very long time or you run to Moscow, those are your choices. Hezbollah and ISIS don't have asylum programmes, Al Jazeera can't put a stamp in your passport. Number two, it won't work. I don't know if you're doing this to get your father freed or because you're pissed at that cocksucker Naseby and his chums for not getting your father released. Either way, *it won't work*. The 'ideological' traitors, and you should be able to hear from my voice that I'm putting quotation marks around that word, they don't make the slightest bit of difference in the long run. The only thing WikiLeaks has achieved is to make sure everybody knows that diplomats sometimes only pretend to like each other and Arab dictators have their ice cream flown in. You really think we've stopped bugging the phones of European politicians? You need to accept your father's not coming home. Even though I'm the least sentimental person in the world, Jonas, I do understand that this is a difficult message to hear, so assume that I am speaking with all appropriate measures of sympathy and respect when I say that I will personally make sure we drop the biggest fucking bomb available on the place they're holding your father if we get even the slightest sniff that you're cooking up some private deal. Leave this to the professionals. Leave this to government. It's cute, that thing on your bedroom wall, all your coloured pencils lined up, looks like something they'd produce in the day care centre at Langley, but we both know you're not a professional, not when it comes to intelligence collection – you belong behind a desk, not out on the street. You're the fat kid struggling in the grown-up end of the swimming pool, you're the cow burning in the barn. That fat ginger prick Naseby wouldn't kick loose your file so we're working up our own one. Our head-doctors are having a field day with you. They're used to dealing with American problems – the jock with anger-management issues, the overachiever who under-eats – but now they've got all this *Downton Abbey* shit to get their heads round: English uptightness, too much education, a religious childhood. I've never seen them happier. I haven't got close enough to see your teeth but I bet they're awful. You certainly look like a mess. I came close, though, didn't I? If only I'd pushed my way into that hotel room. What, were you hiding underneath the bed? Or in the wardrobe like a fucking…like a fucking talking lion? That cut above your eye is going to be nothing compared to what I do to you, you cunt. I'm almost sorry that someone else got to throw the first punch. You'll never know when it's coming. I might be sitting outside your apartment now, I might be inside your apartment already, I might be coming up behind you, swinging my fist —"

Jonas hung up.

# CHAPTER SIX

Jonas stood on his balcony. He was first made aware of the sun by the birdsong, and later by the shadows that appeared across the flat rooftops around him, crowded with aerials and wires and water tanks and hoardings. The sun began its climb into a cloudless sky. He hadn't been able to sleep. His bruised, bloodshot eye looked so out of control in the bathroom mirror that he suspected the sticking plasters he had applied were being held in place by dried blood, stiff and flaky like rust on a chassis, rather than by any adhesive quality they had retained. He was surprised at how effectively a simple plaster could evoke childhood memories. It was that feeling of playing at doctor, he thought, of cutting with clumsy fingers strips from a bundle of rough, sweet-smelling material like something from a field hospital, and camouflaging the wounds against his skin. He watched Desmond Naseby's Audi complete its third pass of the building and pull into a spot opposite the entrance. The knock at the door came just under a minute later. Naseby gestured for him to step into the hallway.

"God knows how, Jonas, but the Yanks – Jesus Christ, look at your eye!" He lowered his voice to a conspiratorial whisper. "Didn't I tell you these were dangerous waters? Looks as though a shark has been having a nibble at you. You can tell me about it later. I've got a coffee waiting for you in the car. The Americans have somehow learned of your...situation. We need to talk. No, not inside – I wouldn't be at all surprised if they've had your place bugged from top to bottom."

Jonas followed him down the stairs. He hadn't expected to go outside – he was unwashed, his hair was uncombed and he was wearing an old, oil-stained pullover of his father's with patches at both elbows. Naseby was dressed in pressed beige chinos and a blue cotton shirt; a pair of expensive sunglasses held back his sweep of red hair. As they stepped out of the building he reached above his ear to tap them into place.

"Don't worry about the car," he said. "You can speak your mind in here."

It was oddly cluttered, given that Naseby had only recently arrived in Beirut: an Arabic newspaper on the passenger seat, a pile of Lebanese and English coins, a shopping bag with flowers sticking out the top, a map of Syria marked with half-obscured circles and scribbled notes in red ink, a buff-coloured file with a rubber band around it. He tried to take it all in. There were two Starbucks coffee cups in the holders, each with the name "Richard" written on the side. Everything revealed something potentially useful. Having spent so long turning over the same old information, Jonas was greedy for something new, however incidental it might be, and he wanted to make sure he retained it all. He remembered a childhood game his parents would play with him when he was sick or it was his birthday in which he would be given thirty seconds to memorize a selection of objects on a kitchen tray before it was covered up. He had quickly learned that certain items – scissors, an egg timer, Sellotape – would always be used, because of their convenient size and the fact they were kept in the same place as the tray. He assumed the items in the car had been placed there to create a particular impression on him. If there had just been one or two things – the Fayrouz CD by the gearstick and the slim volume of religious poetry in the pocket of the door, say – he could believe that they were there by chance, but it was difficult to imagine that the pandemonium of detail on show to someone in his position could be anything other than deliberate. He remembered Naseby's three passes of the building, unaware that he was being watched from the balcony. From this point onwards, Jonas told himself, he should assume that everything was deliberate.

"An odious man named Harvey paid me a visit yesterday," Naseby said as he fiddled with his seat belt. His freckles seemed to have darkened since their last meeting. All that tennis, Jonas thought. "It's not just happening here. It seems the Americans have got a bee in their bonnet, they're sticking their oar in all over the shop. Wanting to know what intelligence you've had access to, what jobs you've worked on, what high-level US reporting you might have seen. Not to mention what the hell it is you're doing out here. The Foreign Office has had some of it, No. 10, our place, your place – I'm told it's what they call a full-court press. Ever heard of one of them?

No, me neither. More like pressing all the bloody buttons at the same time, like someone who doesn't know what they're doing."

"What does he look like?" Jonas asked.

"Eh?"

"Harvey."

"Oh, very…average." Naseby started the car and pulled out. At some point, Jonas noticed, he had put on a pair of beige driving gloves. He took a turning that led in the direction of the sea. "He spoke to me as though I was his lackey – do this, do that. You know what I can't understand? How they have the nerve to lord it over the rest of us when the single biggest theft of intelligence in history has just taken place right under their noses. On their watch, one might say. But rather than putting their own house in order they wag their fingers at us as though we have a problem of the same magnitude. And we don't, do we, Jonas?"

"What did he want you to do for him?"

"I really shouldn't say." They took a left and then a right into a scruffy narrow street edged with plastic rubbish bags. The indicator of a black Toyota behind them was flashing repeatedly even though there were no turnings in sight. Without thinking about it Jonas memorized the number plate. "But since you ask." Naseby lowered his voice to a whisper. "He wanted us to run traces on some-one called Father Tobias Hoffman. A Catholic priest who has dabbled in the hostage game. Defrocked, actually – or rather laicized, I think that's the word for it. Practically ordered me to go to the Swiss and see what they have on him. He has this theory that you're somehow in cahoots with the priest, that you've got him running errands on your behalf." Naseby looked across to evaluate the effect of his words. "To be frank, Jonas, he sounds like the last person someone as sensible as you would go to for help. Got your head screwed on the right way. I'll tell you what we've found, though, if you like, just in case you do ever run into this chap. Forewarned is forearmed, et cetera, et cetera."

He made these words sound like a piece of obscure Latin wisdom. The traffic had thickened and slowed. Jonas opened his window to let in the sounds of the street, busy like an orchestra tuning up, the engines and radios and pedestrians and horns, and the smell of the sea. His head pounded and his left eye was partially closed by the swelling. He would have asked where they were going but didn't want to acknowledge that Naseby was in control. There was a plan, he knew that much. At some point in the past few weeks he had crossed the line that separated the general public from that small group of individuals for whom there would always exist a secret strategy.

"There's really no need," said Jonas. "Thomas Hoffman, is that what you said his name was? I've never heard of the man."

"Turns out we hadn't either. There's some stuff on Google about a big success he had a year or so ago getting three aid workers freed. Saintly priest secures release of hostages, that sort of thing. In interviews he took the usual kind of anti-government position, Iraq war, Bush and Blair, blah blah, we've all heard it ad nauseam. A

European service told us he had stumbled into the middle of a release they had already arranged – one of these countries that pay ransoms behind the scenes. If anything he slowed the process down, added a few new layers that had to be smoothed out, and then the papers heralded him as the architect of the whole thing, whereas the truth was that he almost brought the house down."

They had pulled on to the Corniche and were driving by the sea, glittering in the sunshine like a thousand tiny camera flashes. The wide pavement was crowded with walkers, runners and cyclists.

"Come to think of it, grab that file off the back seat and take a look, Jonas. It's for Harvey's lot but I suppose there's no harm in you having a peek. I've never been much of a stickler for the rules, me."

Jonas continued to look out of the window. He didn't want to give any indication that Tobias's name meant anything to him. In any case, he had already read every available newspaper article that mentioned him, and he knew there was no prospect of Naseby showing him any real intelligence. Anything in the file masquerading as an official report would have been dreamed up overnight by back-room staff in London.

Naseby continued, unperturbed. "He had clearly developed a taste for publicity because he decided to have another go at it six months later, except this time the hostages ended up dying. Because of his cock-up. He says the wrong thing to the wrong person, Jonas, or he gets the politics mixed up. Negotiation is a complex business – it's more than telling people what they want to hear. He just hasn't got the temperament for it. But I expect he has learned this by now, and the hard way, after what happened last time. God knows what they did to him, but you don't come away from an experience like that without a few screws being shaken loose. Of course, his drinking will rule him out of any similar escapades in future."

"I don't know why you're telling me about someone I've never met and have no connection to," Jonas said.

"There are a few other bits of tittle-tattle, but I won't tell you about those as it's all a bit seedy – hand in the offertory box, getting a little too close to the prettier members of his flock, that kind of thing. I'm not one for gossip. Suffice it to say there's a reason crackpots like him end up in these remote places."

Jonas found himself getting angry. How many times had he denied Tobias now? It felt like an act of disloyalty to let this pass unchallenged. "Couldn't a statement like that apply just as well to you and me?" he asked, and immediately felt disappointed that he hadn't found something better to say.

Naseby continued as if he hadn't heard anything. "If we wanted anything other than gossip we'd have to go to Le Corps de la Gendarmerie in the Vatican, and I can tell you from experience that's like getting blood from the proverbial stone. Now *there's* an organization that could teach us something about secrecy. I'll take lessons from the Vatican, not the bloody CIA." He reached for the CD box and tried for several moments to open it with one hand. "Let's have some music," he said. He pressed the plastic case against his thigh to hold it in place and pulled at it with his fingertips until the case popped open, sending the disc spinning into the footwell on Jonas's side. "Be a good chap," Naseby said, his eyes on the road.

The first track was a ballad, sung in Arabic. It might have been that the sun was shining and he was by the seaside, or that he didn't know where he was being driven but sensed everything was in hand; either way, Jonas found himself thinking again and again of his childhood. He barely thought of England any more, except when he spoke to his mother. He felt increasingly disconnected from his past. It came back to him now as a series of frozen images: a vicarage, its carpets in shades of brown; a stained-glass window leaking smudged, waxy light; and a solitary, serious, dark-haired boy with a frown on his face, arranging his toy cars in a long line and inching them forward one by one. He had been an only child with few friends. There had been no one with whom he could explore the wildness inside himself. He saved his pocket money, did what he was told and found his modest portion of the things that boys long for – adventure, mystery, danger – in those hours when he took his father's keys and slipped into the empty church on his own. He would wander methodically between the stiff-backed pews and kneel to explore with his hands and his eyes the uneven stone floors like those of a long-lost temple, and when he felt brave enough he would climb the twisting stairs to the pulpit, spinning like a rocket that had just taken off, lifting through the pale light where galaxies of dust drifted. Sometimes he would pray, too. After careful consideration he had concluded that prayer in a church must be especially effective. Imagining it, he saw a rope bridge stretched across a yawning black abyss filled with poisonous spiders and woolly mammoths and sabre-toothed tigers, and he would have to consider each word carefully so as not to stumble and say the wrong thing by accident and change the world in a way he hadn't intended, and he would get eaten by all those wild animals. He only felt safe when he was back in his bedroom, managing the traffic jam that snaked across the floor.

"Do you know Fayrouz?" Naseby was saying. "I first saw her perform in 1975 – a young case officer, fresh out of training and sopping wet behind the ears. Not the old camel you see before you now." He moved his hand as though he was conducting the music and sang along in Arabic for a few lines. "I was on the hunt for my first recruitment and had zeroed in on a disgruntled minor Saudi royal who was in Beirut for the summer to pursue his passion for prostitutes and single malt. Oh, we had some enjoyable nights, I can tell you! This was in the days before all the bureaucracy that's got us tied up in knots now, you understand." They were driving into the sun. Naseby pulled down his visor and reached across to do the same for Jonas. "Abdullah worked in the Ministry of Petroleum and Mineral Resources – it wasn't so long after the 1973 oil crisis; it's hard to imagine now what a clamour there was for intelligence on OPEC's next move. Problem with Saudi in our line of work is that there are no secretaries to target, that's the difference with the Soviet bloc. Anyway, I sold him to my superiors as the next great white hope and got us a pair of extremely sought-after tickets to a Fayrouz concert. Baalbek or Beiteddine, I can't remember which one it was. He blubbed his way through the concert, promised to work for us and took ten thousand of Her Majesty's pounds. Hugged me at the airport like I was his nanny. Sentimental lot, the Arabs. I never heard from him again."

Naseby sounded his horn as a scooter swung in front of him with inches to spare. The rider's face was covered by a helmet, but to Jonas there was something familiar about his muscular build, about the red T-shirt visible beneath his sweatshirt. He touched the bruise above his eye.

"Bloody fool. Point is, Jonas, the Service gives out second chances. I got dragged over the coals for that one, as you would expect, but they're not going to let a good man get away. I don't want you to feel you've burned your bridges with everything that's happened. In fact, the message I've been feeding back to London is that you've a darned sight more vim, more chutzpah to you than anyone expected. We want people like you – we're not like the rest of Whitehall, we want people with a bit of light and shade in them."

The scooter held its position several metres in front of the car, its rider stealing glances over his right shoulder to maintain a consistent distance. When Jonas leaned forward he could see a second and third scooter in his side mirror weaving their way aggressively through the traffic towards them.

"I'm pretty sure I can smooth any ruffled feathers and get you back in," Naseby was saying. "Why don't we start with some part-time work at the embassy to see how it all feels? That way you can stay in Beirut while we sort out the situation with your father. We'll find you a quiet corner somewhere, get you back on the payroll. Shame to let all those degrees go to waste."

Jonas thought through the implications of being followed by Hezbollah, if in fact it was them. Four days had passed since Raza had told Jonas to call him if he intended to stay in Beirut. On the second day he had returned home to find a small printed doctor's appointment card, all the details left blank except for Raza's number, in his mail box in the lobby. On the third day it was a small cardboard box left just outside his front door. Jonas had already carried the box inside and set it on the kitchen table when it occurred to him that it might not be safe. The idea proved hard to dismiss. It hadn't felt particularly lopsided or heavy for its size, and when he closed the window and door and pressed his ear against it he couldn't hear any noises. There was a smell, though, something sweet and sharp. He considered – and quickly discounted – various options: constructing a pole from wire coat hangers so that he could open the box from around a corner, throwing it into a bath filled with water, leaving it outside his front door.

In the end he dropped it from his kitchen window on to the empty street below. Two grey puppies hurried out from beneath a nearby parked car to investigate the commotion. By the time Jonas got downstairs they had decided there was little of interest in a box filled with fruit, other than the unexpected hostility of the pineapple, and they soon gave up on that to chase a passing taxi. A typed note was stapled to the inside lid of the box. "To speed your recovery. Please do not be frightened of a visit to the doctor. It will not be as painful as your last visit, I give you my word. Call me. R." On the street the puppies bounced along behind the taxi like tin cans tied to the back of a honeymooners' car.

"These chaps are getting a bit close, don't you think?" Naseby asked.

The two new scooters had moved into place on either side of them. Jonas had said that he didn't know anyone in Beirut and yet here he was, four days later, being driven around by a British spy. There was no way he could agree to meet Raza now. They would know exactly who Naseby was. By his own account Naseby had spent a lot of time in Lebanon over the course of his career, and the group was known to take counter-intelligence seriously. A story had broken in the media several years earlier claiming that Hezbollah had identified a network of double agents inside the organization because of the poor tradecraft of their American handlers, who chose to meet their sources in the same Beirut pizza restaurant each time. Standard practice in such situations was to name the diplomats so that they were forced to leave the country. Things were different for the people doing the actual spying, though – they were rarely seen again. Raza had looked at Jonas's passport. He knew he didn't have diplomatic status, which meant that there wouldn't be too much fuss if he fell victim to a traffic accident or a violent street robbery.

Before Naseby had time to brake, a fourth scooter appeared directly behind them. After that everything happened within a matter of seconds. The ones at each side carried passengers on their pillion seats. With their hands they seemed to be pointing at the chassis of Naseby's car. There was the sound of smashing glass on one side and then the other. Naseby swerved and knocked into the pair on the right, who wobbled and steadied themselves before accelerating away, at which point the scooter on the left crossed over the central reservation and raced off in the opposite direction. In the wing mirror Jonas watched the third scooter turn and disappear into the oncoming traffic. That just left the man who had hit him, who waited patiently to see that his colleagues had made their escape before waving to Jonas and Naseby and peeling off down a side street.

They pulled in next to the wide pavement that separated them from the sea. Two elderly ladies in matching purple velour tracksuits marched past, their arms pumping.

"Christ almighty," said Naseby. He was breathing hard. "Are you all right?"

They got out to see the extent of the damage. Shattered glass from both rear windows covered the back seat and a single yellow stripe had been spray-painted all the way down each side of the car.

"Well, that's a first," he said. "Hooligans. Teenagers, no doubt. The car will need to be repainted, not that you'll have to worry about that. Are you sure you're all right?"

To Jonas it looked like the same yellow that formed the backdrop of Hezbollah's flag.

"Syrians, probably; they've flooded into this country since the war started. You must be shocked. I'm used to this kind of thing – someone tried to run me off the road in Baku in '86. Listen, I'll get a car to come and pick us up. We'll head to the embassy, have a proper chat in the safe speech room about next steps. Maybe even have a drink to calm your nerves. Pick out a desk, discuss a particular project we'd really like you to help us with, agree on a salary. How does that sound? There's all sorts of perks you get for being overseas, Jonas – flights, entertainment allowances, private healthcare. We'll get you out of that dingy flat for starters. And you can have that eye looked at by the best doctors in the city. The last thing you want to do is take any chances with your eyesight."

"I'm not going to the embassy," said Jonas.

It wasn't that he was afraid of rendition or his passport being seized under the Royal Prerogative. The embassy was not sovereign British territory; other than being inviolable by the host country, it didn't enjoy any special status in law. He wasn't afraid of arrest either. The British government was in the peculiar position of suspecting that he was about to cause great harm to national security but having no proof of wrongdoing. The way things stood they couldn't detain him, and it would be both highly embarrassing and legally impossible to ask the Lebanese to arrest him without providing any evidence of a crime. As for being killed or kidnapped, that was the stuff of movies.

None of which meant there was nothing they could do. Civil servants might be panicking at the limited range of options open to the government, he thought, but spies would be in their element. In situations like this they would calmly gather intelligence, identify an opening and throw a handful of deniable sand into the machinery. They would slow things down and make them difficult. They would rely on human weakness, on people's inability to stay the course, on their need for an eye specialist they couldn't otherwise afford.

Jonas took off his shoes and his socks and his father's pullover with the oil stain and the patches at each elbow. The touch of the sun on his bare skin was startling. Several people stopped at a distance to watch the peculiar man with the pale lean body getting undressed.

"What in hell's name are you doing, Jonas?"

"Going for a swim." He smiled at Naseby. "Come with me. There are no microphones out there."

"Are you mad? It'll be freezing! You don't have trunks on! And this isn't a public beach!"

"There are people swimming —"

"They're street kids, Jonas. They'll swim anywhere!"

He unbuckled his belt and took off his trousers. Dressed only in his underwear, he walked to the railings and stood above the glittering sea. He was tired of it all – of himself as much as of Naseby's efforts to control him, of the guilt he carried for deceiving Tobias and the anxiety about his father that stained every hour of every day. The water was ten feet below him. The children swimming there saw him and began to wave, encouraging him to jump.

"Jonas, we need to talk," Naseby called out. "It can't go on like this. We have to —"

He jumped.

The water was cold and he felt the breath rushing out of him. He had the sudden, curious sensation that he had sloughed off a skin, that he had been cleansed in a way that went beyond the simple effect of the water on his body, the froth of bubbles around him like a hard coating of dust that had cracked upon impact and crumbled into the sea. His descent continued. All around him was dark but he wasn't afraid. He saw himself as a child, swimming in the sea with his father and mother, and then as a young man, his head bent as though in prayer. It had not been a difficult transition to make, from churches to libraries – the atmosphere of boredom and solemnity, the deep hush. He remembered his university supervisor explaining the rules on the first day. Bold statements are bound by their very nature to be wrong. Prevailing opinion is not overturned in one fell swoop; rather it is coaxed, one inch at a time, in a new direction. A good paper should contain only a handful of novel sentences. He lived alone in a studio flat in Cambridge, cycled to his part-time job in a bookshop, spent his free hours and weekends researching the Suez crisis or the League of Nations. He would sometimes stop for a drink at a quiet pub with a fireplace and original wood beams near the station. He puzzled over whether he was in fact going out with a pretty German student writing her PhD on ice-mass distribution and post-glacial rebound until she settled the matter for him by getting engaged to her supervisor. Not once did it occur to him that his life had become subject to the same constraints as his academic work, that his conversation was footnoted and cross-referenced, his character edited of anything that might raise eyebrows, his body dust-wrapped.

He rose to the surface and gasped for air. The sun was warm on his face and around him was the sound of children laughing.

# CHAPTER SEVEN

**1**

Jonas hadn't been at all shocked by Naseby's suggestion that the Americans had bugged his apartment. In fact he thought it was likely they had, and possible that the British and maybe even Hezbollah had installed eavesdropping devices of their own. He wondered whether technicians in this field had certain locations they favoured, whether they had stumbled across each other's handiwork while lifting a floorboard or unscrewing a light bulb. It seemed an implausible notion. But his visual memory was good enough that he had spotted, coming back from a walk early one Monday morning, a pile of books that had been moved slightly to the left, and after visiting an internet cafe on Tuesday to see whether Tobias had sent him a message he noticed a new, thin film of dust across a coffee table, as though something high above it had been disturbed. On Wednesday it was a lingering smell in the toilet.

The only explanation he could think of for multiple break-ins, with the accompanying risk that a neighbour would call the police or Jonas would return early and disturb them, was that it had taken several visits to complete a full technical installation, which seemed unlikely given the size of the place, or that it was a different team – from a different organization – each time. It was also possible that they were looking for something rather than installing a device. He couldn't imagine that a search would take more than five minutes. He had taken down and burned the sprawling chart that covered his bedroom wall on the same day that Hezbollah had stopped him, and aside from his clothes, a handful of books and a family photograph he didn't have any personal possessions.

This may have contributed to his ambivalence about being spied upon. He certainly didn't feel that he had any sort of privacy that could be violated. Indeed, he was surprised at odd moments to find that the interest in him was a welcome thing, that it acted as an antidote to his acute loneliness, as though a kind of warmth was generated by those people who had gathered around invisibly to follow him on the streets, collect details for their psychological profiles and listen to him sleep, as anxious as new parents, waiting to hear what his first word would be.

Jonas knew what he was up to; he would find it impossible to criticize anyone who had concluded that he should be watched closely. His former colleagues in London would have been told in general terms of the seriousness of his case, advised to delete his number from their phones and instructed to notify the vetting department if he tried to make contact. He couldn't blame them; it was difficult to go against the prevailing culture in a community that was closed to outside influence. It wouldn't be long before his story, suitably embellished, was being circulated widely as a vaccine against a violent, transatlantic bout of disobedience rumoured to be doing the rounds. He remembered other such stories he had heard. The surveillance officer caught moonlighting for a security company. The promising young graduate who got so drunk during an official dinner in Washington that she threw up on the table. There were still plenty of people around who remembered Michael Bettaney, the member of staff who delivered a file to the KGB London resident in 1983 revealing the secret intelligence that had led to the expulsion of several Russian spies.

The saddest story of all, Jonas had always thought, was that of an audio transcriber who fell in love during the Troubles with an Irish cigarette smuggler whose telephone line she was monitoring. Over the course of a year, during which she listened to his calls every day and was turned down twice for promotion, she found herself charmed by his turn of phrase, sympathetic to his experience of a sexless marriage, moved by the account of his teenage nephew being beaten up by a British soldier and incensed by the authorities' unwarranted seizure of his two Transit vans. She engineered their meeting on the night ferry from Liverpool to Belfast. She smoked his brand of cigarettes and wore a dress of emerald green, his favourite colour. He couldn't remember meeting someone so completely on his wavelength. Their affair didn't last long, and neither did her career. She was caught when she burst into tears after hearing him on the phone to another woman just three weeks later.

**2**

Jonas returned to his apartment one evening to find seven missed calls and four voicemail messages on his phone. They were all from Maryam, the Syrian woman he had promised to help. The last message, already two hours old, was the most alarming: "I have been calling you all day, Mr Jonas." She made it sound like Mr Jones. "I need to speak with you. Tobias Hoffman gave me your telephone number but perhaps it is not working, I do not know. Can you call me? Are you at the embassy? I am using a public phone, I will be waiting here at each hour exactly." She read out a local landline number. He called her back immediately, even though it was only 5.40, but no one answered. There was no answer at six either, or at five past or ten past. At 6.20 he spoke to a Filipino maid expecting a call from her daughter in Manila and at 6.33 to a man who shouted at him in Arabic. At 6.50, Jonas's phone rang. A Lebanese mobile number showed on the screen.

"Everything is settled," Maryam said. Her voice was strained and she sounded tired. "The man said I do not need to speak with you and that he —"

"Which man?" Jonas asked.

"The man who is helping me. He gave me a mobile telephone and money for a hotel. I must meet him again at the embassy in thirty minutes. You left the country, this is what he told me."

"My flight was cancelled. What was this man's name?"

"I don't know."

"Desmond?"

"No."

Jonas remembered the coffee cups in Naseby's car. "Richard?"

"Perhaps."

"With red hair?"

"Yes."

"Can we meet now? If I ask you to, Maryam, can you come to meet me right now?"

It was getting dark when they met at the statue in the centre of Martyrs' Square. Jonas wondered if he would be able to recognize her from the small black-and-white photograph he had seen in Tobias's New Testament. Three couples were sitting on a long bench and an old man in a shabby suit was trying to sell them yellow roses from a plastic bag hanging from his bicycle handles. Jonas had worn his suit, too, thinking that it might confer some small measure of respectability on the wilder elements of his story, seeing as he didn't have Naseby's advantage of an actual embassy to bolster his version of things. He started to walk around the statue and the old man set off after him at speed. Jonas could hear bicycle wheels squeaking behind him.

"Is one of you Mr Jones?" he heard someone ask.

He hadn't known what to expect of Tobias's girlfriend, if that's what she was. He noticed that she was dressed in jeans, that she was very pretty, that she was smoking a cigarette. Thinking she had spoken to him, the old man raced towards her, the back tyre of his bicycle hopping furiously between the uneven paving stones. He used both brakes to squeal to a stop. She kept her eyes fixed on Jonas as he approached.

"When I asked him to describe you, he said that you wear a suit when you are trying to persuade a person to do something they don't want to do."

Her voice was soft and he struggled to hear her above the sounds of traffic.

"I can see why you thought it could be either of us," Jonas said, looking at the flower-seller.

"I was joking. I knew it was you. He said the suit doesn't fit."

The old man stood with his plastic bag held open so they could see the full selection of roses. He looked from Jonas to Maryam. From a distance it might have seemed that the three of them were engaged in a conversation about his shopping. She was in her early thirties, he guessed. Her dark hair was pulled back from her face and her eyes were red as though she had been crying, although it was hard to be sure of anything in the lovely crumbling light of early evening.

"I'm sorry for taking so long to call you back, and for the confusion over the embassy," he said.

"Confusion? There is no confusion. I only came to give you this." She held out what looked like a white envelope wrapped in tape. "The other man, Richard, he is helping me. I have to meet him now."

There was something theatrical about the setting, he thought, about being watched through the gloom by an audience of lounging couples and impassive stone figures while an old man sold flowers in the aisle. This was an important moment. The audience could see it too: one of the young men untangled himself from his partner and leaned forward with his elbows on his knees to give them his undivided attention. Jonas knew he was supposed to be playing the part of the capable, efficient diplomat, friendly but impartial, trained to smooth away the wrinkles of distress and confusion and hostility, but he didn't know what to say, as though he had forgotten his lines, or the whole thing was in fact an improvisational workshop he had wandered into by mistake.

"Wait," Jonas said. He took a deep breath and steadied himself. His apprenticeship had come to an end; he had to find a way to take control of the things that were happening to him. "The man you met, Richard, he isn't aware of the agreement I made with Tobias. He may have offered to help but he won't be able to do anything for you, whatever he might have claimed. It's important you understand this."

"He told me that you have some personal problems," she said, nodding, as though Jonas had just confirmed this element of Naseby's story.

"I asked him to field anything urgent that came up because I was called away. But that was before I knew that you had arrived. I'm not going anywhere now." His heart was racing. With a single phone call she could confirm Tobias's suspicions that he had been lying. "We tend to say 'personal problems' to stop people asking questions. You know, a sick aunt or something like that." She glanced at her watch and pulled her thin grey coat around her. "Look at it this way," Jonas said quickly. "Tobias told you to speak to me. Tobias asked you to put this letter in my hands. Tobias told you that I would help you with visas and anything else you need. You know that I am the person he was talking about because of the description he gave you. He didn't mention someone called Richard because he has never met him. Of course Richard said that he would help you, because it's his job to be helpful. But he doesn't understand the situation we are in. Once he realizes that, he won't be able to help you. I owe Tobias for what he is doing for me, Maryam – I owe him, and I don't want to see you waste your time."

The old man, grown impatient, held the open plastic bag between them and shook it violently. A flurry of yellow petals fell to the ground. Jonas wondered how he could have mistaken their tone for that of lovers. He pulled out a few dollar bills to get rid of him, but the old man insisted on selecting the freshest rose from the bag and pressing it into Maryam's hands.

"Why don't we all discuss this together?" she suggested. "You and Richard and me. Come with me to the embassy."

"Richard isn't aware of my agreement with Tobias. It's important it stays that way. This must sound strange, I know, but this is such a sensitive area that unfortunately it's necessary. Did you say anything to Richard about why you were here?"

"That I knew Tobias and that you had agreed to help me."

"Did you mention – do you know, in fact – what Tobias is doing for me in Syria?"

"Something to do with a church council. He refused to say anything more. He promised me it was not dangerous."

"Give me ten minutes of your time," Jonas said. "Walk with me a little."

"I agreed to meet Richard at seven o'clock."

"He's always late. It's what he's known for in the office – always being at least half an hour late for everything. Believe it or not, he was even late for his own wedding. Valerie, his wife, I don't know if he mentioned her, she's what we call long-suffering."

"Ten minutes," Maryam said.

They walked away from the statue. He wondered how Tobias would react to a call from Maryam telling him that Jonas was not who he claimed to be. She would no doubt be angry with Tobias for having placed her in such a position, and in turn he would be furious with Jonas. There was no way he would continue with his efforts to contact the kidnappers. Putting to one side the question of Maryam not being given a visa, it was inconceivable that he would be prepared to put at risk his own safety and that of the people who were helping him inside Syria, to destroy any future possibility of negotiating for hostages, all to help out someone who had lied so consistently and whose motives remained so thoroughly opaque.

"What did you think of Richard's Arabic?" Jonas asked. They were walking in the direction of the central business district. Two soldiers stood waving a steady stream of cars through a checkpoint. "He learned it here in Lebanon, you know, back in the 1970s. We shared an office for a while in London a few years ago and he would cover his computer screen with little pieces of coloured paper with Arabic words on, to help him memorize them. Or he would play the same Fayrouz song endlessly until he could sing it himself. I've always admired that side of his character."

"His phone plays a Fayrouz song when it rings," she said.

When they came to the road Maryam stepped directly into the flow of traffic and began to make her way, one lane at a time, to the other side.

"I worked with him more recently on a project that required his Arabic skills." He had to shout to make sure she could hear him against the roar of the traffic. "I was looking for someone who could help us tackle the problem of terrorist funding. You'll know as well as I do how much financial support for Daesh comes from the Gulf and how important it is – if we want to protect communities like yours – that we cut off that flow of cash." He looked across at her. She was walking half a pace in front of him with her arms folded and appeared uninterested in what he was saying. He tried to adopt Naseby's easy manner. "I had zeroed in on a disgruntled, minor Saudi royal visiting Beirut to drink whisky and chase women. We were very close to the point where Abdullah would have agreed to measures that would have regulated money transfers above a certain amount from Saudi into Syria. I asked Richard to help me with the technical details because of his Arabic. He joined us late in the evening, took one look at our table – it was covered in bottles of whisky, bottles of wine, overflowing ashtrays, you name it – and marched right out again. He said afterwards it was too smoky for him. But I heard from other people that he had filed a complaint about the way I was handling things." Jonas took out his cigarettes and offered one to her. She took it and they stopped while he fished for his lighter. "He's a bureaucrat at heart, Maryam, that's the problem." The glow from the lighter flickered across her face. She wore a trace of lipstick and her eyes were a pale hazel colour. "I'm extremely fond of him but he's just too cautious. Wants to do everything by the book. I have no doubt he will try to block your visa and cause problems for Tobias if he hears about this; that's the only reason I'm reluctant to share any details with him. He's fine to share an office with or for a game of tennis, but not for the rough and tumble of the real world."

"He was wearing a tennis uniform when I met him."

"Everything white, clean shoes, racket in a case? He doesn't like getting dirty."

"I will talk to anyone who can help me," Maryam said.

"That's most definitely not Richard. If anything, he —"

"I want to talk about the visas."

"Yes, your British visa," Jonas said. "There is a tempo-rary —"

"Not just for me. I want my mother to travel also."

"But everything is ready." Jonas patted his jacket pocket as though he had brought her a passport and ticket. "I've booked you on to a flight leaving at midday tomorrow."

"I will not leave without my mother."

"I talked about this with Tobias. If she has trouble walking it's going to be impossible —"

"Can you imagine what it is like to live in Syria today? To be a Christian in Syria? Please you must try. If you leave your house you will be stopped by men with guns who will say that you must choose between becoming a Muslim, paying a tax or being killed immediately. So nobody leaves their house. This means they cannot work and so there is no money for food, fuel, clean water. Everything which has value has been taken. My mother is sick. She needs doctors, she needs medicine, she needs to live in a house with heating and electricity. What about your parents, Mr Jones? Will you abandon your mother and father if you know they are living in these conditions?" She stopped and turned towards him. A uniformed guard watched them from the doorway of a fashion boutique across the road. "I know this is not what you agreed with Tobias. I don't have any money to give you but maybe there is another way." He had forgotten that she was still carrying the rose until she lifted it to her face. "Maybe there is something else I can do for you," she said hesitantly. One of the petals fell to the ground. In his confusion and embarrassment Jonas bent to pick it up, as though she had dropped a coin or an earring. He didn't know what to do with it. "This is the first time that somebody gives me a flower," she said.

The yellow against her skin made Jonas think of butter, of buttercups. It occurred to him that he was in a position to help her after all. If he called Naseby and told him that the price for stepping back from the edge, giving up on his father and going home was that Maryam and her mother should be given safe passage to the UK, Naseby would agree to his terms. There would be some grumbling, but the political pressure from No. 10 and the US to resolve the matter quietly would be overwhelming. Nobody would care about two extra refugees. It made him feel a little less of a fraud that he had this power, that there was an element of their relationship that was as she imagined it.

"Do you have a girlfriend?" Maryam blinked away the single tear that suddenly appeared in the corner of her eye and took a half-step backwards. "If you want, I will… I will be your girlfriend."

How had Tobias described him, Jonas wondered, that she had thought it necessary to make such an offer? What had happened to her in Syria that she was desperate enough to make such a suggestion? He repeated to himself that he was not responsible for her situation, that the worst that would happen to Maryam was that she would suffer disappointment, that his father was in a far worse position. It was essential that he resist the temptation to see the situation as complex. It might appear so, like a chessboard halfway through a game, but in fact all the squares were either one thing or another, and each piece had adhered strictly to its own law in its pursuit of the king, walled in by pawns, defended by castles. He let the petal fall to the ground.

The mobile phone in her pocket began to ring.

"It is Richard," she said. "He is waiting for me at the embassy. What should I tell him?"

He considered the options. That she didn't need Richard any more? That Jonas was going to help her instead? Neither of those would work.

"I tell you what," he said, the answer suddenly becoming clear, "why don't I speak to him? We need to discuss a couple of things anyway."

She handed him the phone.

"Richard, old boy."

There was a brief silence.

"Put her on the line, please," Naseby said. "This has got nothing to do with you, Jonas."

"Fine, fine. Listen, thanks again for stepping in while I was away. I owe you one. Maryam was just telling me how kind you've been."

"What the hell are you playing at? Why did she come looking for you at the embassy? Did you tell her you're still in the game?"

"That sounds reasonable," said Jonas. "Let's sit down in the office tomorrow morning and work through the details, shall we? I'll be in around nine. By the way, I had a quick five minutes with the ambassador today. He wants you to stand in for him at that meeting on tax reform this weekend and wondered whether you could catch a flight tomorrow afternoon."

"Listen, wait – Jonas, don't do anything stupid. You can't go dragging innocent people into this scheme of yours. It's just not right."

"What do you mean, get rid of *this* phone? The one I'm speaking on? What's wrong with it?"

"You stupid prick, Jonas. I'm the only person left on your side. I'm the only one telling London that you'll come round, that you're just overwrought, that there's no way you'll do anything reckless."

"Okay, I'll change it for another one. Listen, I'd better run. Please thank Valerie again for the meal on Sunday. Her cottage pie is the best. Let's try to squeeze in a game of tennis when you're back from Brussels. What's that? Yes, of course I'll say goodbye to her for you."

"Fuck —"

Jonas hung up.


**3**


It was later on that evening that Jonas opened the letter, once he had taken Maryam to a nondescript hotel on the other side of the city and replaced her mobile phone so that Naseby couldn't contact her. It was written on the back of pages torn from a hymnal, and what Jonas had mistaken for an envelope was in fact a carefully folded page from an Arabic Bible. The handwriting was cramped and smudged in places.

Dear Jonas,

It is midnight and I am inside a church near Aleppo. It is safer for everyone that I stay here. It is very cold and there is no electricity. In any case, all the lights have been stolen, as well as the pews, the floor tiles, the water pipes, the doors and the curtain from the confessional booth. Broken glass is across the floor in many different colours like gemstones and rain is coming through a hole in the roof. It feels right for someone like me to stay in a place like this, in a church without windows or a roof. I do not know if this makes sense. This church is also in poor condition, this is what I am trying to say. This church is defrocked. My lights have all gone out.

Can you tell that I have found a bottle of communion wine? I still know the priest's tricks, the places they hide things. They can't take that from me. A bottle of communion wine and a small piece of candle in the cupboard with the fuse box. I will allow myself one more drink and then I will stop. Please do not be angry with me. You could be my son, and yet always I feel your disapproval.

You are impatient for news, I can see it. Enough of the drunken old fool. Put him in a church and he starts to preach a sermon.

Two days ago I spoke with someone close to the church council and this morning he confirmed that he has passed them our message. He said they wish to speak with me and so early tomorrow morning I will go to meet with them. This is good news. This is very good news. I don't know why I feel so scared. I have done this before. The car, the hood and the bumpy road. If there is an opportunity I will ask to see him, to pray with him. I will explain that people he has never met are making themselves thin and tired and sick worrying about him.

The candle is almost finished. Forgive me, Jonas, I must be direct.

I wish to make peace with you. Still I do not know what to think. Have you lied to me from the first day? Your story is such a strange one. It does not matter. I do not blame you for what happens next and you must not believe that things could be different. My trust is in God, not in your codes or your helicopters. You must not believe that I am being saintly. More than most people you know that in my heart I am the worst kind of sinner. The truth is that I do not have any choice but to forgive you. When I was still a priest people would come to me each week with their sins, and because of the language that we use to speak of faith (confession, witness, testimony and so on) I would feel like a minor court official always deferring to a judge who, so the rumour goes, lets everyone off.

All right, yes, you are right, I have finished the wine.

You are a clever man, you will soon understand why Maryam is important to me. I do not need to pretend with you. I hope you are an honourable man. I don't think I will be able to forgive you if you let her down.

Tobias

# CHAPTER EIGHT

At least Jonas finally knew what time frame he was working towards. The email from the kidnappers, which had arrived at 6.42 that morning, read:

> We have recieved information that you want to negotiate on behalf of the british government for the release of a hostage. The price you must pay for his life is $10 million, not one penny less. This is not up for discussion. Thirty day's or he is executed.

The internet cafe was filling up. Jonas logged into a cloud storage website administered by a Geneva-based company and retrieved images he had scanned and saved before leaving the UK: his passport, driving licence and MI5 identity card. He had been required to return this last item before going on long-term leave. They were normally for use by operational officers who might need to prove their identity in exceptional circumstances but Jonas had been provided with one to allow him to gain entry to a heavily policed conference in Glasgow in early 2012. No one had asked to see it. He hadn't even taken it out of his pocket. He typed a message into the body of the email, attached the three images and pressed Send. It was already 9.14 in the morning, and he didn't want to waste any time.

The message you have received states that I work for British intelligence and that I wish to negotiate with you in secret for the release of your hostage. This is all correct. I am also the son of your hostage. The British government and my employers do not know that I am in contact with you.

In exchange for the safe return of my father I will give you hundreds of documents containing highly sensitive information about the West's intelligence and military campaign against your new state – information I have stolen through my work in the most secret parts of government. The documents contain the names of Western spies in your ranks, details of communications methods you are currently using that are being monitored by GCHQ and the NSA, UK and US tactical and strategic military plans to deploy troops into territories you control, the identities of your operatives in the UK and Europe who are under close surveillance and much, much more. Please do not underestimate the value of this offer. The information I am willing to give you in exchange for my father's life will set Western intelligence agencies back a generation. It will ensure that you are victorious.

I am attaching three documents to confirm my name, nationality and employment in British intelligence. We do not have much time. Please write back immediately.

Jonas sat for thirty minutes waiting for a reply. He logged out, walked around the block four times, returned to the internet cafe and waited for a computer to become free. It had always been clear to him that paying the ransom was not a viable option, even if the kidnappers could have been persuaded to lower their demands. He could have sold all his possessions, his mother could have sold their home, they could have pooled their savings and whatever money they were able to borrow from relatives or the bank, and it wouldn't have amounted to more than a fraction of the total sum demanded. The only parties able to play the ransom game were states, multinationals and insurance companies.

There weren't any other avenues he could explore. A successful approach to the Russians or the Chinese was harder than it looked, as any number of people had learned over the years, and in the early stages of cultivation and assessment of bona fides they would have limited each payment to a few thousand pounds to prevent him drawing attention to himself, raising his expectations of future reward and ruining his career as a potential double agent. Any significant sums would have been held in an overseas accrual account for years. Jonas remembered reading the file of an academic who had approached a Russian trade delegate in London looking for an introduction to someone interested in buying restricted-level research papers from a government-linked foreign-policy think tank. This had been met by a polite rebuff, followed by a cold call two weeks later from a political consultant in Prague who wanted to know whether the researcher would be interested in collaborating on a joint study into the tensions between NATO member states. He had been reading some of her work online, he said, and had been impressed by the rigour of her approach to rational choice theory and her openness to alternate readings of the data. It was how *long* everything took that put her off the idea in the end, she confided to a close friend, along with the frankly ridiculous request that prior to any payment she should send a sample of at least ten per cent of the material, that she should explore her access to other areas of interest to ensure a long-term and mutually beneficial relationship, that she should use phone boxes that smelled of wee. It was harder to betray your country than it looked, Jonas thought.

In the end it was the Edward Snowden affair that made him realize he possessed something of great value to the kidnappers, a currency more sought-after than cash: information. Jonas broke the law for the first time in his life at 11.15 one Tuesday morning. It was nine days after his father's disappearance, thirty-six days before he left the building for the last time.

The first document was a JTAC assessment of the general threat posed by ISIS, filled with the vague language typical of papers distributed widely in Whitehall with the Top Secret classification so gratifying to its readership. From there he moved on to a collection of messages from a pan-European working group about routes used by foreign fighters on their way into Syria. In the middle phase, as he became bolder, he began to focus on GCHQ and NSA capabilities, particularly against different encryption systems. A contact in Defence Intelligence shared US satellite imagery of what were assessed to be the most important ISIS locations in Raqqa. He took surveillance logs, telephone transcripts, psychological profiles, source reports, covert photographs, strategy papers, email intercepts and an internal discussion forum thread about the ethics of drone technology that he had printed by mistake but decided to include because it added a little human colour to the collection, along with a blog about Islamic theology and a guide to the principles of personal protection.

It had been surprisingly easy: he had natural access to all the information he took. Counterterrorism was characterized by the principle that whenever possible intelligence should be shared widely, both internally and externally, since it was accepted that no single team, agency or country could tackle the issue on its own. It was often said that there was no such thing as a local terrorism problem. It was also the case that everyone was terrified of not sharing something they should have shared, of the personal and professional burden of having known – and failed to pass on – something that could have prevented an attack. This meant that in gathering together his collection of documents Jonas was able to draw from a deep well of information: national and international, current and historic, speculative and corroborated, harmless and threat-to-life.

He had avoided technical methods of copying and removing the documents. Instead he had chosen to print and hide them on his person when leaving the building.

He imagined that somewhere in the basement details of his printing habits, along with those of every other member of staff, were being collected and analysed for anomalies, and so he began slowly and only picked up pace towards the end, once he had seen that no action was being taken against him. The downside to this was that he was restricted to taking hundreds rather than thousands of documents. He was also limited by the capacity of the secret compartment he had created in the space between the lining and the leather exterior of an old briefcase bought on his lunch break from a charity shop near London Bridge, which could not take more than twenty-three pages before they became faintly discernible to anyone doing a fingertip search of the interior. He considered simply carrying the documents out of the building with no attempt at concealment, on the basis that searches were infrequent and the only explanation for a hidden document was that he was stealing it, whereas one left in plain view could be forgiven as absent-mindedness, especially given the pressure he was under. But this line of defence could only ever work once, and so he went with the covert option.

At that point he didn't know what he would do with the documents. He still had some faith the whole thing could be resolved through the involvement of local church networks in the Middle East, or the payment of a small ransom by the Church in the UK. He was able to justify the theft of the intelligence to himself because he had no intention of using it. It was a theoretical last resort, a barely plausible option whose real value was that it allowed him to imagine he was doing something practical to help his father.

His plan to ask the Church of England to pay the ransom had seemed like a good idea up until the moment he had rehearsed what he would say. Then it seemed like a terrible idea. Then he thought: if I want to save my father, I am going to have to betray my country. It was his first street bump. It had been difficult to find the right person. The nearest thing he could find to a head of security was a brief mention on www.churchofengland.org of a paper submitted to the chief legal adviser to the General Synod entitled "Encryption Keys and Mortise Locks: The Challenges of Security in the 21st Century", written by a Harold Turnbull, Human Resources Director (Security and Estates). His LinkedIn profile, created two weeks before the submission of his paper, revealed a plump, bald man in his late sixties with a passion for baking and gardening but not much more than that, as though the whole laborious exercise of creating a profile had proved too exhausting a cyber challenge to overcome.

Jonas had called ahead to see if he was at work that day. He told the switchboard he was a reporter for the *Church Times*, and hung up when he heard Mr Turnbull introduce himself. It was drizzling and his newspaper was getting damp. He had stood for far too long in the same place. To pass the time he tried to decide which character from the Bible would make the best Human Resources Director (Security and Estates), whether it would be David, armed with his sling and five smooth stones, if the threat was a physical one, or Samson, who slayed an entire army with the jawbone of an ass. The Apostle Paul would be more of an interrogator, he decided, questioning staff who stumbled over the Nicene Creed or used too much incense or printed reams of documents at odd hours, and sending anyone without the right answers down the corridor to Ehud the left-handed, whose sword disappeared into the belly of the massively fat King Eglon and made his excrement leak on to the floor.

He almost missed Mr Turnbull when he emerged just after midday in a brown suit that flapped around his wrists and ankles. There was a crust of dried toothpaste at the corner of his mouth. Mr Turnbull looked unsettled, he looked panicked. He looked as he must have looked just before abandoning his LinkedIn profile – overwhelmed, saddened by this new world and its complexities. He put his hand on Jonas's shoulder and leaned in to speak with him. Jonas listened carefully ("This must be so awful for you and your mother, we are praying for you every day, I don't think what you are proposing is the most sensible path to follow, in any case we are in step with the government on this extremely difficult issue") and found himself nodding in agreement. It *was* a crazy idea. It was a *crazy* idea. But couldn't Mr Turnbull see that it was the kidnappers who were forcing this craziness upon him, that any solution to the problem of a father being held hostage in Syria was always going to sound ridiculous, that following a sensible path was all well and good if you wanted to go to Great Smith Street in the borough of Westminster, but what if you wanted to go to Syria, what if you wanted to go to Raqqa, what if you wanted to go into the heart of the Islamic State?

Of all people, Jonas thought, certainly more than his own employers, Mr Turnbull should have understood that being sensible has its limitations. After all, there were no sensible people in the Bible, at least not in the stories that everyone remembered – the ones about criminals, kings, prophets, murderers, hermits and saviours. Where would Mr Turnbull fit in? Where would Jonas himself fit in, with his pens neatly lined up, with his carefully ordered life? A nobody in the crowd, most likely, or a tax collector. The only person living boldly enough to deserve a place in the Bible was his father, he thought.

During the period in which Jonas stole 287 documents his bag was searched just twice – on a cold and foggy January evening when he wasn't carrying anything at all (but only because his printer had run out of ink), and then on his very last day, when he was escorted out of the building after being told by the director of personnel that he should take some time off. It was on this occasion that the security guards discovered the secret compartment in his briefcase. It was empty. He told them he had created it to frustrate thieves and muggers. There wasn't much they could say to that.

Late that night he removed all the documents from their hiding place in an envelope taped to the underside of his freezer drawer, scanned them one by one on to a laptop and burned the entire collection in his bath. It took him until dawn. He had turned to Snowden for advice on how to store the data securely. In the end he used a combination of TOR, manual encryption and an online cloud storage service that followed a "zero knowledge" policy of hosting and processing content without itself ever having access to the uploaded information. Jonas had previously been scornful of such companies. It had struck him as perverse, in a world where the threat of terrorism was real, to create an infrastructure that would not allow access to the information it hosted even if served with a warrant signed by a government minister. It was hard to avoid the conclusion that rhetoric about rights and freedom had become in part a marketing slogan used by profit-making companies rushing to exploit the alarm caused by the leaks. But all sides market themselves, he thought: the government generates fear of WMDs to sell a war, media companies generate fear of mass surveillance to sell newspapers. Everyone is to blame or no one is to blame. It all seemed hopelessly muddled – the public debate, his own position, Snowden's motives. He remembered seeing the footage from the Hong Kong hotel room of the large red hood Snowden used to hide himself and his laptop from secret cameras, of his paranoia that the hotel's fire alarm test was a ruse to get him out of his room – and this at a time when the US government hadn't yet even realized he had gone anywhere or done anything. It was as though Snowden's understanding of intelligence operations came largely from the films he had watched on the flight over. But Jonas had just hidden his own collection of stolen intelligence beneath a lasagne and some frozen peas, so he was hardly in a position to judge anyone. He listened to the sound of traffic on the street outside. Was that a bin lorry? Did they normally make a collection this early? Should he have worn a hood too? Did it have to be red?

It was early that same morning, while bin men were rattling lids and he was scanning documents, that Jonas learned for the first time of the existence of Father Tobias Hoffman. Or Father Tobias HOFFMAN, as it was rendered on the Cabinet Office letter. He hadn't had time to read everything properly when selecting which documents to steal. In fact, he had only chosen that particular document because its title included the words "kidnapping" and "solutions" and its first sentence made a reference to "alternative strategies which might enable a hostage-release scenario". He hadn't got any further than that.

The letter began by reaffirming the British government's position that "a ransom payment of any kind made to a terrorist organization engaged in kidnapping would i) encourage future attempts to seize British nationals; ii) be used to fund the preparation or execution of terrorist attacks, possibly against British targets; iii) assist the terrorist organization in improving its general capabilities, such as the recruitment of additional members; and iv) provide them with a perceived 'high status' that follows from being seen to negotiate successfully with a legitimate government." It moved on from this to explore the idea, described as a piece of "blue-sky thinking", that certain individuals could be asked to act as "linchpins in the public debate within the region, galvanizing opinion and building momentum towards a hostage-release scenario that does not require the payment of a ransom." It said something about the author's belief that Tobias was a

136

realistic candidate for this role and not just there to make up numbers that in the list of people given, which ranged from politicians to pop singers to sportsmen, Tobias came eleventh out of twelve, just ahead of an Egyptian poet Jonas happened to know had died ten months earlier after a long battle with lung cancer.

The paragraph about Tobias was short, certainly shorter than the poet's – possibly indicative of the fact that Tobias didn't have a Wikipedia page that could be copied. It said that "HOFFMAN, a German-speaking Swiss national, joined the priesthood as a young man and went on to have a high-profile career as a lecturer and writer in Oxford, Berlin and Rome. He turned his back on academia in 2005 at the age of forty-five and took over a small church located within the Apostolic Vicariate of Aleppo. The circumstances leading to his laicization two years later are unclear, but rumours persist about a complicated personal life and a problem with alcohol that he has struggled to control for much of his adult life. HOFFMAN remained involved in local church networks in Syria after his formal expulsion from the Catholic Church and since the start of the war in 2012 has participated with mixed success in the negotiations for at least three groups of hostages. Currently living in Beirut, his personal circumstances are likely to render him unsuitable for a public role in any campaign."

A computer terminal finally became free. He wondered whether his message had been clear, whether it had been too businesslike or patronizing. He worried that the line about ensuring they were victorious might sound sarcastic or even blasphemous. Jonas didn't think the kidnappers knew that their hostage had a son in British intelligence as it would most likely have featured in the group's public statements, and he suddenly realized that they might deprive his father of food and water, force him into stress positions or beat him as punishment for withholding such an important piece of information.

There was an email waiting.

OK, you need to send us those documents so we can see your genuine. Also youll need to take his place. This doesn't change anything. Clocks ticking. Thirty days and he dies.

# CHAPTER NINE

## 1

"Good morning."

"Who is this?"

"I am telephoning to arrange an urgent appointment to check that your eye is healing correctly."

Jonas had only answered because he thought it might be Maryam. He had taken to ignoring calls from numbers he didn't recognize after Harvey had phoned him in the early hours of the last three nights, from a different number each time, to read aloud those parts of the US Espionage Act that dealt with the theft of government property, unauthorized communication of national security information and wilful communication of classified intelligence to an unauthorized person, as well as a report by Amnesty International describing the US practice of incarcerating prisoners in long-term or indefinite solitary confinement.

"Who is this?" Jonas repeated.

"Your doctor. You came to my office for treatment after a certain…regrettable incident occurred." Jonas heard the French accent, he remembered the smell of mint and garlic on Raza's breath. "We talked about your plans here in Beirut."

"My eye is fine. It seems to be healing on its own."

"It is prudent to allow a professional to make that judgement. We are sometimes able to identify issues that the layman is not aware of. Headaches, nosebleeds, insomnia – there are many ways that a problem can manifest itself. A colleague of mine saw you by chance the other day. I don't know if you recall the encounter. He said you looked most tired and stressed."

"The bruising has almost gone," Jonas said. "There'll be a small scar, but aside from that everything is fine. Really, there's no need —"

"I am not being clear. This is my fault entirely. The eye is a very delicate organ. There may be a subconjunctival haemorrhage or an orbital blowout fracture – we simply do not know at this stage. You wouldn't want to lose your eyesight, would you? I am afraid that if you do not attend the appointment I cannot be held responsible for what follows. It may well be…life-changing, shall we say. Now, what time today would be convenient for you?"

"I'll call you if things get worse," Jonas said. He hung up.

He admired the simplicity of Raza's code. It was so effective that even Jonas couldn't have sworn at every moment in their brief conversation that they weren't actually talking about his eye. He looked at it in the mirror. A red weal the size of a worm stretched from the middle of his eyebrow towards his ear. The phone call had at least cleared up the question of how persistent Raza would be, whether he could be ignored on a permanent basis.

It was not that Jonas was unwilling to meet him again. Any contact with Raza would send Naseby and Harvey into a tailspin, which was a good thing. But it might also derail his own plans, which were at that moment rounding a corner at speed, given the recent email exchange with the kidnappers.

The problem was that he didn't know what Raza wanted. If he genuinely thought Jonas was an agent for the British, why was he merely asking for a meeting, why was he making it plain in advance that he was interested in Jonas rather than grabbing him off the street like the German with the secret girlfriend? The problem, too, was that Jonas would not be allowed any control over their next meeting. Raza would choose the time and the place, Raza would ask the questions, Raza would decide whether he was allowed to walk away.

In case it came upon him suddenly, as was the way things traditionally happened in Beirut, Jonas had done what he could to prepare. The day he had first met Raza, as well as burning the chart that covered his bedroom wall, he had piled up all his possessions – clothes, books, phone, passport, wallet – and gone through them as though he had been tasked with examining the personal belongings of a suspected terrorist whose property had been seized as evidence by the police. He listed all the journeys recorded in his passport, each item of wallet litter, every call and text on his phone, and slowly, painstakingly, began to construct a story that would explain the data. He made up a terminally ill friend in Kenya to justify three trips to Nairobi in late 2012 and a brief stint as a volunteer with an international charity to explain a week in Irbil just nine months earlier. He stored Maryam's number in his phone under the name "pizza", and over the coming days began to pad out his call log with the numbers of local takeaways ("spicy pizza", "cheap pizza", "chicken"). Every time he got in a taxi he would ask for the driver's business card, call his number and store it under his first name. He bought an introduction to Arabic and a handful of guidebooks and filled them with handwritten notes. He went to the National Museum. He sat in a minibus full of Japanese tourists on a day trip to the cedars. It would not be enough to confuse a well-resourced intelligence agency, he knew that, but it might just slow down anyone briefly rummaging through his life for incriminating evidence. The only downside was that when his phone rang these days he could never be sure whether it was Maryam looking for an update on her mother's visa, Harvey wanting to read him a description of what it felt like to be water-boarded or Ahmed the taxi driver asking whether he was still interested in that tour of the Beqaa Valley.

He didn't call Raza back. Perhaps that was a mistake, he thought, two days later, as the cream-coloured Mercedes turned a corner and nosed down the street behind him. By then it was too late. It was a quiet neighbourhood. Other than a group of children playing football in the distance there was no one Jonas could look to for help. He turned back and saw two men walking towards him. Ten metres ahead, the car eased on to the pavement. When the back door was opened fully it touched the wall of the building to Jonas's left, blocking his path. Everyone was smiling at him. They showed him their empty hands, they held out their arms as though they were preparing for a hug. History was on their side. Ninety-six foreign hostages snatched off the streets of Beirut in ten years of civil war. They had done this before. They knew how it worked.

So why did he decide to fight? Even afterwards he couldn't have said. He had always walked away from confrontation. But surrounded by three large men with experience of violence he felt an anger that surprised him as much as it seemed to surprise them. He bent to pick up a rock and swung it upwards into the startled face of the one nearest to him. Blood spurted from his jaw. The best he could do was describe it as an anger towards men who believed they were entitled to take a person and do with him what they wished. It didn't matter that they were the enemies of those men who had kidnapped his father. They were their enemies in the same way that politicians who shout at each other claim to be enemies but are indistinguishable to the rest of us.

It didn't last long. At first he tried to push past them and run, but when that didn't work he pinned his back to the wall and threw futile punches into the armour of their leather jackets before adjusting upwards and swinging for their eyes, for their throats. They stood around, unsure what to do, until one of them decided to take matters into his own hands and headbutt Jonas somewhere between his right eye and the bridge of his nose.

It was clear they hadn't expected him to put up a fight. The driver got out to open the car boot but the others shouted at him and he closed it. They pushed him flat on the floor. After a heated discussion, the two in the back seat took their shoes off and held them on their laps so that it was only their socks that made contact with his back and legs. It took a few minutes for them to find something – an oily rag from the glove compartment – to mop up the blood streaming from his nose. Even then he continued to struggle until one of them finally reached down to show him a handgun, in the same way that a distracted parent might absent-mindedly dangle keys in front of a restless baby.

From then onwards he was quiet. He could smell fuel, feet, smoke. In the square foot of car floor beneath the driver's seat there were three Pall Mall cigarette butts, twenty-seven pistachio half-shells, four unopened pistachios, seventeen splintered sunflower seeds and a chocolate-bar wrapper. They drove for forty-six minutes and made thirty-three turns, nineteen to the left and fourteen to the right. The driver only used his indicator for six of them; Jonas guessed that these were busy cross-roads where traffic policemen were stationed. Two turns before they stopped, someone slipped a hood over his head and everything went black.

**2**

"I can only apologize for the unpleasant way your day has been interrupted." Raza was seated in his wheelchair behind a desk, wearing a grey collarless shirt buttoned up to the neck. He shouted angrily in Arabic at the driver standing behind Jonas in the doorway, as though the whole thing had been *his* idea, as though Raza had been taken aback to learn that Jonas was being brought to him. "This is not how I had hoped we would meet again."

They were seated in a small, windowless, book-lined office. Jonas blinked several times, pressed the bloody towel to his nose and looked around. Framed medical certificates on the walls awarded to Raza Yazbik by the Paris Descartes University. A photograph of a young woman holding two small boys dressed in tiny suits. Shelves crammed with books by Peter Kropotkin, Joseph Conrad, Frantz Fanon, Noam Chomsky and Albert Camus, with titles such as *Combat Medic Field Reference, On Violence, Survival in Auschwitz, Guerrilla Warfare* and *The Israeli Military and the Origins of the 1967 War.* An artillery shell in the corner with Hebrew writing on the side.

Raza watched him taking it all in. "I am curious, why did you refuse to come when I telephoned you?" he asked.

"Because my eye is fine." Jonas's voice was muffled by the towel pressed against his nose. "At least, it was fine until your men attacked me again."

"What else?"

"Because of your reputation, I suppose. Because of what happened the last time I was here." Jonas touched the scar above his eye. "How is the other man?"

"It is very kind of you to enquire. He has a broken nose. I treated him after you had left. He has been disciplined. He behaved very badly, hitting you for revenge, purely because he was upset. This is not how we do things."

"You don't believe in revenge?"

"Not against someone with their arms pinned to their sides."

"How the hell do you think your men got me here?" Jonas asked. He was surprised by the anger in his voice.

"But this is not about revenge. Precisely the opposite, in fact. I wish to present you with an opportunity. First of all, though, permit me to examine you."

He angled the lamp towards Jonas, rolled his wheelchair around the desk and gently pulled the towel away from his face.

"Your nose is broken. I'll give you some painkillers before you go." He tutted. "I am forming the impression that you are not one for doctors. You are fortunate, though – no sign of infection around the eye. You really should have had stitches."

"I didn't want to spend my holiday in a hospital waiting room."

"You have decided it is a holiday, have you? Does this mean you will go home soon?"

"I think so. I've seen almost everything I wanted to see, apart from the Beqaa Valley. But I've made it up to the cedars, finally, and there's an exhibition of Phoenician artefacts at the National Museum that —"

"Please forgive me, Jonas. This is my fault entirely." His tone was light and matter-of-fact as though they were discussing something of no consequence. "I did not mean that you should tell me about the touristic activities in which you have been so energetically engaged. I know about the museums, I know about your day trip to the mountains. Let us place all of this to one side. I do not wish to put you in the position of lying. It will begin our conversation on the wrong note. You see, I know very well that you are not a tourist. In fact, this is exactly why I have asked to see you."

Raza directed Jonas's right hand to the bloody towel pressed against his nose and drew his left hand to rest on the arm of the wheelchair. His fingers sought out Jonas's pulse. "I have sent them to get some ice," he said.

So he would be accused of spying after all. The case against him was weak: that he had wandered into Hezbollah-controlled territory without a plausible reason for being there, that he hadn't been able to provide satisfactory answers to Raza's questions, that he had been observed with a known British intelligence officer. Mistakes, all of them. But what did it mean to catch a spy? A slip-up while using an alias, stolen documents, a confession. Being caught on an eavesdropping device dropping cover to pitch a recruitment target. A camera with photographs of sensitive locations or a piece of everyday equipment modified in some inexplicable way. He remembered the CIA man paraded on Russian TV by the FSB with a bag of cash, two wigs and three pairs of sunglasses. Jonas's only real vulnerability was his contact with Naseby, and he had concocted a story involving a distant aunt, a failed marriage and a coincidental meeting on the streets of Beirut to explain that away.

"Jonas, I know who your father is," said Raza quietly. "I know he was taken prisoner by Daesh last year." There was a vulnerability about the way Raza sat so close to him. He hadn't expected this. His anger returned, and he wondered how much harm he could do before the other men burst through the door. "You can see that it is out of the question for me to accept that you are here to look at ruins," he heard.

Jonas looked everywhere except at Raza. He hadn't expected this. He wanted to remember everything, he wanted time to think. *War Surgery in Afghanistan and Iraq: A Series of Cases, 2003–2007*. The initials RY stamped on the old-fashioned doctor's briefcase. *À la recherche du temps perdu, Shakespeare: The Invention of the Human*. A child's drawing in crayon of a man riding a horse through a forest. A bloodstained piece of cotton wool in the bin. A pair of wooden crutches —

"Jonas?"

"What are you talking about?"

"You have the same surname. You —"

"It's common enough."

"It says in newspaper articles that he has one child, a son in his mid-thirties."

"There are thousands of people who match that description."

"What does your father do?"

"He's retired."

"Don't be evasive. From what?"

"Teaching."

"You had a photograph in your wallet the last time you were here."

It had been taken at Halloween. Jonas was eight years old. His parents had tried to talk him down from his insistence that he should dress up as Frankenstein's monster or Dracula or best of all Freddy Krueger, because it trivialized evil, it turned it into entertainment. Even at that age

Jonas was serious. He didn't make friends easily. He felt sympathy with the view that some things should not be laughed at. But he had studied the life-sized cardboard figure in the local video shop and picked out a striped pullover, borrowed a cowboy hat and fashioned five metal blades from card wrapped in aluminium foil, and to him this argument was more compelling than anything his parents might say. They settled on a compromise, finally, and Jonas's father brought a white robe down from upstairs. His mother pinned the bottom so he wouldn't trip on it. They told him he looked like a scary ghost and he told them through his tears that he looked like his father on a Sunday morning.

He was laughing by the time the photograph was taken. His mother is holding him in her arms. Although his father is not in the picture Jonas can tell that he is there because their eyes are turned towards him, because he is the reason for their laughter, because their love for him is so apparent. His father is not there but he is everywhere, which is how Jonas used to think of God, which is how he hopes he will think of people when they are dead.

"Your father was a priest," Raza said quietly. "This was his robe." His fingers were intelligent, expert. They understood without hesitation factors such as bones, pressure and temperature. "Jonas, I do not accuse you of doing something wrong. You did what any normal person would do. You came to Beirut to feel that you are *doing* something, because the alternative is to sit in London and observe inaction from a government that will condemn with empty words the kidnapping of your father but take not one single step towards freeing him. You came to Beirut to be closer to your father. You came to Beirut to put pressure on the embassy and show them that there are real people suffering as a result of their failures.

"But they do not want you here, do they? You are already beginning to learn this. You can see their impatience, their frustration, their boredom with the whole thing. It is becoming more difficult to contact them on the telephone. They are busy with other matters or they are unable to meet with you. When you do speak with them they give you the same answers as the last time. They are unable even to pretend that they are making progress.

"The truth is that your government is indifferent to the people who elected them. They serve the elite and the interests of corporations and banks. You are a meaningless irritation and your father has already been forgotten. But we can help you. We are on the side of people like you. We are sending our young men to die in the war against Daesh, we are not standing by to watch. We are the resistance." He let go of Jonas's hand and sat back in his wheelchair. "We also have access to information in Syria that may be of interest to you," he added.

Had he come to Beirut to be closer to his father? If that was his plan, it had been a failure. He had never felt further from him. He struggled at times to remember the simple things: what his voice sounded like, how tall he was. Sometimes he thought it would have been easier if his father had died, if there had been a nothingness, a slow oblivion. Instead he was being held in a context so powerful that it had come to contaminate Jonas's memories.

He couldn't remember his father's smell, but things he had never even seen, such as the thin mattress his father slept on or the bucket of human waste in the corner of his cell, were as vivid to Jonas as his own surroundings. In his dreams he would see his father bruised and beaten at the family table, he would see him standing in the pulpit wearing an orange jumpsuit.

"Jonas?"

"Yes."

"Do you recognize any of these people?"

Raza reached across his desk and picked up a file. He placed it on his lap and handed a colour photograph to Jonas. It had been taken at a distance but clearly showed Naseby and a woman of around the same age entering a hotel.

"What are you asking me?"

"Tell me who you recognize."

"This man is Desmond Naseby."

"Do you know who he is?"

"He's a diplomat with the Foreign Office. He's come here from London to work on my father's kidnapping."

"Would it surprise you to learn that he is a senior MI6 officer? We were merely welcoming him to Beirut the other day – you can imagine my surprise when they told me you were in the car with him. He has served in Riyadh, Washington, Damascus and Cairo. Married with three children. An Arabist, currently second in command of their Middle Eastern section. OBE in 1994. You will understand it is impossible that someone of his rank comes to Beirut solely in order to assist you. What about this man?"

The photograph was of a short, athletic-looking Chinese man in his mid-forties with closely-cropped hair. He was getting out of the back of a black SUV with diplomatic plates. Jonas remembered seeing him on a payphone across the street from an internet cafe he had visited.

"He looks familiar, but I don't know why," he said.

"Have you spoken to anyone from the US embassy here?"

"A man called Harvey."

"Harvey Deng. Ex-military, veteran of Iraq, single, now a case officer posted to the CIA station. What about this woman?"

Jonas had never seen her before. At first glance she looked English. The picture was out of focus. Grey bob, glasses, dark clothing. He shook his head.

"You may not have had the opportunity yet; she arrived only two nights ago. Her diplomatic passport is ten years old and very nearly full, so we can conclude that she is not junior. She went directly to the British embassy, even though it was close to midnight. Mr Desmond Naseby was still inside."

Raza took the photographs from Jonas and replaced them in the file.

"I will come to the point," he said. "The British send out the deputy head of their Middle East division. He claims to be here to assist you, but this is merely what we call in our line of work his cover. He sees you every few days and at other times he engages in his true mission, whatever that is.

"At precisely the same time we observe a dramatic increase in activity in the CIA station. Cars coming and going, additional personnel arriving, everyone is working longer hours. And then from nowhere a second senior British officer arrives and goes directly to the embassy to meet with Mr Naseby, even though it is the middle of the night. Isn't it obvious? Something is happening – something big. And if something is happening on this scale in Lebanon it will affect us, one way or another."

"I don't understand," Jonas said. "Why have you brought me here? What has any of this got to do with me?"

"We will help you with your father. And in return, you will spy on these people for us."

# CHAPTER TEN

**1**

"Jesus, finally. Today I'm hat in hand, Jonas – I need a favour. Your office has decided to send us that report we've been asking for. Paragraph three is the relevant bit, you have to wade through a long and frankly unnecessary build-up about how much we respect each other to get to the cum shot, which is this: security personnel conducted a comprehensive search upon his final departure from the building at 1642 on blah blah blah they discovered a concealed albeit empty compartment among his belongings. Fucking Brits. Why you can't just speak normally. A concealed albeit empty compartment among his belongings. What, were you carrying a chest of drawers out of the building? Was the intelligence hidden in your top hat? The question is this, where was the compartment and what was its capacity? Are we talking matchbox or shoebox? Would it hide a camera or a laptop? What about a hard-drive tower? I'm not asking you to tell me, Jonas, I just want some help drafting our response. I've been sitting here for hours trying to make it look pretty. Paperwork is not my thing, and I want to make sure I get all the diplomatic niceties correct. To be absolutely honest with you, if it wasn't that we needed to know the potential size of the intelligence stash you're planning to sell Hezbollah in return for your father's ransom I'd favour a little plain talking. The question I always come back to is this, what do we lose by saying exactly what we think? British intelligence is going to turn the faucet off? If it's a faucet it's one of those rusty ones in the yard that trickles like a kid pissing. So far I've got this: we are requesting urgent clarification about or on – I'm not sure which is correct – the size of the compartment and its location among his belongings. It's impossible to write in this style and not sound a little prissy myself. A little prissy oneself. We also urgently request a list of the documents accessed by LEAKY PIPE in the period between his father's kidnap and his final expulsion from the building. Capital letters, right? That's how you guys do code names? We might have gone for something a little closer to the bone, something like WANDERING ORPHAN or MARKED MAN. But then we do go for more dramatic names. We called the war against the Taliban Operation ENDURING FREEDOM. You guys? Operation HERRICK. What does that even mean? What the fuck is a HERRICK? Is that a fish? We understand from our own recent experience the challenges and complexities involved in ascertaining the scale of an intelligence theft – I'm pleased with that sentence, that one'll keep the diplomats happy – but cannot urge you strongly enough to divert more resources towards a rapid and comprehensive investigation of LEAKY PIPE's treasonous activities. Our coverage indicates that he has not yet delivered the stolen intelligence in his possession to his Hezbollah contacts. As a result, we are exploring options around kinetic action with partners in the region as a tier-one priority. That's clear enough, right? Do I need to spell it out that this is going to get messy any day now? There's really no need for your employers to feel embarrassed about this, Jonas – there's no need for them to bury their heads in the sand. We've been in the same sinking boat as you are now on many occasions: Aldrich Ames, David Henry Barnett, Robert Hanssen, Jonathan Pollard. It comes with the territory. Snowden's a bit different, though. Some people in the agency will tell you that's because he's created a new category of threat, the human rights extremist, but I think that misses the point about Ed, it gives him too much credit, which is that he's as mercenary as any of the others but wants to be paid in celebrity moments rather than in cash. Awards from minor European countries, fawning interviews, honorary degrees – that kind of thing. He wants to be told that he's *changed the world.* Let's get back to it. We have informed our Israeli counterparts of LEAKY PIPE's presence in Lebanon and provided them with his biographical details, address, pattern-of-life and known selectors, as well as an assessment of his likely intentions with regard to Hezbollah. They share our extreme level of concern. We are working on all channels to secure a commitment that they will consult Langley before pursuing any unilateral disruption strategies. We had to tell them, Jonas. Mossad and Shin Bet are on the front line when it comes to Hezbollah, and if you're planning on putting a dent in their capabilities they have a right to know about it up front. I'm not trying to alarm you. We both know that nobody in London or Washington is going to agree to have you killed. That's not the way the world works these days. The question is whether the Israelis are prepared to roll the dice and take the chance that you won't sell Hezbollah something damaging. You know what they're like when it comes to protecting their interests. I was in your shoes I'd avoid opening car doors, using cell phones, walking around in your apartment at night with the lights on. Not that any of that'll slow them down. Looks like I haven't got any choice with the last line of this thing. It's part of the template, I don't even know if you can delete it. We appreciate your Service's assistance on this and other matters and look forward to working together to ensure the safety and prosperity of our two nations blah blah blah. Jesus, it's like one of those automated announcements at stations that apologizes for your train running late. Ah, you can delete it. How about this instead? We would appreciate a more proactive and forceful approach from your Service but will deal with this ourselves if full cooperation is not forthcoming. Too punchy? Screw it. Turns out I didn't need your help after all, you fucking retard. Send."

## 2

It was difficult to think of a reason to put off seeing Maryam. She called Jonas at least once a day to ask for news of her mother's visa. Soon after their first meeting he had agreed, in the face of her repeated threats to inform Tobias that Jonas was not keeping to his side of the bargain, to help get her mother out of Aleppo. He couldn't deploy any of his team, he said, citing a little-known prime ministerial injunction against diplomatic staff or their proxies crossing into Syrian territory, but he could access Treasury funds, and if she used the money to pay smugglers to bring her mother across the border that was her business entirely. It was his own fault for using the word Treasury – he had no choice but to agree to the sum of $1000 as though it made no difference to him whatsoever. In reality it left him with £243.62.

The visa was a different matter. He could have promised her anything, since in reality none of it would come to pass. All he needed was to keep her from telling Tobias that he had refused one of her requests. But for a number of reasons he didn't want to let Maryam down any more than was absolutely necessary. And so he had explained that the case he was putting to London on her mother's behalf required that he spoke to a number of government departments to bring them on board before even thinking of making a start on a draft of the official telegram, that the Home Secretary and Foreign Secretary would eventually both need to approve the arrangement in writing, that the Foreign Secretary's schedule – newspapers had published pictures of him that week taking part in a ceremonial dance in a former Johannesburg township – meant this could not be rushed. He tried to pre-empt her frequent outbursts by expressing his own frustration with a system that was needlessly archaic and labyrinthine and that presented so many obstacles to actually getting anything done, in the form of private secretaries, permanent secretaries and undersecretaries, all of whom turned out to have a view on the matter in hand.

She began to insist on seeing him after a week of this. "Did Richard return from his visit to Brussels?" she would ask him each time he mentioned Whitehall. "You said he is a bureaucrat. Maybe he will be better than you at writing letters to the secretaries in London. Maybe we should ask him for help."

The truth was that he didn't want her to stop calling him, and he was glad for the opportunity to see her again. The fact of his loneliness might have gone some way to explaining this. It was certainly the only plausible reason for the intense pleasure he had begun to take in the most fleeting instances of human contact, in his morning visit to the bakery and the words he tried to exchange on the stairwell with his elderly neighbour, to the point he suspected she had changed her routine to avoid his increasingly tiresome attentions. He even took some pleasure in Harvey's calls, in the way he addressed Jonas by name and with such particularity, in the intimacy he had been surprised to discover lurking in the ungovernable space between a bully and his victim. The calls reminded Jonas of the time he had spent his pocket money phoning a sex line. He had listened thoughtfully to the obscene endearments being whispered at him. Although he knew they were wholly imaginary they seemed more real to him than anything he had heard before, anything he had ever seen or touched. For weeks he carried around memories of the things that woman had done to him.

But loneliness could not explain everything about his wish to see Maryam again, and the argument he made to himself that the illusion of the visas should be maintained at all costs was a weak one now that he was in direct contact with his father's kidnappers. There was little damage Maryam or Tobias could do at this point. She didn't know enough to tell Naseby anything of importance, even if she did contact him again, and Jonas had already admitted to the kidnappers that he was acting on his own. Tobias and Maryam had each served their purpose and could be set to one side. But still Jonas checked for emails from Tobias every day, and he found himself thinking about Maryam at odd moments throughout the day. Things such as, I wonder what Maryam is doing right now, I wonder what it would feel like if Maryam was walking down this street at my side, I wonder if there is anything I can buy that would make Maryam smile again. Thoughts that carried more of a gravitational force than their bright, weightless appearance might have suggested. For the most part he skirted a frank admission of what would have been immediately apparent, if only he'd had someone to talk with, in order to avoid sharp-edged feelings of guilt and betrayal. It was only in the very early hours of morning, somewhere in the deniable space between sleep and wakefulness, that he was able to come anywhere near the idea that he had already betrayed Tobias so completely, so flagrantly, that a second betrayal could not add to his guilt in any meaningful way. "In for a penny, in for a pound," he said aloud one of these mornings, to no one other than his invisible listeners, before rolling over and falling asleep with a sigh.

It was the prospect of not seeing her again that made him prepare so thoroughly for their meeting at a cafe near the fairground. The last thing he wanted was for her to realize he had been lying all along. He combed his hair, put on a tie, attached a luggage tag to his new briefcase to suggest he'd recently flown in from somewhere and downloaded an app that would make his phone ring at a prearranged time, at which point he planned to apologize for the interruption and turn away to speak with Richard or the ambassador or one of the many secretaries in London who were working so hard on Maryam's behalf.

But Jonas was surprised to find that she was in no mood to discuss her mother. She hadn't even sat down and she started firing questions at him.

"What did you do to Tobias? Why did you make him go to Syria? Did you know that Daesh arrested a priest?"

The cafe was across the road from the Corniche, and beyond it the sea. A huddle of old men talked fishing rods at the railing. Behind them a group of teenage boys slouched in folding chairs, their legs long and bent like those of a spider, waiting to see what passing girls they could trap. Where it touched his shoulder, Jonas could feel the window vibrating with the dance music from their car stereo.

"A British priest has been held hostage since last year," he said. He stood and tried to pull out a chair for her, but she was in the way and wouldn't move. "Is that who you mean? I haven't heard anything to suggest —"

"People are saying there is another one – a new one. This week." Her arms were folded. "When did you hear a message from Tobias the last time?"

"The letter you —"

"The letter I gave you? What? This was the last time? But he wrote this more than ten days ago!"

"The fact we haven't heard from him doesn't mean he's in trouble," Jonas said. He was standing next to her. He could see fine lines around her eyes and mouth that belonged to a happier person. At the table next to them four school students argued over a laptop. "I advised him not to send messages unless it was absolutely necessary. There are always rumours floating around. Most of the time they come to nothing. Please, Maryam, sit down and tell me what you've heard."

She remained standing and shook her head to repulse the advancing waiter. Her dark hair was tied back with a rubber band and she was wearing jeans and a loose blue shirt. She held a mobile phone clenched tightly in her right hand and with the fingers of her left hand she scratched violently at her thumb until blood showed.

"The caretaker of Tobias's church heard it from his neighbours; they have a nephew who is married to a woman from Raqqa. And I have a cousin who was forced to become a Muslim and join Daesh." She closed her eyes as though she wanted to remember everything. "He tried to leave but they will not let him, he needs permission even to travel to the next town. He is not allowed to speak with his parents because they are Christian, but he hides a telephone from everyone around him. He told my uncle there is a foreign priest in the prison in Raqqa, he knows this because he saw him three days ago, he is not the very old one who was on the television before. It was the first priest he saw for a long time. He wanted to say something. He wanted to smile at him and ask for a blessing but he is afraid because the other fighters will kill him if they know he is still a Christian." She opened her eyes. "I told my uncle to find out where the priest is from."

This is real intelligence work, Jonas thought admiringly, this is the way to run a network: understand the sourcing chain, take into account motivation and access, task and re-task in search of greater clarity. "Has your cousin seen the other priest – the older one?" he asked.

She waved away the question. "What are you doing to help Tobias?"

"Even if it was Tobias that your cousin saw, and we can't be sure that it was, it doesn't mean that Daesh are holding him hostage. Remember that he has been there before. He knows what he's doing."

"What is so important that he must go back there? What is he doing for you that no one else can do?"

Jonas wasn't sure he knew the answer to her question. He hadn't heard from the kidnappers for four days. Everything had gone quiet after he had sent them three sample documents in response to their demand for the entire collection. He had tried to make sure that the samples were of high enough value that they would demonstrate he had access to intelligence of real interest and relevance, without giving away anything too important. But with each day that passed he found it harder to resist the conclusion he had somehow made an error of judgement.

The first document, much of which Jonas hadn't fully understood, had been a paper outlining the technical countermeasures being developed by the Five Eyes community to protect government websites from the ISIS cyberattack programme, which had taken down the US CENTCOM Twitter account. In what he imagined would be a useful conclusion, the paper identified those official websites its authors judged remained most vulnerable to attack, particularly of the "cross-site scripting" or "format string vulnerability" types. He added to this a GCHQ sigint report that contained verbatim transcripts of an ongoing email correspondence between one of the kidnappers and a Cyprus-based facilitator who was in the process of buying five specialist rifle scopes through a criminal associate. Jonas felt the final document should focus on something human, something that would appeal to the kidnappers on a personal level, and so he chose a surveillance report detailing the movements, on a given day, of a young man at least one of them had grown up with in London who had tried and failed to join them in Syria on a number of occasions, as he went between a gym, a bookmaker's, a mosque, his girlfriend's flat, a Poundland shop and the Camden High Street branch of Chicken Cottage. "I have hundreds and hundreds of documents similar to these but of much greater value," Jonas wrote in the accompanying email. "Please seize this opportunity. Nothing will be the same after this."

"When will Tobias come back?" Maryam asked.

"It's very hard for me to make those decisions for him," he said. "The thing to remember is that he has been there before and spoken to those people before. It's a difficult position he is in, I accept that. But this was something he felt he could do."

"You keep on saying this. You think that if everything happens this time like it happened last time, Tobias will be fine. You think that because he went there and came back everything was all right. Do you know what happened to him? Do you know what they did? The guards wore masks. They gave him electric shocks all over his body and they hit him more than one hundred times with the generator belt from a truck. They put him in a position called the scorpion. One hand is pushed behind his back and the other hand over his shoulder and they put on handcuffs so he stays like this for a long time. Now tell me, do you still believe that he will be all right? Do you think he will survive that again?"

Jonas sat down. If he turned one way he could see the old lighthouse; if he turned the other he could see the Ferris wheel. It looked as though they both belonged to the fairground, as though the lighthouse was a helter-skelter ride, nestled at the edge of the city.

"We don't know that this is what's happening, Maryam," he said. "We have your cousin, someone under an enormous amount of pressure, who has seen someone he thinks is a priest in a Daesh prison. Was this person wearing a priest's collar? Was he being held for an hour or a day or a week? Was he being mistreated? Is he still there? We don't know the answers to any of these questions." It didn't cross his mind any more to ask himself whether he believed his own words. Whatever moral equation he had been trying to balance had long since collapsed, leaving him with a jumble of elements but nothing to connect them, no plus or minus or equals. "What I can tell you is that I wouldn't have asked Tobias to go and he wouldn't have said yes if we didn't both believe that it was important enough to justify the risks."

"Tobias will always say yes if you ask him for help. He is not the right person to say if he can do this again." Maryam took a step towards Jonas. The blood on her finger had marked her jeans. There were tears in her eyes and she was shouting. "You know this. This is how you work. You find people who are in a difficult position, you make them say yes and then you tell yourself that they are doing it freely. Does Tobias look like a healthy person? Does he look like a person who sleeps properly, does he look like a person who is happy? Does he look like a person who is strong enough to go to the worst place on the earth and make a deal with murderers and torturers and rapists and slave traders? Do you think it will be a problem when he vomits because he hasn't had a drink, that he won't be able to think clearly because his head is hurting all the time and he can't sleep? Do you think it will be a problem if they smell alcohol when he sweats?"

My father is going to die, he wanted to tell her. The world is not allowed to proceed as normal. "This is how intelligence works," he said quietly. "The targets are damaged, we send damaged people after them."

"What kind of person are you? Why don't *you* go there?"

"I *am* going there."

Tears flooded her eyes. Everyone in the cafe was looking at them. He watched her pick up a glass and then pause, uncertain as to what she should do next. He nodded imperceptibly as though giving her permission. The least he could do was accept unflinchingly whatever pain she wanted him to experience. She flung the glass at him. It caught the side of his head and spun off to skitter across the neighbouring table, cracking the screen of the children's laptop on the way.

As she walked out, Jonas's phone began to ring. The thought that there would be no one at the other end made him feel very alone.

**3**

There was an art to the practice of the dead letter box. Raza had chosen the location carefully. Although it was dark, Jonas knew that he was walking in the right direction because he could see the old lighthouse ahead of him, rising above the buildings that surrounded it. Its white stripes floated like smoke rings into the late evening gloom. Somewhere behind him a car engine started.

The road narrowed. Other than a Filipino maid walking two small dogs there was no one around. He had received instructions in a typed note pushed under his door that morning. "From now on this is how we will communicate with each other. Memorize the map." A detailed pencil sketch of the neighbourhood was on the back of the piece of paper, along with a new mobile number and the instruction that it should only be used in emergencies. "Make sure to visit other places before and afterwards. Near the bottom of the lighthouse is a wall with a circle of green paint. Pull out the stone that is three to the left of this. There is a metal lamp post at the end of your road. Someone will tie a piece of red string around it each time we put something there for you. Check at least once each day. If you have left something for us, place a piece of chewing gum on the same lamp post at head height. There is something there now. Go tonight."

The headlights of a turning car strafed the trees and the buildings and allowed him to pick out, even at this distance, a momentary burst of green near the base of the lighthouse. He thought about a cover story. Taking photographs, treasure hunt for a friend, for a child, for the child of a friend. Geocaching. Historian, amateur archaeologist. A cat trotted parallel to him on a wall, its head upright and its back arched as though performing dressage. Jonas knelt to tie his shoelaces. The stone came out easily. As he walked away he pushed the bundle into his pocket. No one shouted at him, no one came running after him. No one shot at him.

He didn't look until he was inside his apartment. It was hard to make the bills lie flat. Two hundred dollars in twenties. "We are getting something for you," the note read. "Proof that your father is still alive. Look for the signal."

# CHAPTER ELEVEN

## 1

Jonas recognized her immediately from the photographs he had been shown by Raza. In person she looked a little greyer, a little older, in her mid-sixties at least, as though she had aged in the few days since the picture had been taken. The door to the embassy interview room clicked shut behind him. On the wall was a notice reminding applicants that any false statements would result in their visa being denied.

"We've not met before, have we?" she asked in a soft Edinburgh accent. Her hair was cut in a severe bob and she was wearing a black roll-neck sweater. "Not properly, anyway. The odds are we've passed each other in a corridor once or twice. My name is Meredith. I hope you won't mind if I dispense with formalities and call you Jonas. I'm afraid we've been a little incoherent on our side. Lacking clarity, generating more heat than light. That's why I'm here. To slow the conversation down, give everyone a chance to say what's on their mind, allow us both to draw breath." Her eyes crinkled at the corners like cigarette paper when she smiled. "How does that sound to you?"

"I'm not sure I know what you mean," said Jonas. A camera watched him from a small black dome in the corner of the ceiling. "Before he turned up at my door this morning I hadn't seen Desmond Naseby for over a week. There's a CIA man called Harvey who sometimes phones in the middle of the night to threaten me, but I wouldn't call it a conversation."

"You're taking what I said literally." Her smile widened as though he had said something funny. "I'm characterizing what has happened as a conversation. You taking the documents tells us something. It's a form of communication. It says, I am angry because you are not doing enough, or I think you can do more with the resources at your disposal. Both of those are legitimate reactions to your father's situation. Desmond coming round to see you at your flat, putting to one side what he said to you and the way that he said it, that was our first attempt at a reply." She leaned towards him. "We were *trying* to say: we are worried about you, we want to know what is happening, we want you to understand the seriousness of what you may be thinking of doing."

"We know where you live. We can reach out and touch you whenever we choose."

She sat back in her chair. "I am not suggesting it was a well-scripted reply. It was rushed, it was muddled, it must have been upsetting to hear. My point is that we are in the middle of a conversation, not that we have been conducting it particularly well. On either side."

Jonas felt a little giddy. The glass Maryam had thrown had left him with a large purple bruise just below his hairline and a headache that wouldn't go away. Halfway through his second sleepless night he had gone to an all-night pharmacy and been sold a packet of pills by the teenager on duty that had left him feeling theatrically light-headed, unfocused, half asleep all the time rather than asleep half the time. His heart raced when he climbed the steps to his flat. The persistent drone of the doorbell that morning had worked its way into his dreams in the form of a dentist's drill, then as a scooter being driven away at speed and finally as a quiz-show buzzer that he kept on pressing even though he didn't know the answer to any of the questions he was being asked.

"That's a very modern way of looking at it," he said. "The thief steals in order to communicate something to his victim." He felt dangerously talkative – he would have to be careful. "That might be the case with a crime of passion like assault or murder. But maybe the thief just wants what he's stolen. Maybe he had hoped it would never even be missed."

"If the thief and his victim are strangers, perhaps. But one friend stealing from another? A child from his parents? An employee from his employer? Perhaps we can agree that there's more than one motive at work. I'm a great believer in complexity, Jonas. Complexity and mystery. It's the old-fashioned churchgoer in me. I've come to the conclusion rather late in life that if something looks simple, it's because you can't see all of it." She beamed at him. "What do *you* think?"

He looked for the buzzer. Another question he couldn't answer. He tried asking one himself.

"What exactly is your role in all this?"

"We've wandered a little off track already, haven't we?

That's probably my fault. Why don't I tell you how I see our conversation unfolding today? I am going to do two things for you and in return, Jonas, I want you to do two things for me." He tried to shift in his chair and discovered it was bolted to the floor. "Number one: I will give you as much of an update as I can on your father, his current situation and our rapidly evolving plans on what we might do to help him. I won't give you any fabricated intelligence reports, any news articles dressed up as CX, any weather forecasts. I won't pull any punches. Number two: you will tell me exactly how many documents you took. At this stage I don't want to know where they are or whether anyone has seen them. Number three: you will press pause on any discussions you are conducting with third parties concerning the documents. Number four: we will agree on one reasonable thing that we can do for you. It might be money, it might be a plane ticket and a comfortable hotel so that your mother can come out here. It won't be a desk in the embassy or your old job back. It won't be immunity from prosecution. We both know those are out of the question. Now, what do you think about all that?"

"It's an ambitious agenda," conceded Jonas.

"We'd better get started, then."

## 2

Raza's blurry photograph had failed to capture the spirit of twinkling amusement that lay just beneath the surface of her character. Jonas might have thought it was something she was doing for his benefit if she hadn't clearly been so concerned to keep it in check herself. Her hands, whenever he said something that pleased her, would flit towards him like a pair of swallows, and her smile would broaden until it triggered a sudden frown, cast forth like a spring-loaded net to keep her native exuberance under control, and she would look serious for a minute or two at the very least. It might have been sympathy that she was trying to express. His appearance had the potential to confuse the issue at hand. It was not just that he looked like a victim (the purple of one bruise, the yellow of another), but that it would be easy to conclude from the evidence on show – the unwashed, mustard-coloured T-shirt, the pair of beltless suit trousers cinched at the waist, flip-flops – that he was failing spectacularly to cope. The truth, however, was that he felt more himself than he had for a long time.

She was talking about his father.

"We are presented with an unexpected opportunity. A window that may or may not open just the tiniest wee crack, but wide enough for us to slip through. I'm not going to give you much more detail than that, Jonas, because of the situation we are in, but I will say that we believe your father is being kept in one place and that he may be moved to another place in the next week or so. The place he is in now is one that we cannot get to. The place he will be moved to is one that we believe we can get to. This is the good news. The bad news is that he is being moved because he is very unwell. It's quite possible he won't survive the move, and it's more than possible he won't survive any rescue attempt we make. These things tend to be fairly…chaotic. Lots of noise, more than a few flash-bangs." She clapped three times to illustrate her point. He noticed that she wore a digital watch, that she wasn't wearing any jewellery on her hands, that her nails were painted black, as though they had been trapped in a door. "There's no way of doing this kind of operation gently, and it'd be unfair to ask the soldiers to try to find one. Now, I would normally ask if you had any questions, but since I won't be able to answer them, shall we move straight on to number two?"

"What's wrong with him?" Jonas asked.

"Wear and tear. How many documents did you take?"

"Two hundred and eighty-seven."

The smile disappeared from her face. "Thousand?"

"No. Two hundred and eighty-seven."

He didn't mind telling her. It wouldn't take her long to realize that in its own way two hundred and eighty-seven was just as dangerous a number as two hundred and eighty-seven thousand.

"Well! That's…" She sat back in her chair, tilted her head to one side and looked at him as though seeing him for the first time. "I'm at a loss for words, Jonas." She laughed suddenly in a way that made him want to join in. "We had been bracing ourselves for a larger number. After Snowden."

He shrugged. "Americans tend to do things on a bigger scale."

"You've restored my faith in humanity," she said. This time one of her hands made it all the way across the table to rest on his forearm. "That's my strictly off-the-record reaction; I don't think I'd get the Chief to put his initial to it." Her grey eyes twinkled. "We had been working on the assumption that the secret compartment in your briefcase was for USBs, CDs, portable hard drives, all positively brimming over with gigabytes of our most precious data. But you're telling me" – she gave Jonas her broadest smile yet – "that you smuggled *pieces of paper* out of the office, have I got that right? How wonderful! How absolutely wonderful!" She leaned back and clapped her hands. "I was sure that the age of such finesse and delicacy was behind us. Wiser heads tell me the future of intelligence work lies in harvesting data and putting the algorithms to work like threshers. We obtain data in bulk and people steal it from us in bulk. Snowden can't have read the tiniest fraction of what he stole, which is why so much of it was dinner menus and parking directions." She sat back in her chair and frowned as she thought it through. "But you chose what to steal with *care*, didn't you, Jonas? You selected which documents to take and which to leave behind, you considered the market and curated a collection that would meet its needs. At the end of the day it doesn't really matter how big that collection is, does it? A dozen pieces of paper could set us back years."

**3**

"I'm one of the lucky ones," she was saying. "My career started in the golden age of espionage. In twenty years the business will be unrecognizable. There'll be no cultivations demanding years of persistence and guile, no moonlit infiltrations by boat. Tradecraft will be about passwords and IP addresses. There won't even be alias names. Instead we'll pay our agents with bitcoins, email them equipment via their 3D printers, debrief them by encrypted text message. That's if we even need agents any more. You only have to look at how criminals are evolving. Imagine…a robbery. A jewel robbery. You start with the preparation: reconnaissance, recruiting an insider, assembling the team, a dry run the week before. Think of how many factors conspire to make it a success or a failure: the traffic, the weather, how well the locksmith slept, whether the driver can hold his nerve. And then, assuming the whole thing goes off without a hitch, the massive police operation that begins immediately: the physical evidence, the cameras, the question of how to offload the jewels. Now compare all of that to the cybercriminal operating from the basement of his parents' house, crossing time zones and jurisdictions at the click of a button, launching hundreds of raids every single day, at no cost and with next to no personal risk. That's the direction we're moving in. That's the future of spying, Jonas. It'll all be done online – by programmers, by teams of social engineers. If you want to know where someone's been, ask their phone, ask their car, ask one of the six million cameras around the UK. If you want to know how long they've been away for, ask their fridge how full or empty it is, ask the central heating when it was last switched on. If you want to know their sexual preference, ask Google.

They call it the internet of *things*. Show me a human agent who can deliver on that scale. Did you know half of all the vehicles stolen in London last year were broken into *without* the use of force? That's computers. That's the future right there."

It was over in a second, but Jonas fancied that he saw her make a fist and tilt her hand as though showing off her digital watch, as though to Meredith there was no better proof of the future.

**4**

"We're making good progress. Thank you for bearing with me." She smiled. "Number three. Negotiations to be put on hold."

Jonas could barely imagine she existed beyond the small interview room. He wondered whether she had grandchildren, a husband waiting at home, neighbours she greeted each morning on her way to the Whitehall department where she performed a vague set of administrative duties that were frankly too dull to talk about. There was only Raza's blurred photograph to prove that she wasn't a product of the chemicals acting upon his overheated brain.

"You need to press pause for me," she said.

She had made the same request three times. Why was it so important? His agreement wouldn't mean anything, and he knew that she knew it wouldn't mean anything. She would have been trained to treat the word of someone she believed to be sincere with suspicion – the word of a traitor like Jonas would be less than worthless. The only way it might mean something was as a test of his good faith, and that was a test they could only adjudicate on if there was some form of independent corroboration – if they could expect to learn from another source whether or not he had kept his promise. British intelligence and their allies had agents inside Hezbollah, inside ISIS. Had Meredith recruited one of Raza's men? Was there an agent close to the kidnappers? Is that why she didn't want to know if anyone had seen the documents, because she already knew the answer? It was possible they were closer than he had expected.

"We need to talk about this, Jonas," she said. "You're not in a strong position."

"And yet you've flown all this way to see me."

"To give you a way out. After all, you've just admitted breaking the Official Secrets Act."

"There's no case against me," he said. "We both know that. It's hard enough to convict people under the OSA when you catch them red-handed. There's no physical evidence other than a compartment in an old briefcase, and it'd be difficult to use this interview as proof of any-thing – you haven't told me who you are, you haven't informed me of my rights." He slipped his feet out of the flip-flops and was revived by the feel of the cold tiles against his skin. "Besides, let's not forget that my father is a hostage. It would look bad."

"I'm an intelligence officer, not a police officer," she said. "I'm not interested in evidence or prosecutions.

I appreciate you telling me the number of documents you've taken, but what I really want you to do is to stop looking for a buyer."

"And in return?"

"What do you want?"

"Pay the ransom."

"You know we can't. The government's position is that it would be wrong —"

"Wrong has nothing to do with it," he said. That warming anger again, like a new friend. "Who in government even uses words like 'wrong' any more? Necessary and proportionate, that's how we justify what we do. That's why we distort intelligence for political purposes, that's why we listen to the conversations of innocent people, that's why we break into the hotel rooms of foreign diplomats doing nothing more than serving their country in the same way that we serve ours. Your argument is that the downside of paying ransoms, which is that it will lead to more kidnappings, is greater than the upside, which is that it results in hostages being freed. But that's clearly not the case in this instance. If what you are accusing me of is true, the upside is that the government avoids a catastrophic leak of the most sensitive intelligence imaginable. The balance has changed."

"The government cannot pursue a private course of action that is completely at odds with its public position."

"What are you talking about? What's SIS *for*, then? Look, use an intermediary. A wealthy businessman from the Gulf, a charitable foundation in Pakistan or Indonesia, the government of one of those European countries that isn't so squeamish. There are countless options. It'll be a little messy, but nothing compared to what will happen otherwise."

"Whitehall would have to agree, No. 10, the Foreign Office. It would mean going back on a long-held position. It's just too…complex an idea."

"Maybe that's the difference between us, Meredith. I'm a great believer in complexity. It's the old-fashioned churchgoer in me."

"Listen, Jonas, the prime minister is not going to stand up in Parliament and lie, nor is he going to say that he has reversed the government's position since time immemorial because he was put under pressure by a single individual. But we are getting ahead of ourselves. We have been discussing a possible rescue operation. This should be an easy decision for you to make. Press pause on negotiations and we will see what happens over the next few days. In the meantime," she said, "make a reasonable request and we will grant it. Number four."

Press pause, press pause. The phrase must have been written into her script by the psychologists. She had said it so many times now that he could see her gleaming black fingernails tapping against the controls of an old stereo as she filled mixtapes with data about fridges and cars and central heating systems. He wondered if there might be something slightly hallucinogenic about the medication he had been given. He wiggled his toes on the cold floor. If his father was as ill as Meredith claimed, he would have expected the kidnappers to be rushing to trade him for Jonas. But he hadn't heard anything from them since he had refused to send the entire collection of documents in advance of any exchange. It was possible his father was already dead. He wondered how he would learn of it, whether Meredith or Naseby or Twitter would get there first. Harvey would take some pleasure in being the one to break the news, he expected.

"There is something you can do," Jonas said. He suddenly felt very tired. He fought the urge to lay his head on the table.

"Good. What is it?"

"Two British visas."

"That's the second time today you've taken me by surprise," she said. "Who are they for?"

"A Syrian woman and her mother."

"Out of the question. We're not going to do anything that might in any way enable or move forward this madcap plan of yours."

Jonas could feel the medication take a physical hold on him. Drowsiness billowed up behind his eyes as though his head was stuffed with the softest bed sheets imaginable.

"They're not involved," he managed to say. In the silence of the interview room he could hear his eyelids clicking each time he blinked. "It's got nothing to do with them."

"This woman *is* involved, though, isn't she? Desmond has mentioned her. She's linked to the Swiss priest in some capacity."

"She knows nothing about this," he said. "She doesn't know what I am doing, she doesn't know about my father. She hasn't consciously or unconsciously done anything to contribute to where we are today. They're a Christian family – they won't have links to ISIS or any of the other extremist groups. I don't know what else to tell you." He held the seat of his chair with extended arms to prevent himself slumping. "If you give me some time, I'll pay you back for their flights and as many of their other costs as I can."

"Speaking personally, Jonas, I was hoping you'd ask us to bring your mother out here. I had a son around your age. He —"

"This is not open to negotiation, Meredith," he said. "I won't talk to you after this if you don't agree. There'll be no deal on anything."

She was quiet for a while.

"I'll have to talk to London," she said. "We'd need to screen them. An interview, background checks. And if we found anything remotely questionable there'd be no way —"

"This week."

"I'll see what I can do. No promises." She looked at her watch. "You look tired. That's probably enough for today. I'd like us to stay in touch, Jonas, if you don't have any objections to that idea." She reached across and stroked his hair. Her smile was filled with sadness. "You poor boy. Shall I tell you about your mother? I went to see her before I came out here. She's lost the two men in her life all at once. It's not easy for her. She made me tea and showed me pictures of you as a bairn."

He couldn't keep his eyes open any longer. His mother had come to London to see him before he left. He remembered packing his bag while she stood anxiously in the doorway trying to persuade him not to go. She only half believed his story that it was a routine work trip. She was crying. Shirts, socks, trousers. Sweaters. He knew the Beirut winters could be cold and wet. He found it difficult to listen to her and focus properly on what he was doing at the same time. He knew that he had forgotten something. She told him she didn't know if she was angry or sad. She told him that she didn't want to lose him as well. Part of the problem was that he didn't know what he might need, or how long he would be away for. He went through his cupboards. Hiking boots? A guidebook? A torch? His father would need clothes to wear once he was released. Jonas took a suit from the wardrobe and folded it into his suitcase, and when he turned round to ask his mother a question she was no longer there.

# CHAPTER TWELVE

## 1

On Tuesday night it wasn't there, on Wednesday morning it was: a piece of red string tied around the lamp post at the end of his street. Jonas had barely walked for five minutes in the direction of the lighthouse before he was forced to turn away by the team that aggressively followed his every step. They were not making the slightest effort to remain hidden from view. It was a tactic he had never come across in his career. In the intelligence world secrecy was prized above all else, even success. An unsuccessful intelligence operation was not one that failed to achieve its goals, since it was accepted that this would happen on a regular basis, but one that revealed itself to the opposition. And yet deliberately revealing itself was what the team seemed to be doing. He felt at a huge disadvantage. He had learned in recent weeks it was possible to lose surveillance that wanted to remain covert – they had to rotate personnel, they had to keep a certain distance. But he had no idea how to lose a team that behaved like this.

He struck out for a different part of Beirut. The man following him was stocky, dark-haired, in his thirties. He looked Mediterranean. He kept a distance of between fifteen and twenty paces as long as Jonas remained clearly visible. When they entered a busier neighbourhood a second man of a similar profile came forward and together they narrowed the gap to around ten paces. They were not content to watch from the opposite side of the street but would step into traffic the moment that Jonas showed signs of crossing the road, so as to prevent him building up even the smallest advantage. After thirty minutes the individual in the lead position was replaced. They made cursory attempts to avoid third-party interest by pretending to check their phones or look in shop windows when forced to stop or slow. The first time Jonas flagged down a taxi they called forward their own vehicle, a black Honda SUV with three aerials and a broken front-left indicator, but when he tried the same tactic an hour later, this time using Beirut's one-way road system to prevent the Honda getting into position, a dark green scooter appeared from nowhere to pick up the man who had been on foot.

It wasn't until early evening that he spoke to one of them. By that point, he calculated, they had spent over five hours and forty minutes walking through six different neighbourhoods, and he had seen nine of them closely enough that he would remember their faces. At no point in the twelve or so miles had they come close to losing control of him. Jonas turned abruptly to enter a restaurant in the Hamra district. The man in the lead position, further back than he should have been and sensing that something had just happened, rushed forwards. Jonas stood off to one side and watched the man hurry around the room, looking at each of the diners in turn, until the young waitress approached him to ask a question in Arabic that he didn't answer. When she suggested in English he might like a table by the window he just shook his head at her, as though by remaining silent he had successfully concealed his origins.

Jonas stepped into the man's path as he headed for the door. "Who sent you?" he asked. "Do you work for Harvey or Meredith? Remind her that we had an agreement —"

The man pushed past him with such force that although he had been braced for it Jonas was spun around and lost his footing. The marble floor was cold and smelled of lemons. The room had gone quiet. For a moment, staring at the floor, he thought about leading the team towards Raza, but he knew that none of this would make any sense to him, that more than anything Raza would want to know why a full surveillance team had been deployed against the unimportant son of a hostage no one cared about, and everything would begin to unravel. A replacement was waiting on the pavement outside. Jonas smiled at him and he nodded back; they continued onwards.

In the end he just ran for it. Concluding that the scooter was the team's greatest asset, he walked from Hamra down into the central Solidere district, where soldiers stood guard around a network of pedestrianized streets filled with shops and restaurants and offices. He knew the area well from previous night-time walks. This might give him a slight advantage, but only until the team realized their vehicles were useless, at which point he expected them to close in around him on foot. And so he started running as soon as he had turned the first corner, and he was able to make it round the next corner seconds before the man behind him realized what was happening. There was a shout and the sound of footsteps. He turned left and right and left, trying to put as much distance as he could between them, and ran down some steps and behind another building until he arrived, breathing heavily, at a row of bars that had spilled their drinkers into the warm evening air. It was starting to get dark. He wiped the sweat from his face. He tried to control his breathing. He went into the third bar and pushed his way through to a set of double glass doors at the back that opened on to a small, busy terrace where he stepped into the flower bed, ignoring the cries of the waiter, to pull himself up and over the wall and into a narrow side street.

Changing taxis every ten minutes, watching for any sign of the Honda with three aerials or the dark green moped or anyone looking hurried or frantic or lost, Jonas zigzagged his way towards the lighthouse. He didn't have any time to waste. He covered the final few hundred metres on foot. Three Filipino maids stood talking in a huddle while the dogs they were supposed to be walking danced a maypole around them. Later on it was so quiet that he could hear the bubbling of a water pipe on a balcony high above him. A small Syrian girl aged around seven or eight came up silently, tapped him on the arm and asked for money. By then he had recovered Raza's package from the base of the lighthouse, and the only thing he could find in his pocket to give her was a roll of six fifty-dollar bills, but he had to persuade her they were real, and even then she walked away as though holding something worthless in her tiny hand.

**2**

– Read this.

  – What is it?

  – Your statement.

  – What do you mean? *My* statement? What does it say?

  – Just read it.

  – Sorry, sorry. I'll do my best. It's difficult without my glasses. They were broken, you might not remember. And my eye has been —

  – Is it. Then hold the paper closer to your face.

  – Is the camera on?

  – All these questions. Don't you worry about the camera, old man, I'm just sorting out lighting and stuff. First time's a – what do you call it – a dress rehearsal. It's a dress rehearsal. Just read the statement.

  – As the representative of the Archbishop of Canterbury, I call on the worldwide Church to cease its support of the brutal Assad regime and its oppression of Muslims. I was sent here to tell the Syrian puppets that the Church supports its crusade against Islam and against the – what's this word? Indiscriminate? – indiscriminate slaughter of Muslim families, schools and hospitals. I now condemnify – you do know that's not a word, don't you? And this isn't how you spell tyrannical. I'm sorry to be so fussy, but —

  – Man thinks he's marking homework or something. If you want to change bits, change bits. Got to sound like you. That's why we're doing a dress rehearsal.

  – Can I ask…do you know if the medication I requested is available?

– Requested. Huh.

– It's just that I'm finding it very hard to sleep at night. The headaches are getting worse, sometimes I can't see because the pain is so fierce, and my breathing gets —

– Doctors are busy with people whose skin was burned off by British bombs, with children who've got no arms or legs. And you're talking about getting a good night's sleep. Hurry up and read the statement, old man. The others will be here soon. I said I'd get you ready. Maybe one of these —

– No, no, I'm sorry, I'm sorry, no, no – there's no need for —

– Plenty more where that came from. Now get on with it.

– I'll read it, I will. I'm sorry to be such a bother. I'm not trying to be difficult, really I'm not. I'd be happy to write something that expresses my feelings on this subject, something about the illegal war in Iraq, something about the importance of good relations between religions, the things we can all learn from each other. This just sounds like propaganda. With the utmost respect to you and your colleagues, people in the West will just see a hostage reading something against his will and you'll lose any support you might otherwise have gained. You're British, you know what British people are like.

– I'm British? You got that wrong. I burned my passport when I got here. Who gives a shit about British people anyway? It's Muslims we're speaking to. Muslims are not British, they're not French, they're not Chinese – they're Muslims, simple as that. Anyway, you lot take hostages too.

But you call them detainees. Guantanamo, Bagram, Abu Ghraib, Belmarsh. Where do you think we got the orange jumpsuit thing from, eh? Now read the statement from the first word to the last word so we can see how it looks. Any more questions and you'll be getting more than a slap, old man. Haven't got all day.

He pressed Pause.

Someone had walked in. It was just after midnight. Jonas was seated at a terminal in the far corner of a half-empty internet cafe. A fluorescent tube flickered above his head. The streets were quiet and the only sounds he could hear were those of teenage boys at war: furious bursts of clicking and tapping, whispered gunfire, yelps of delight and disgust. In addition to three hundred dollars, Raza had left him a USB stick containing a single video file lasting eight minutes thirty-three seconds and a note asking him to write a report on his recent contact with British and American officials.

The man walked back out on to the street. Jonas went back to the beginning and pressed Play. If he had been asked to describe the footage after the first viewing he would have commented on the bare light bulb and the black flag against the far wall that had slipped to reveal a crudely boarded-up window. He would have described the way the door had been reinforced with rough planks of wood. He would have said that the kidnapper came from London, that he was distracted by a task he was carrying out behind the camera.

It was only on the second viewing that he saw the rest of it. His father's left eye socket appeared to have been smashed and the damp purple flesh had swollen up like an airbag to close the eye itself. There was a coloured stripe under his white beard that was either a bruise or a burn. He held his arm at an odd angle. Jonas recognized the collar of a shirt he had given his father for Christmas three years earlier, the year that it had snowed, the year they had argued about something unimportant, the year Jonas had left early.

– This focus ain't right. Do you know how these things work? All these buttons. No, just keep sitting there. Read the statement again without those mistakes but do it louder this time. Can't hear a thing, your voice is so quiet.

– I'm sorry, I really am. You've gone to all this trouble to set everything up. But I can't say these things about the Church. Can we change a few more words? Please don't look at me like that. I just don't want to play a part in making people think that their Christian neighbours are the enemy, that there's some sort of crusade against Muslims. Things are already bad enough. Do you think that sounds ridiculous? You're laughing. I just don't want to make anything worse. We only came to show our solidarity with Christian communities caught in a terrible position, that's all.

– I'm laughing because it's funny how naive you are. Let me ask you this. What about Muslim communities caught in a terrible position? Did you come to show solidarity with them? Did you come to ask Assad to stop dropping barrel bombs on civilian neighbourhoods? No, wait – you guys let him get away with *murder*. Literally. Nobody bombs *him*. Cameron makes some half-arsed attempt then says oh well. Truth is, Assad's helping you fight us. You two is on the same side. You came here to say well done old chap, keep it up, go easy on the Christians but keep on sticking it to the Muslims. No, no, wait, listen, tell me this: if there's no crusade, how do you explain George W. Bush and Tony Blair praying together before sending their armies into Iraq? How do you explain the Tea Party? How do you explain four thousand Jews staying home on 9/11? Just because you're paranoid doesn't mean they're not trying to kill you. Know who said that? Malcolm X. Point is, racism is everywhere, Islamophobia is everywhere. You're like a fish doesn't know it's swimming in water.

– I, I…I don't know what to say. The last side in the world that I am on is Assad's side. And I'm not on the side of the British government either, I'm really not. I would rather Blair had never been prime minister and I think Bush should be locked up. I don't want the British and Americans to be fighting you, I don't want Assad to be fighting you, I don't want you to be fighting the world. None of this is any good, none of it is any damned good. Didn't you see all those people marching through London against the war in Iraq? We tried to stop this. We tried, we really tried, but, you know, it, it —

– It fell on unpopular ears.

– Exactly. That's exactly what happened.

– This is boring. Listening to you, it's like listening to the news or something. The brothers'll be here soon and you're still talking.

– I'm sorry. I don't get the opportunity to talk to many people these days. I suppose I am going on a bit.

– Thing is, at the end of the day you're always going to think life in England is fine because it works for you. There it is. You're like the people on the TV or, I don't know, the banks. Life's different for people like me. Getting stared at because you've got a beard, because you wear these clothes, getting stopped at airports by the feds asking you questions about where you pray, where you travelling to, what do you think of terrorism young man, would you be prepared to talk to us about your friends and what they're playing at.

– They've got jobs to do just like everyone else.

– Why are you defending them? You forgot where you're at, old man?

– I don't know. They get criticized from all sides, don't you think? It's hard to imagine... Shall we go back to the statement? Shall I tell you which bits I agree with? The bit about the bombing of homes and schools and hospitals being utterly wrong. The bit about the Assad government being reprehensible. The bit —

– The bit where it says we're going to cut your head off if we don't get our money? It'll be over so quick, scrawny old man like you, maybe we'll get one of the kids to do it, like cutting the neck of a chicken. Little spurt of blood like a chicken. Don't...sit down, sit down, stay in the chair. Don't throw your marbles out of the pram, man of your age. Have some dignity. It's hard to take you seriously. Piss stains on your trousers. You sniffle like a baby when you're falling asleep, kneeling on the floor talking to yourself. Truth is, I don't care about you or what you say one bit. You're nothing to me or my people. Talk till you're blue in the face and it's not going to change nothing. Let's get on with this. All that talk of chicken's made me hungry. I want to go and eat.

Where had Raza got this from? The Syrians, most likely, either from an agent of theirs inside ISIS or from some kind of technical coverage. His fingers crackled against the computer screen. His father was close enough to touch. The camera had been positioned to take in his torso, his bruised face, the black flag behind him. It was as though he was speaking to Jonas, especially when he looked directly at the camera, as though Jonas was the one responsible for his distress, as though Jonas was the one making him cry. He wanted to say something. He didn't know what to say. I'm sorry that I've been such a poor son, I'm sorry that I've let you down. He was no better than the armchair warriors around him, fiercely brandishing their joysticks and consoles. He played games like they did – he stepped into flower beds, he jumped over walls. He watched events on a screen and pretended he had some control over what would happen next.

– I don't know why we're still talking. Wipe your eyes and read the statement or things are going to get pretty bad for you. That's the truth.

– I don't see how they can get much worse.

– They can get worse. Some of the brothers here. I mean, they're expert at that stuff. Can you hear a car? Is that… Maybe they got held up somewhere. Listen, if you read it your family will know you're okay, they'll keep looking for ways to get you home. It's in your interest. If there's no statement after a while people think you're dead and that's it. Game over. Might as well finish it now.

– I've accepted I'm going to die here. I know I'm not going home. No one's going to rescue me from here, wherever here is – Mosul, Raqqa. No one's going to pay a ransom of ten million dollars.

– Don't say that; only Allah knows what's going to happen. It's just a simple statement condemnifying, I mean, what is it, condemning things that are happening. I don't know about you, for Muslims it's a sin to despair of Allah's mercy. Stop doing the everything's hopeless thing, stop talking about dying. You're just, what's it called, playing the thingy.

– Playing the martyr?

– Whatever, just do it for fuck's sake.

– Since when do you and your friends think playing the martyr's a bad thing?

– Come on, they'll think I can't… Tell you what, just read it through to see how it sounds and if you don't like it I'll delete the recording.

– Can I speak to my family?

– What?

– If I read the statement.

– Are you crazy? Quickest way to get yourself killed round here is to pick up a phone. Hundreds of drones in the skies, some of them look just like real birds. They'll be scraping us both off the floor. Just read it, man. You can put something at the end for your family, let them know you're okay, how you're doing, like a DM.

– What about your family?

– What about them?

– Do you talk to them?

– Nah, my family is out here. People in England are nothing to me. My mum kicked me out when I was fifteen. She's a Christian, my mum – like you. Bet your mum didn't do nothing like that. She called the feds on me one time, another time she tried to get a priest to do a thingy, what's it called, like in that film. My dad and my uncle was holding me down, I had to call the brothers round. They sorted that shit out quickly, gave the priest a proper scare, put him in hospital.

– What a horrible experience to go through.

– She's got type 2 diabetes, has to take medication every day, makes her feet swell up.

– That priest sounds as though he comes from the Middle Ages.

– They're so boring, priests. Always going on. I used to hate church. Who gets up at that time on weekends? At least you don't preach at me.

– I think my son feels the same way. He would —

– I only used to go for the girls, to be honest.

– How old are you?

– Nineteen. Twenty next week. Muslims don't celebrate birthdays though. So, what, you're not going to do it?

– I'm sorry. I thought I could do it, I thought it would be all right. Like an interview, right? You've got everything ready, I'm wearing my favourite shirt. Turns out it's not that straightforward.

– We'll see about that when the brothers get here. If you're not going to do what we tell you then there's no point in holding back. Chuck you off a building, burn you in a cage – they'll come up with something that makes a splash. I like my idea. Get one of them young cubs to take your head off. Seriously, do you think they'd show that on the BBC?

– It does feel as though I'm missing an opportunity, that's the funny thing. That camera there. It's my chance to say goodbye.

– Here they are, here they are. Finally. As-salaamu alaikum, where you been all this time?

– What's that light? Turn that thing off, akhi.


**3**


Dear R.

Firstly, thank you so much for allowing me to see that footage of my father. I am at a loss for words to explain to you what it meant, especially after not having heard any news for so long. It might come as a surprise to hear that I had some doubts at first about working with you. But this has convinced me of your good faith and your ability to help me out of a situation that my own government has failed so miserably to address. Can we meet in person as soon as possible to discuss this? I'd like to do whatever I can to help you, and I'd like to know what other channels you might have access to that could help secure my father's release.

On to my recent contact with British and American officials. This whole world of private signals and hidden messages and secret reports is completely new to me – you'll have to forgive me if I don't focus on the information you want or go on for too long about unimportant things. I'll try to put down everything I can remember.

The other day Desmond Naseby came to my flat to ask if I would accompany him to the embassy. He took me in the same car I've seen him in before, a maroon Audi (the number plate ends with 565, I think – I can try to remember the whole thing next time if you think that would be useful. I don't know what diplomatic plates look like here but there didn't seem to be anything official-looking about them, which might support your theory that he's here in a secret capacity). I noticed a real change in him. He is clearly under a lot of pressure at work and commented a number of times that he hasn't been getting much sleep. He looks tired, too, for what it's worth – he kept trying to disguise his yawns. When I asked him about this he said he was being "run ragged" by "some harridan" (I don't know if it's useful for you to know the exact language that he used) who had just arrived in Beirut and who was making some of the staff work through the night.

Anyway, he was very apologetic for the way that he had been neglecting "my case" (I know it's not important, but the language he used really made it clear that he sees me as a work problem and has no real interest in how I am feeling) and put it all down to some crisis (I can't remember if he used that word – he may have said "emergency") that has occurred and is taking up all his time. Naturally I asked him what the crisis/emergency was, but he brushed aside my question by saying something in Latin that I think I recognized from my schooldays as "in pace, ut sapiens, aptarit idonea bello", meaning something like "the wise man prepares for war", which sounds a bit ominous.

The reason he had brought me into the embassy, it turned out, was to sign some legal documents related to the repatriation of British nationals after their death. He insisted it did not mean they thought my father was dead, but that it was merely a detail that needed to be cleared up. (A detail! My father's death is a detail! I'm sorry, but it just makes me so angry.) He said they had no new information about my father's status, health, location or prospects. The British government, he said, was in exactly the same position it was several weeks ago. It's clear to me now that what you said is true, that he hasn't been working on this at all, that he doesn't really care – that no one in government does. You have made me see things in a completely different light.

He left me in an office – I don't know whose – to read and sign the documents. I was in the middle of doing that when the older woman whose picture you showed me came into the room to collect a book from the shelf.

(I wasn't able to see the title but it was next to a Who's Who of Lebanese politics and a map of the border with Israel.) I know that you are interested in her and so I tried to engage her in conversation by asking if she could answer a question about the documents I was reading. She couldn't, but she did tell me that her name was Meredith and that she was with the Department for International Development (I don't know if this means that she isn't a spy after all) and that she had just arrived in Beirut. She told me that she wasn't here on a posting but had come to "coordinate a project". When I asked her what her field was she said it was "international water disputes", and we spoke for a while about the disagreement with Israel over rivers in the south of the country. I thought she sounded very knowledgeable on the subject – she mentioned various international treaties and UN resolutions about the right to water, although at one point she referred to Nahr el Kalb (she said it meant Dog River) being in the south of the country whereas my map shows it as being north of Beirut. But I probably misheard her.

When Desmond Naseby came back, soon after she had gone, I told him I had met his "harridan" and he looked at the door she had come from and gone back through, which suggests to me that she is the one making him work all hours.

A few other scraps, finally: they're short on desk space in the embassy because of new people who have come out; apparently the Americans are just as busy as the British (I asked after Harvey), but Desmond wouldn't say whether they were dealing with the same crisis or something different; and Meredith is staying at a hotel (she didn't say which one).

I've been thinking about what to do next. It seems to me that Desmond doesn't like Meredith – do you think this will make him more willing to speak about her behind her back? If I invite him for a drink, do you think he might tell me more about this project she's forcing everyone to work on? Also, I realize now that there may have been an opportunity to look through the drawers in the office. If I get the chance next time, should I do this?

Please write back soon. I'd really like to meet up in the next few days to hear what I can do for you and to discuss any other information you might have about my father. Thank you too for the money. It's been much appreciated.

Yours,

J.

# CHAPTER THIRTEEN

That same night Jonas checked into a cheap hotel on the other side of Beirut under the name Clive Dashwood. When asked for his passport he told the receptionist that his girlfriend had suddenly flown home to Sydney after learning that her grandmother had taken a turn for the worse and in the confusion of packing in a rush had taken *his* passport as well as her own, but it was currently with DHL and would, he had been promised, be back in his hands within a matter of days. As proof of his identity, instead of a driving licence or a bank card, he offered up a letter on headed notepaper from the Australian embassy confirming that he was the holder of passport number M6395629, issued on 11 August 2011 and expiring on 11 August 2021, and a tea-stained, dog-eared copy of his flight booking that looked as though it had sat untouched in his back pocket for several weeks. They had taken well over an hour to prepare; the man barely glanced at either. If he looked suspicious at all it was only because of Jonas's implausible claim that he'd never met a single one of the man's five cousins, who between them owned a car showroom, a juice bar and a series of successful dental practices all along the Gold Coast.

Over the next few days Jonas kept himself busy. He bought new clothes and had his hair cut by a barber around the corner from the hotel. He pored over maps of Beirut and the border with Syria. He rediscovered his appetite and ate five or six meals a day. He slept every afternoon and woke up each time to see in the cracked mirror that his bruises had healed a little more. He exercised morning and evening with the same unhurried attention to detail that a prisoner on death row might bring to their workout, and climbed up to the hotel rooftop before sunrise each day to do pull-ups from a rusty pipe that fed into the water tank and look for cars that had been parked overnight with a view of the hotel entrance.

And after dark he would go out, wearing a baseball cap, a pullover beneath a loose shirt to change his shape and a pair of glasses he had bought from a local pharmacy. He used taxis and buses and followed carefully planned routes that skirted busy areas. Unable to check the lamp post near his apartment in case the surveillance team were lying in wait, he would visit the lighthouse to see whether Raza had left him a message and then find an internet cafe – a different one each night – to check the email accounts he used with Tobias and the kidnappers. He couldn't understand why they were taking so long to respond.

One evening there was an email waiting for him.

OK, listen, we want that stuff but there is no way of knowing if its real or not, send half now, when you come over to us bring the other half. We'll settle for that.

Jonas replied immediately:

I'm pleased that you want to exchange my father for me and for the documents. This is good news – you will not regret your decision for one single moment. You will understand that I cannot send you half the documents now. That is not how an exchange of this kind works. But I have all the documents with me and I am ready to place them in your hands and surrender myself to you on whatever day and in whatever location along the Syrian–Lebanese border you choose. But you must understand that as a fugitive from my government I am under significant pressure. I cannot hold out much longer. They know the significance of what I am planning to do and are trying everything in their power to stop me. I need to know what you want me to do. Time is running out.

Please confirm you have not detained the man who delivered my message to you. He did it as an act of kindness and is not connected in any way with this.

Jonas found another internet cafe and waited for a reply until it closed at midnight. He followed a foot route that took him in the opposite direction to the hotel before looping round through a number of quiet residential neighbourhoods; he crossed the road to avoid street lights and bright shopfronts; and when he heard the whine of a scooter he stepped into a doorway until it passed. Nobody paid him any attention. He might have been Lebanese, with his dark hair and beard and his skin browned from long hours in the spring sunshine. As he neared the hotel he focused on parked vehicles – at this late hour there would be nowhere else for a surveillance team to lie in wait. He stood in the shadows and listened for whispered conversations or mobile phones or car doors and tried to catch the smells of coffee, cigarettes and fast food. It took him over an hour to cover the last few hundred metres.

The next day there was a message from Raza in the dead letter box.

Go to the McDonald's restaurant in Ain El Mreisseh this evening. Eat a meal. At precisely 7.15 according to the clock above the counter leave through the main exit. Stand on the street as though you are looking for a taxi. The vehicle that approaches you will be a light blue Mercedes and the registration will end with 892. Ignore any other vehicles. Say to the driver that you want to go to the American University and get inside. If you are one minute late the vehicle will not be there.

If anything, Jonas was early. It worried him to be out before dark, and in such a public place. An overweight fair-haired man playing a game on his phone joined the queue behind him. Jonas ordered his food, checked that his watch matched the clock above the counter and carried the plastic tray upstairs to a corner table with an oblique view of the street. Three taxi drivers waited with their cars. He picked at his food. A row of scooters painted with the McDonald's logo were constantly arriving and departing, like cards being shuffled, and at any one time up to five cars were nosed in towards the entrance to collect takeaway orders, slowing the passing traffic to a crawl. The blonde man walked off down the street, the game on his phone briefly audible.

At 7.14 Jonas stepped outside and saw almost immediately, still about fifty metres away, a pale blue car slowly making its way towards him. To pass a moment or two and make it all seem as natural as possible he asked one of the drivers how much it would cost to be taken to the American University and then smiled and shook his head at whatever price was suggested. He stepped away from the renegotiations as the Mercedes rolled into position, and stuck out his arm, said his line and found himself being driven away more quickly than he would have thought looked natural.

The meeting took place thirty-five minutes and two vehicle changes later inside a blue Ford Transit van in the far corner of an underground car park. It was empty apart from a car blocking the entry ramp and a group of three men who stood smoking about fifteen metres away from the van. They didn't look at Jonas once. When the door had been pulled shut only the weak watery glow of two electric lights allowed him to see Raza, seated opposite with a pink blanket folded over his legs. The black doctor's case was by his side.

"We do not have much time," he said. "Please, tell me again about the embassy and the woman called Meredith."

He pronounced her name as though it was French. Jonas repeated his account of the meeting. Nothing could be less convincing than an identical version to the one he had put down in writing and so he left out some details and added others, such as his impression that Naseby might be a drinker and a description of the clothes Meredith had been wearing. Raza was quiet. Jonas could hear the three men speaking in low murmurs outside the van. He had to tread carefully. Despite the gifts of money and the footage of his father they would be viewing him with suspicion, they would be considering the possibility that he was a dangle. If they judged this was the case they would look to send back a strong signal that such games carried a price.

"The item she removed from the shelf. Was it a book or a folder?"

"I don't know," said Jonas.

"She would have been holding it in her hands throughout your conversation with her. You looked at her closely – you recalled the clothes she was wearing without any difficulty."

"Maybe it wasn't very big. That's probably why I can't remember it."

"The Latin phrase that Mr Naseby used. What was it?" Raza tilted his head as he asked the question. He was wearing a grey shirt and a green knitted tie. The scarring down the right side of his face made Jonas think of heat and machinery and the surface of the moon.

"The man who prepares for war is wise, something like that."

"In Latin."

"Oh. I can't remember exactly. It starts 'in pace, ut sapiens' and then something about 'bello'," said Jonas.

"I am impressed by people who know Latin. You are very fortunate. Do you know it well?"

"Not particularly."

"But well enough to recognize the exact phrase that Mr Naseby used."

"I suppose so, yes."

"So if he had used any number of Latin phrases you would probably have understood him. It was not mere good fortune that he used the single phrase you knew. Please tell me which other Latin phrases you know."

"Non omne quod nitet aurum est. That sort of thing?"

"What does that mean?"

"All that glitters is not gold."

"What else?"

"Delphinum natare doces."

"What does that mean?"

"Something about teaching a dolphin to swim. Why are you —"

"What is this new contusion on your face?"

"What?"

"The bruise. By your hairline."

"I slipped and hit my head."

"On what?"

"On the edge of a table. Can I —"

"Really? Poor Jonas. You seem very prone to accidents. Come closer, lean forward." Raza took Jonas's head in his cold hands and turned it towards the light. "You know that it is possible to obtain a lot of information from a simple contusion? The colour, for example. Typically it will go from red as the fresh blood leaks into the tissues, to blue and purple as the red blood cells break down, and then finally green and yellow as the chemicals biliverdin and bilirubin are released. So we can certainly tell how old it is from the appearance. Does this hurt? I would expect the edge of a table to have broken the skin, but there are no abrasions or lacerations." He was quiet for a moment. "No," he finally concluded, "I doubt this was caused by the edge of a table."

Instead of releasing his head Raza pulled it towards him and downwards so that Jonas was looking at the ridged metal floor. He could see Raza's bare feet poking out from underneath the pink blanket. They were larger than he had expected, white and bony and stiffly whiskered like a pair of catfish in the watery gloom of the van. Raza spread his hands into Jonas's hair and with gentle, persistent fingers began to work his way over the crown of the skull and down towards the base of his neck, tracing the landscape of bone and cartilage as though following the swirling contour lines on a globe.

"What really happened?" he asked.

It was pseudoscience, Jonas knew that, phrenology had no basis in fact, but part of him wanted it to be true, in the same way that he wanted every implausible article of faith to be true. His own experience had left him sympathetic to belief, like an athlete who cheered on a competitor attempting a leap they themselves hadn't quite been able to make. He was aware of his failure every day. That's the problem with having faith and losing it, he thought: you build the largest frame conceivable and then spend your entire life looking for a canvas high and wide enough to fill it.

Raza pressed hard, as though he might succeed in breaking through to the truth on the other side. Jonas felt that he was being enlightened, clarified, in the way that a vague thought might be clarified by the pressure of argument. To his surprise, the thought taking shape in his head was that he no longer felt afraid.

"Jonas?"

He lifted his head and peered through the gloom into Raza's face but saw no news there of his character, no news of his fate.

"I had an argument with a woman," he said. It was always possible they had witnessed the scene with Maryam. "She threw something at me."

"A woman? What is her name?"

He shook his head.

"What is her name, Jonas?"

"I'm not telling you."

"There are ways to get this information from you."

"You can do what you want with me but I'm not telling you anything about her. She's got nothing to do with this."

"You are not permitted to speak to me like this."

"I came here to exchange information about British officials for information about my father, that's it."

Raza stared at him. "You wish to talk about something else? Are you sure? Then we shall talk about something else. But let us be clear that you have told me one lie today and I will not tolerate a second. Is that understood? This is not a game, Jonas, neither is it an 'exchange'. You have already accepted our money and in return betrayed your country. Do not think that there is a way out for you."

He opened the doctor's case by his side and took out a brown paper file. Gleaming instruments – scissors, tweezers, forceps, scalpels – were held tightly in their narrow pouches like knives and forks in a picnic hamper. He handed the file to Jonas. It contained thirteen black-and-white surveillance photographs. Three of the nine men pictured he had never laid eyes on before; the other six had followed him around for the best part of a day earlier that week. In the photographs they were speaking on their phones, buying food from roadside stalls, driving. There was useful information here. Jonas memorized the details of those vehicles and men that were new to him.

"What do you notice about these pictures?" asked Raza.

He could see where this was going. "That I'm in them?" he asked. In only four of them, to be accurate, but he imagined this was what Raza was getting at.

"You don't seem very surprised."

"Well, I'm confused rather than surprised," said Jonas. "I remember seeing some of these men. I assumed they were yours."

"Why would I send men to follow you?"

"They weren't really following me. I don't know. It was more like they were protecting me – they came very close at times. Who are they?"

"Oh, British, American – a mixture. But this is not the question. The question is why they were following you."

The men outside had stopped talking. Scalpels and scissors glinted at Jonas from the open case.

"I don't know."

Better to act dumb than to come down on one side or the other, he thought. That talk about Meredith and Latin, this business with the photographs – Raza might have his suspicions, but he didn't have proof of anything. If he had proof he would have produced it by now, or shot Jonas in the back of the head and dumped him outside the city.

"You will have to do better than that," said Raza. "There is something you are not telling me."

He could see the way it might go. A threat, followed by a slap. The men outside would be asked to deliver a beating. Perhaps a scalpel would come out of its tight pouch. He didn't much care as long as he was allowed to walk away once it was done.

"Jonas? Can you think of a single reason why British and American agents would be following the son of a hostage? Or is there more to this whole thing than you have told me?"

"Maybe they know I'm talking to you. Maybe they're worried I'm going to harm myself. Maybe they were practising on someone who doesn't know what he's doing before the real target turns up. Maybe they weren't following me, maybe they were following your men, the ones who took these pictures. Maybe —"

"All right, that's —"

"I don't know what I'm doing, Raza. None of this makes any sense to me. I'm just trying to do what I can to help my father. All this other stuff – surveillance, MI6, CIA, you – I don't know anything about it. If you want me to do something for you, tell me. You've given me the only real help I've got since I arrived and I'm grateful for that. But don't show me pictures of people I've never met and expect me to tell you what they're doing. I don't know what *I'm* doing most days."

Raza was quiet.

"Well," he said finally. There was a knock on the side of the van. "We don't have much time. Return to the embassy tomorrow. It will be easy to find a reason. Perhaps you wish to review the legal document you signed, perhaps you wish to make a statement to the media. And while you are there you will spend some time with Mr Desmond and Miss Meredith and see what information you can gather. Do you think you could do that for me, Jonas?"

"What about my father?"

"Keep your eyes and ears open. I will leave you a list of questions in the usual place."

"My father, Raza? Have you got any news about him?"

"We must learn to be patient. It will take time. For now let us focus our attention on the things we can do, like teaching the British government there is a price for interfering in Lebanon. Your father will still be there next week."

They dropped him on a backstreet behind one of the main highways and he started walking in the direction of his hotel. It took fifty minutes to make sure he wasn't being followed and fifteen minutes to find a DVD shop with a handful of internet terminals at the back. The wall above him was covered with posters of *Apocalypse Now, Eraserhead, From Russia with Love* and *The Blues Brothers.*

The latest email from the kidnappers had arrived at 11.42 that morning.

You havent proved anything to us yet. Its not enough to send 3 documents. Even 50 wont prove anything if I'm honest. You either need to send us PROOF like the names of british spies over here NOW or you need to do something to show us that this is not a TRAP and you are willing to cross a line once and forever. Got it? Do something. Do an attack that we can see on the news or kill someone and send us proof. Then we'll know your serious. Then we'll talk time and place. Your fathers ok but you better hurry. We got the Swiss guy to. Its the first time anyone sent us a hostage so easy lol.

Afterwards he couldn't be sure how long he had walked for or in which direction. The thought of what he had done was intolerable. But when he got back to the hotel he found a note from Meredith pushed under his door that simply read "We're getting him out", and he knew that everything had changed all over again.

# CHAPTER FOURTEEN

**1**

"I haven't got time to see him right now," said Meredith.

Jonas could hear her voice through the closed door. It wasn't the welcome he had expected. Naseby had left him standing just inside what appeared to be a makeshift operations centre on the second floor of the embassy. The room, no more than five metres across, was filled with enough workstations for at least a dozen people, although there were only half that number in there at that moment: three young men typing at computers; a woman in headphones dividing her attention between an Arabic dictionary and a laptop; another woman with bright red shoes talking into one of several secure telephones about the impact of weather patterns on aerial surveillance; and a young man holding aloft a crowded kitchen tray, dipping and curtsying to clear empty drinks from wherever they had been abandoned. Seven mugs, three Starbucks cups – all with the name Charlie written on the side – and five Coke cans. A lot of drinks for six people. Perhaps they had been left by the day shift, although this group looked as though they had been working straight for quite a while – uncombed hair, shirtsleeves, ties pulled askew, no make-up. Jonas had never seen any of them before. They had glanced his way when he appeared in the doorway with Naseby but otherwise ignored him. Three framed posters of cars in various stages of assembly suggested that the business attaché had been moved into temporary accommodation for the duration of Meredith's stay.

"He only wants to know what's going on, I expect." Even through the door it was easy to hear the impatience in Naseby's voice. "Can't blame a chap for that. You did send him that bloody note, for God's sake, so it's hardly —"

Another phone started to ring. One of the young men muttered into it. Jonas heard a reference to "Cyprus" and "0400" and "emergency medical facilities…standby". Sandwich wrappers and crisp packets spilled out of the rubbish bin. Meredith and Naseby's voices had dropped to an unintelligible murmur – the ringing phone must have reminded them how easily sound carried through the closed door.

Jonas stepped into the room. Large maps of Deir al Zour, Raqqa and the border region near Kobani covered the far wall. Nearer to him a collection of sixteen images taken by surveillance drones had been crowded on to a large cork noticeboard, each one stamped in the bottom right-hand corner with the time and date they were taken. He saw some of the more notorious ISIS locations – police stations, a court house, a former local government office – but also what looked like residential buildings and stretches of desert road that were new to him.

He stepped closer. The woman discussing weather patterns on the phone clicked her fingers at him and shook her head vigorously, indicating that the pictures were off-limits, but he ignored her and turned back to examine them. They had all been taken in the last seven days. There was nothing to indicate why those particular stretches of desert road might have been chosen, Jonas thought, other than that they all appeared to focus on areas where the roads curved sharply, where vehicles might naturally be forced to slow down. Three of the images showed a low huddle of white buildings around a small courtyard. In two of the pictures the same vehicle – a dark-coloured pickup truck – was parked outside, and in the third a group of people were crossing the courtyard.

"You shouldn't be looking at those!" the woman called out.

Jonas leaned in further. Up close the photographs were blurred; it was only the number of legs that made it clear there were three people. From the waist upwards they merged into each other as though the man in the middle was being supported or restrained by his companions. He was either wearing a pale head covering of some description or had white hair. And it was impossible to ignore the fact that he was dressed in orange.

The woman took hold of his arm and pulled him away from the noticeboard.

"I *told* them you shouldn't be allowed in here," she said. She was short and overweight and her fair hair was thinning at the front. Jonas suddenly remembered seeing her at a conference on East Africa in Vauxhall Cross nineteen months earlier that had only been memorable because of a long-winded and frequently inaccurate presentation on the Shabaab given by the Americans. She had sat three rows in front of him, lifting the edge of her Afghan shawl to cover her mouth when she yawned, her long hair twisted into a bright coil that caught the auditorium lights as though glazed like a bun. "I know people who used to work with you. Your colleagues, your friends. *Nobody* understands this. No, what I mean is, *everybody* understands this, everybody has asked themselves what they would do if it was *their* father, *their* husband, *their* child. You know what it's like in our line of work. It's difficult, lying to everyone you meet, lying to friends and family. My children think I put stamps in people's passports like the ones they make in school with old potatoes." Tears came into her eyes at the mention of her children. "I'm only willing to do that because the job is important and the people I work with are like my family too, and when a person does what you're doing, whatever that is, it feels as though someone has joined my family, had a good look around and said: no, this isn't worth it. I'm not making any sense – I've been up since four this morning. But, I mean, stealing intelligence? Really? Do you know how much damage that will do? How many people will die? How many other sons will lose their fathers?"

Jonas didn't know what to say. Everyone was looking at him. "Who's this in the picture?" he asked.

"Are you serious?" The door to the office opened. "Do you really think you've come here for a briefing? Anything I tell you will probably end up with Hezbollah or ISIS or God knows where! The last thing —"

"All right, that's enough," said Naseby. "End of round one." His shirtsleeves had been rolled up to reveal a pair of freckled forearms and an expensive wristwatch. "There's nothing here" – he nodded at the pictures – "that he's not going to find out about from Meredith in the next five minutes anyway. Back to work, everyone."

He drew Jonas to one side.

"Everyone's a bit on edge," he whispered. His hair had recently been dampened down with water and was drying stiffly in thick red shards that came to a point as though painted by an artist's brush. "You can't blame them for that. What is it, well after midnight? We've been cooped up in here for five days straight. A diet of takeaways and coffee is hardly good for the sanity, not to mention the tennis. Mens sana in corpore sano and all that." He patted his stomach. As though spurred on to physical exercise by the mere mention of sport, he took aim with his foot at a nearby rubbish bin and looked surprised when its contents scattered all over the floor. More sandwich wrappers, all bought from the same shop, more coffee cups with the name Charlie written on the side. "We've royally pissed off the embassy staff with our comings and goings," said Naseby. "They've even turfed some poor chap out of his office to make way for us. Like most embassies they're geared up for eight to three and then we come along, burning the midnight oil, having pizzas delivered at all hours, running our staff ragged. It'll be ten times this size in London, mind you. They've taken over a whole floor there."

"What's going on?" asked Jonas. "Is that my father in the photograph? Meredith's note said that you're getting him out."

"I'll let her ladyship explain it to you." He took Jonas by the elbow and led him towards the door in the corner of the room. He dropped his voice. "A health warning before you enter the lion's den. She's not in the sunniest of moods. This whole thing has spiralled out of control to such an extent that the odds of her making chief have lengthened considerably. Oh yes, didn't you know? That's what they were saying – first female C. But now, what with No. 10 breathing down her neck, questioning some of her operational calls…" He tightened his grip on Jonas's arm. "I can speak a little more frankly now that this whole unfortunate episode is drawing to a close. It goes without saying that I disapprove of the way you've gone about things, Jonas. I'm not so much of a maverick that I'm in favour of theft, but the loyalty you've shown to your father and your willingness to think outside the box are admirable. One word of advice: get yourself a good lawyer. If I bump into you when we're back in London I'll slip you a couple of names – good chaps, know their way round the system. Truth is, faintest whiff of anything really secret is usually enough to guarantee any charges are kicked into the long grass. If your lawyer knows which cards to play and when, that is. Loopholes galore. Think of the potential embarrassment to the government. Think of the stories you could tell! Right, you ready? That way. She's waiting for you. Don't say you weren't warned."

"Desmond told you I was in a bad mood, didn't he?" asked Meredith. "Nonsense. I might be a wee bit exasperated with him, but I'm very happy to see you, Jonas. How are you? How are those bruises? You're certainly looking better than you did the last time we met."

She stood up and smoothed her severe grey bob into place. She appeared older, somehow – he wondered if it was the absence of make-up or the tired wobble in her voice. The desk in front of her was empty apart from a laptop, a coffee cup, two mobile phones and a notebook, arranged with geometric precision. She was dressed in black jeans and a black silk shirt, and as she came around the desk to shake his hand he saw that she was wearing a pair of black and white striped slippers.

"Oh no, you've caught me," she said. "These aren't meant for public display. You're not going to judge me, though, are you? I came away from our last meeting with the distinct impression that you're not one for unnecessary etiquette. Flip-flops, wasn't it? Well, there's no way I'm wearing heels after midnight." Her good nature broke through whatever layers of fatigue, stress and frustration had settled since their last meeting with a laugh that was sudden and musical. "That makes me sound a little like Cinderella, doesn't it?"

He had come straight to the embassy after finding the note under his door and was still in the clothes he had worn to meet Raza: old jeans, a pullover beneath a dark shirt. The hotel receptionist had tried to stop him checking out, complaining that he would get into trouble with the manager if he didn't have a photocopy of Jonas's long-awaited, much-discussed passport, supposedly stuck in a DHL depot somewhere between Lebanon and Australia, but when Jonas paid in cash for the rest of the week by way of an apology the matter seemed to become less urgent.

"They're a present from my grandson," she was saying. "He's determined to wean me off the colour black. These are as far as I'll go – I've made that very clear to him. He's unaware yet just how rare it is for anyone to force me into a compromise, but having said that, here I am talking to someone who has managed to pull off the same feat. You're in a very exclusive club of two, Jonas, alongside a nine-year-old boy called Tommy who collects spiders and wants to play for Rangers when he's old enough."

## 3

"Let's make a start," said Meredith. She was seated behind the desk and held her hands folded in front of her throat as though she was praying. "Firstly, our deal. We located Maryam Khoury and her mother in a hotel on the other side of Beirut three days ago. They have been issued with UK visas. It wasn't straightforward, but we managed to persuade the Home Office that the case was a compelling one, given the circumstances."

"Really? I would have expected her to contact me if that had happened. Can you prove she is in the UK?"

"What do you mean?"

"Can you show me copies of the paperwork?"

"I am no longer in the business of trying to prove anything to you, Jonas; it doesn't make the slightest difference whether you believe me or not. However, if you had been listening properly you would have heard that I didn't say she is in the UK – I said she and her mother had been issued with UK visas. Her *mother* flew into London two days ago, but Maryam herself has refused to leave Beirut. She says she won't go without Tobias Hoffman." She sat back in her chair and studied Jonas. "She phones the switchboard every day in case we've been trying to get hold of her. Sometimes she waits on the street outside and gives her number to embassy staff on their lunch break in case they hear anything. We've had to ask security to move her along several times. We tried to explain that there's nothing we can do, that she should contact the Swiss authorities, but she wouldn't accept this. She became very emotional, quite understandably. It's an awful, awful trick you played on her, Jonas."

"I didn't know."

"Did you really expect her to contact you? She knows that you lied to both her and Tobias. We had to tell her."

He hung his head not out of any sense of regret or guilt but for Meredith's benefit, because he wanted her to believe she was capable of manipulating him. It was not that he didn't feel anything. He knew better than anyone that what he had done was wrong. But he had finally assimilated the rules of the game and was applying them to his situation as ruthlessly as in other circumstances he might apply Alekhine's Defence or the Danish Gambit. That any piece could be sacrificed in the interests of victory, that any sacrificed piece could return to the board through promotion. Maryam might have been sidelined, but as long as the game was live she remained in play.

"Jonas?" said Meredith. "Are you all right? Let's move on, shall we?" She had an agenda to keep to but smiled to soften the impact of her words. "I am simply informing you that I have honoured our agreement, something that you have not yet decided you are willing to do."

He hadn't honoured their agreement, Meredith was right about that: he had continued to negotiate for his father's release. But did she *know* that to be the case? There was a world of difference between her knowing it as a fact because GCHQ had shown her transcripts of his emails to the kidnappers and her assessing it as a likelihood because a surveillance team had seen him meet with Raza. There was the possibility, too, that she knew very little other than that Jonas was behaving oddly and so had decided to throw out an accusation to see how he would react. He wouldn't waste much time on that theory; it paid to assume the worst when weighing up your opponent, and it would be a mistake to underestimate the agencies' collective ability to sift the facts and accurately assess the situation. After all, that was what the machinery was built to do. Intelligence work was all about fragments and whispers, which is to say that it was all about assessment. At its best it was capable not just of picking up the pieces after something terrible had happened, whether a bomb or a betrayal, but of preventing it in the first place.

The one thing Jonas could be confident Meredith knew for certain was that whatever deal he was negotiating had not yet been concluded. Any sale of stolen intelligence would cause a flurry of activity – phones dropped, agents executed, bugs torn out – that simply hadn't happened yet.

"What do you mean?" he asked. "I told you how many documents I took. Is this because I ran from your surveillance team?"

"My surveillance team?" She gave a low chuckle. "Now you're just being silly, Jonas. When have you ever heard of a surveillance team walking five paces behind their target? They weren't following you, they were trying to keep you safe." She sighed and shook her head. "I had real hopes that we'd established a level of trust in our last chat. There was no need for any of this, Jonas. No need to run, no need to subject yourself to bedbugs and cockroaches and whatever other beasties you encountered in that grotty hotel."

"Keep me safe from what?"

"The Americans have informed us – after the fact, unfortunately – that they've invited the Israelis to the party. We felt there was a small possibility, given their track record, that they might try to intervene directly. We don't have the capacity to monitor all their local personnel but we thought that at the very least we could put some sort of cordon around their likely target. You'll appreciate the anxiety you've caused, Jonas. Nobody knows which documents you've got, which country owns the original intelligence, who you're planning to sell it to. As a result

we've had to brief this out fairly widely as a precaution-
ary measure to all sorts of liaison services, although for
the most part you shouldn't let that bother you. After
all, there's little prospect of the Belgians or Norwegians
dispatching a hit squad to track you down." Her eyes
crinkled at the corners. "But the Israelis —"

There was a knock at the door and one of the young
men hurried in with a notebook under his arm, waving
a piece of paper.

"You need to see this," he said.

Meredith read it in silence. Something isn't right,
Jonas thought. He was being bothered by a visual detail
that had lodged in his eye like a speck of dust. He tried
to blink it loose.

"Paragraph three is the important bit," the young
man said.

"Hush," said Meredith.

A plant was slowly dying on the windowsill. A tartan
ribbon was tied to the handle of a small black suitcase
behind the door. The walls of the office had been painted
in magnolia and hung with pictures of Buckingham
Palace, the Houses of Parliament, Trafalgar Square and
Windsor Castle. It was a world that had grown foreign to
him, the pictures like propaganda advanced on behalf
of Class and Order and Money, every bit as sinister as
smiling peasants and successful factories. The bookshelf
carried a *Who's Who*, a 2010 cricket almanac, a collection
of *Flashman* novels and a framed photograph of an Indian
couple and their three children. Two flies took it in turns
to throw themselves against the window. He felt his mind

doing something similar as he tried to understand what was bothering him.

The young man lowered his voice – pointlessly, since Jonas was barely a metre away – to whisper: "Bill wants to speak with you. He's already phoned twice. The Cabinet Office have asked for —"

"I'll call him in ten minutes," she said. "No more interruptions, please. Make sure everyone out there understands I mean that in the literal sense."

In his haste the young man banged his leg against the edge of the desk, spilling some of Meredith's coffee, and as he reached to clean up the puddle the notebook under his arm dropped to the floor. It landed a few feet away from Jonas. He began to rise out of his seat to retrieve it. But the young man was taking no chances, even though it had fallen open at an empty page, and he kicked it away from Jonas and picked it up on his way to the door.

"Didn't I say you were making people anxious?"

"Can we talk about my father?" asked Jonas.

Meredith looked at her watch. "Goodness, it's almost one o'clock," she said. "No wonder you're getting impatient. Let's do just that, and then you can be on your way back to your hotel."


**4**


"We are going to attempt to rescue your father in the next seventy-two hours," she said in a voice that was flat and businesslike. "I am going to tell you two things only about the operation. Firstly, that the military assesses there is a twenty-five to thirty-five per cent chance of success. Success in this context means that no Special Forces personnel are killed and that the hostage is recovered. It does not necessarily mean that he survives, given his age and physical condition." She cleared her throat and took a sip of what was left of her coffee. "Secondly, that the commanding officer on the ground has the final say as to whether this goes ahead or not. They will not deploy if they judge the risks to be unacceptable. I am saying this in case you decide to make further threats to release or sell information once the military operation begins."

Jonas listened carefully enough that he would remember everything afterwards, every word and inflection, but at a deeper level his mind was at work trying to identify what it was that had struck a false note. He tried to remember everything he had seen, in the same way that as a child he had remembered objects on a kitchen tray. Sandwich wrappers, maps of Syria, Naseby's wet hair, aerial surveillance images, Meredith's geometric desk, the notebook, the tartan ribbon —

"If they succeed in rescuing the hostage," she was saying, "he will be taken directly to a British military base in Cyprus. We know that he is very unwell. It is likely he will be in worse condition when he arrives. The question I have been asked to put to you is this: do you wish to be there when he arrives? We're all flying first thing tomorrow morning. The entire team. Six hours from now."

One of the flies had given up, but the other one was still hurling itself against the window.

"I'm surprised that you're telling me any of this."

"You're not the only one," she said. "If it was up to me I wouldn't have told you anything. This comes from higher up the food chain." She smiled briskly. He could see her frustration not far beneath the surface and remembered Naseby's warning. "There is one other thing I have been asked to raise," she said. "There is an additional reason you may wish to consider being there, beside the fact that it is a chance to see your father, although personally I don't think this will score very highly on your list of concerns. If your father is conscious, we will want to ask him questions about locations he has been held at, other hostages, and so on. Tobias Hoffman, for example. There will be a very brief window of opportunity for another rescue attempt. Now, do you think he will cooperate? If not, as his son and someone formerly engaged in this field, would you be willing to help us ask him those questions?"

"Why wouldn't he cooperate?"

"Not everybody does. It might be that they have formed a bond with their captors, or that they are too distressed, or perhaps they realize the information will lead to military strikes, civilian casualties, that kind of thing."

"I don't think he'll withhold anything from you."

"I agree, it's fairly unlikely. Most people are willing to cooperate."

"I'll be honest, Meredith, I find it difficult to trust you."

"I quite understand. I'd feel the same in your position."

"If he survives, I'll see him back in the UK."

"Correct."

"It just doesn't make sense for me to go there until I can be sure —"

"That wretched fly, I don't know how they get in here. All the windows are supposed to be sealed." She pushed back in her chair, took off her slipper and hit the reinforced glass repeatedly until the buzzing stopped. "Are we finished here, Jonas?" she asked. "I told them this was a waste of time. I told them you'd say no."

Jonas suddenly realized what had been bothering him.

"I'll come with you," he said.

## CHAPTER FIFTEEN

**1**

It was decided that Jonas should spend the remaining few
hours before the early-morning Cyprus flight at Naseby's
hotel. The stars were out and the city was sleeping. Naseby
was being overly solicitous, opening doors and carrying
Jonas's bag as though worried that something as trivial
as having to endure the wrong temperature in the car
or listen to a Fayrouz song he didn't like might cause
Jonas to change his mind and decide not to fly with them
after all. Meredith changed into a pair of black plimsolls
and came down to the embassy forecourt to see him off.
She gave him a quick hug before stepping back into the
shadows. The car slipped noiselessly past the guards and
the barriers and out into the street. Jonas turned back
and saw her waving, small and delicate and practically
invisible beneath her grey bob. It might have reminded
him of leaving home, of saying goodbye to a loved one,
if only he didn't suspect that she had just lied to him on
such an extravagant scale.

It started to rain. Naseby had clearly decided – or
been advised – that the wrong kind of conversation was
as perilous as the wrong kind of music, and he was quiet
as they drove through the empty streets. He put on a

pair of driving gloves at a red light. Once or twice he smiled to himself or pulled a face as though working hard to suppress his garrulous nature. Jonas was grateful for the silence. He closed his eyes and saw the cork noticeboard, crowded with sixteen aerial surveillance images, as clearly as if he was standing in front of it. He allowed himself a minute to take it all in. The police station. The winding desert roads, the pickup truck. The man in orange. He let his mind come slowly to the thing that had bothered him, which was times and dates, which was pinholes.

An old Mercedes swung noisily into the lane behind them, too close for Jonas to read the number plate. The street lamps distorted everything; it took several seconds for him to be sure it wasn't the same light blue colour as the vehicle that had carried him to the meeting with Raza. He closed his eyes again.

According to the timestamps in the corner of each image, they had been taken over the past week, which was approximately how long Naseby said they had been running an operations room in the embassy. So why was a picture from 11 May partially covered by one from 6 May? Why did a picture taken on a Monday obscure the bottom third of one taken two days later? He would have expected to see the earlier picture go up first and the later one pinned on top of it, rather than the other way round. And why was a picture taken just eight hours before Jonas stepped into the embassy almost hidden from view by two *earlier* pictures? This hadn't just happened once or twice. There was no logic to any of it, and the fact that none of the pictures had multiple pinholes in them meant that they probably hadn't been taken down and then put up again in some sort of thematic pattern he wasn't able to detect.

He knew not to read too much into this. On its own it didn't amount to anything more than an observation that the pictures had most likely all been put up at the same time, rather than over the course of the week, and on the same day that Jonas had received a note from Meredith inviting him to come in. There were possible explanations. That until yesterday morning they had been spread out across a desk, for instance, at which point someone had decided it would free up valuable working space to put them on a wall instead. Or that it had taken time to process and analyse the images in London, where the expertise was, and they had only been sent out that day, as a single batch, to the team in Beirut. But it was a loose thread, and once he started pulling on it he found other threads, that laid together made something fine and delicate like a cobweb that you might just be persuaded was actually there if you came at it from the right angle and the light was favourable.

In the course of his career Jonas had spent plenty of time in rooms filled with people who had worked continuously over any number of days. There was something discernible about those rooms: a weary restlessness, a smell of body odour and coffee. There was usually an indication that discipline had broken down at some point, whether a cricket bat and ball, an obscene drawing stuck to the back of someone's chair or a handful of sweets thrown across the room and left to gather dust on the floor until the day that the operation ended and the cleaners were allowed back in. There would be teabags and banana skins and plastic cutlery in the rubbish bins, and someone would have left a Tupperware container or a pair of trainers under their desk, and there would be mugs with mould in and food wrappers from lots of different places, not just one place, because after five days straight everyone would be bored stiff of eating sandwiches from the cafe just around the corner.

It wasn't real. This was the elaborate idea Jonas was spinning in his mind as Naseby raced the car through empty streets towards his hotel. That the operations room was not an operations room, that they hadn't been working for five days straight, that the woman in red shoes hadn't been having a real conversation about the effect of weather patterns on aerial surveillance, that Meredith had only pretended to be annoyed with Naseby. That it was all a trick to get him out of the country. That his father was not going to be rescued.

He saw a possible future disappearing behind him like a turning he hadn't taken. He might have thought it was odd, as the plane's engines started up, that he had been given a seat at the opposite end of the cabin to Meredith and Naseby, that two aircrew sat facing him in the middle. He probably would have wondered why they were climbing to such a high altitude for a forty-minute flight. He would almost certainly have asked when they were expecting to land in Cyprus and been puzzled and then annoyed by their non-committal responses. And when he rose from his seat to ask Meredith what was going on the aircrew would have asked him to sit down and held out their arms to block his path and grabbed him by the wrists and the shoulders to drag him backwards into a seat fitted with restraints that he had seen but assumed were a routine, unfamiliar feature of all military aircraft. After that he wouldn't have had to ask why the plane was changing direction, or why no one would look him in the eye. He would have had time to get ready for the police officers on the runway, for the handcuffs, for the end of hope.

"You look a bit unwell, old man," said Naseby. "It's not my driving, is it?"

They had tried something similar before, Jonas thought, in 1943, but on that occasion it had worked. They should have kept it as simple. The corpse had belonged to a Welsh vagrant. They dressed him in good-quality woollen underwear and the uniform of a captain and filled his pockets with theatre tickets and love letters to make him look real. The sea did the final bit, carrying him and his cargo of top-secret plans for the Allied invasion of Greece into enemy hands. The planners of that operation had the right idea. A corpse can't strike the wrong conversational note, a corpse doesn't drop an empty notebook by mistake.

"Right, here we are," said Naseby. "Home for the next few hours."

Jonas had the beginnings of an idea.

## 2

"I imagine you're shattered," said Naseby. He closed the door behind them. "You drifted off once or twice on the way over here. Want to hit the hay? A car's coming for us at 5.45, which is" – he consulted his watch – "just over three and a half hours from now. Not a proper night's sleep, but not to be sniffed at either. You take the bed, I'll take the couch. No, please – I insist. I can sleep anywhere. Once managed ten hours straight in a car boot all the way from Sarajevo to Vienna."

Naseby moved between his three rooms on the eleventh floor, switching on lights and drawing curtains.

"Have a look at the view, Jonas," he called out from the bedroom. "Best place to stand is in the corner behind the sofa. That way you can see the harbour and the mountains."

As he crossed the room Jonas caught sight of Naseby's reflection in the television screen, kneeling to put something out of sight in the bottom third of the hallway cupboard.

He appeared at Jonas's side. "That's where the old spy school was, give or take," he said, pointing towards the mountain. Its lights pulsed weakly as though they would struggle to make it until dawn. "Started in Jerusalem, moved briefly to Zarqa in Jordan – where Zarqawi was from, incidentally – and finally settled in the Chouf Mountains of Lebanon. Maid's put clean sheets on the bed so it's all yours."

"My mind's racing too much to even think of falling asleep. I might sit up for a bit."

"Are you sure? Things will start moving very quickly when we hit Cyprus. It's a good idea to get some rest while you still can."

"Which military base in Cyprus are we flying to, by the way?" asked Jonas. An easy enough question to answer if the whole thing was real. He decided to add another layer of pressure. "I heard recently that they've closed down one or two of the airfields for repairs."

"Really? Yes, these things do require an enormous amount of upkeep, don't they? Jets these days are fitted with thousands of sensors, I was reading just the other day, where was it now, for everything from air pressure to wind speed to fuel consumption, and I imagine that means every time a rivet pops out the whole kit and caboodle has to be grounded. Health and safety – discuss, eh? For my money it's better to be safe than sorry. I mean, an hour's delay while they check everyone's bags is hardly the end of the world. What do you think?"

Jonas started to reply but Naseby quickly said, "I think I might leave you with the view, if that's all right, while I attempt a spot of Egyptian PT in the bedroom. It's been a long day. What do you say? Television's over there, bathtub's in the bathroom, camomile tea's in the kitchen and pillows are in the hallway – actually, forget that, I'll bring some pillows through in case you change your mind."

"Thanks for everything." Jonas rubbed his eyes, held his arms open and stepped forward. Naseby wasn't the only one who could play a role. "I can't get over how kind you're being after all the things I've done."

"Don't mention it," said Naseby, patting his back. "Now if you'll —"

"I may go for a walk if I can't sleep, but if I do I'll let myself out quietly so I don't disturb you, and I'll either be back up here or downstairs in the lobby – one of the two – around six."

"Quarter to, on the dot. Best aim to be back at half past just to play it safe. Where do you think you might go? Just a quick turn around the block, I imagine?"

"How long would it take me to walk to the end of the Corniche and back?" Jonas asked. "Not more than an hour each way, surely?"

Naseby looked alarmed and then disappointed. He glanced into the bedroom, he eyed the pillows.

"Tell you what, maybe I will sit up with you after all," he said. "Can't have you walking around in this rain."

"It looks as though it's stopped."

"It's very changeable at this time of year. Meredith will take my pension away if you turn up at the airport sniffing and sneezing. After all you've been through recently." He took the pillows back from Jonas and threw them into the bedroom. "Tell you what, you're not a whisky man at all, are you? I've got the remnants of an exceptional bottle of Tullamore Dew in the kitchen. Probably enough there for two large ones. Notes of tar and split logs. Fancy a tumbler? That'll help you to sleep."

"Let me get them," Jonas said. "It'll give me something to do."

On his way to the kitchen he picked up his rucksack from the hallway. He made plenty of noise opening and closing cupboards until he found the whisky and two clean glasses, and with his back to the door he rummaged through the rucksack for the packet of pills he had been given for his headaches. He popped four of them loose on to the kitchen surface.

"One small ice cube for me," Naseby called out from the living room. "Just enough to bring out the caramel finish."

Jonas wasn't sure how many would be enough. He had never taken more than two, and that dosage had made him feel catatonic within an hour. Four should be plenty. He divided the whisky between the two glasses and broke the plastic capsules open above one of them. The powder fizzed and sparkled and settled into a vivid green scum across the surface. He tried to stir it in but the same layer soon re-formed. Naseby would notice it instantly.

"What are you doing in there, digging up some peat?"

Jonas found a can of Coke in the fridge and divided it between the two drinks. For good measure he added another two pills' worth of powder to Naseby's glass.

"Sorry for the wait," he said.

"Christ alive, Jonas, what act of barbarity have you carried out against this poor defenceless whisky? Have you got something against the Irish?" He held it up to the light. "Possibly the worst thing you've done yet," he muttered, sitting back in his chair and reaching for the television remote.

The mess Jonas had made of the whisky emptied Naseby's reservoir of goodwill, previously brimming over at artificially high levels, at a stroke; without a word of consultation he rifled through the channels until he found a tennis match that was just beginning and settled back in his chair to watch it in silence. He ignored his drink out of principle for five minutes. He found it difficult to sit without something in his hands, though, and experimented with wedging them under his thighs, drumming a round of applause on each arm of the chair each time a point was won and inspecting his nails. Occasionally he would look at the glass and shake his head. But by the time the players were concluding the first-set tiebreaker, and apart from one final complaint – "I'd forgotten how godawful Coke tastes" – he was a quarter of the way through it.

It didn't take long after that. The first sign that something was happening was a low humming noise that Jonas thought was coming from the television but turned out to be from Naseby himself. Then for a period of several minutes he struggled to keep his head upright, and when that passed he said out loud, "Unusual to get snow at this time of year" and "Well, that's what I'd expect a Frenchman to say!" He seemed for a while to be recovering a little, mumbling, "I don't know what's come over me" and reaching for his mobile phone, but by the time he remembered the PIN code he'd forgotten what it was he was doing, and he returned it to the carpet with a gentle thud. "You a tennis player, Charlie?" he asked, looking round at Jonas. "I play a bit, don't know if you're aware. Not this kind of thing." He waved dismissively at the television. "I'm of that vintage that was raised to value spin, ball placement, all-round athleticism. The tennis player's most valuable weapon is his brain. That's what my tennis coach used to say." His speech was slurred as though he was drunk. He tapped his forehead. "Out-think 'em and you'll outplay 'em. These days it's all bosh, bosh, bosh, seven-foot Croats firing missiles at you, where's the fun in that? Don't get me wrong, I'll take on all comers. Just last week some twenty-something-year-old kid challenged me to a set. It's six–six, tiebreaker time, and after trading a few from the baseline I draw him into the net with an easy one to his forehand, he sends it back with interest, I deliver a slice sharp enough to take his toes off, he's struggling, I put him out of his misery with a backhand cross-court winner down the right side. No, wait – was it the left side? Maybe it was the left side. Yes, my game's got a bit of finesse to it. Harvey's the opposite. You should see him running all over court, tiny little fellow, grunting like Monica whatshername. Everything's a lob so far as Harvey's concerned. He is tenacious, though, I'll give him that. Like a little dog, like a little Chinese…dog." He yawned. "Spectacular legs, too. Normally a breast man but those legs could convert anyone. Saw her play Steffi in 1990 at Roland Garros." He gave a long low admiring whistle and fell asleep.

## 3

The specialists must look down on the practice of searching a hotel room, Jonas thought: it was so much more straightforward, so much less idiosyncratic, than a person's home. Easier to get into, for one, what with guests having roaming rights throughout the corridors, the ubiquity of cleaners and maintenance men to provide cover and the speed at which a hotel key card could be copied. No alarms, no barking dogs. And then, once you are in, a layout and design that you are already familiar with from the hundreds of other hotel rooms you have seen. Anything that looks out of place belongs to the guest.

Jonas started in the bedroom. It made things easier that there was no need to replace everything in its original position – to put Tom Clancy back underneath *The 10 Habits of Highly Successful People*, or to remember whether the bookmark was at page 42 or 142 of Naseby's well-thumbed copy of *The Thirty-Nine Steps*. It would be immediately apparent to the next person who came through the front door that something significant had taken place in these rooms. No attempt to tidy up loose ends was going to change that.

Suit trousers, jackets, shirts, chinos. One belt, three ties. A neat pile of ironed handkerchiefs. A tennis top with the words "The Buchaneers, 2004, Nulli Secundus" embroidered in gold thread across the breast. Brogues, tasselled loafers and deck shoes. It was evident that Naseby had ended up staying longer than originally expected: four of the eight shirts hanging in the wardrobe had been bought in Beirut, along with a new pair of tennis shoes and three sets of socks that looked distinctly cheaper than the others, which had all come from the same Jermyn Street tailor. He had started to collect assorted receipts in an envelope marked "expenses" that was propped up on the underwear shelf. Most of these were for meals, including what appeared to be a lunch for three people just the day before – the day everyone had supposedly been working flat out – that had covered three courses at a cost of $223.70. Jonas was surprised by how easy it was to build up a picture of Naseby's typical pattern of life, from his mid-morning espresso and biscotti at the Beirut Souks branch of Starbucks to his lunch of grilled chicken with a glass of dry white wine at Al Balad on Nejmeh Square. On the back of the receipt for the tennis shoes he had written "liaison??". Jonas heard a single thud and an increasingly loud noise coming from the living room.

Naseby was sprawled across the floor with the remote control underneath his belly while the crowd applauded the winner of the match at full volume. He switched the television off. Naseby appeared to be breathing normally. Jonas rolled him on his side, checked that his pockets were empty and arranged a cushion under his head. There was no need for him to suffer unnecessarily at this stage.

He didn't waste much time in the bathroom – shampoo, two types of conditioner, teeth-whitening strips – before moving on to the hallway and the wardrobe where Naseby had hidden something when they first came in. He knew before looking inside that Naseby wouldn't have used the hotel safe. It wasn't so much the argument that hotel safes could be opened by any staff member with access to the master key, or that they made it easy for an intruder to know where to focus their efforts. It was more that he couldn't see an old-fashioned professional like Naseby relying on something so obvious. The whole point of being a spy, after all, of daring to risk one's life behind enemy lines in Sarajevo or Moscow, was that one didn't place one's faith in combination locks or three-inch steel but in a well-timed dummy, in nimble footwork, in spin.

Jonas finally found Naseby's diplomatic passport under the basket containing the shoe-shine kit, and a sealed envelope inside the trouser press. The envelope contained a letter written in Arabic on a single A4 sheet of paper. At the top in the middle was a crest depicting a cedar tree with two golden wings coming out of it and a scroll underneath on which something was written in Arabic. Jonas went back into the living room and retrieved Naseby's phone from the floor by his chair. There had been ample opportunity earlier to watch him trying to type in his access code – 0887, 0807, 0007 – and he quickly found the hotel Wi-Fi and logged in. The first line of the letter, he guessed, would be general greetings. He downloaded an Arabic keyboard, chose a medium-length word from the second line and typed it into a translation website as best he could, experimenting until the word looked as close as he could get it to the one on the letter. "Colleagues". Encouraged, he jumped forward a few words and repeated the process. No result. He tried another word. No result. Then "permission" or "approval", followed by "seven". No result. Losing patience, he went to the crest at the top and spent five minutes confirming that the letter had come from the Lebanese air force. Back to the text. "Airport", "direction", no result, no result, "apple", "with", "fantastic", no result, no result, no result, "destination", "London", no result, "Great", "Britain", no result, "peace", "shortly". Signed by "Major General", "Emile", no result.

The phone suddenly buzzed in his hand. A text from Meredith: "Pls confirm cargo intact." Jonas wasn't sure whether he had to reply – Naseby would have been fast asleep in the bedroom if he had been allowed his own way. He scrolled through earlier messages to gauge the right tone and to put her mind at ease settled on "All fine. He is sleeping."

He took the opportunity to see whether there was anything else on the phone that might be of use. It had been active in the Vauxhall area on twenty-two occasions in recent months, and among the dozen photos – mostly of oriental lamps, which he had sent to his wife with comments such as "This one?" and "Yellow would match the carpet" – was one of Naseby and Harvey standing on either side of a tennis net with their arms around each other's shoulders. The chain of messages between them dated back to a week or so before Naseby had first visited Jonas at his apartment. The majority were taken up with arrangements for various tennis matches and subsequent gloating by the winner; Harvey seemed to come out on top more often than Naseby had suggested. Others appeared to refer to work but involved codes, either personal or professional, such as "Give him the PJR treatment" and "Your 116/5 incomplete. Can you resend? On other matter, I'm informed 'clock will strike twice', which is a bloody relief!"

But there were a handful that Jonas was able to match up with specific incidents, such as the day that Harvey had knocked on Tobias's hotel room door ("He's with a Swiss national, first name Tobias, got any traces? Lemme know. Lift broken ffs. All those stairs gd cardio!!!") and several hours before one of Harvey's phone calls to Jonas ("Would you be able to put in a call to our chap tonight? Late-ish, we think. Tell him a horror story. Valerie says thanks for the 'cookies', they're the high point of each day!"). More recently, after Jonas had run from the surveillance team, Naseby had sent the following message to Harvey: "He's slipped our chaps. We're checking usual areas. M still adamant we don't go to locals – pls enforce same policy your end. Can you make discreet enquiries at hotels? Any male foreigners 30–40. Next dinner on me. We'll sting the office for it."

The phone buzzed again. Another text from Meredith: "Pls reply as discussed." He kicked himself; he hadn't even considered the possibility they were using a code. One that involved "cargo". How should he reply? "Cargo safe"? "Cargo in one piece"? "Cargo secure in container"? He mirrored her language and went with "Apologies. Cargo intact." But when the phone started to ring thirty seconds later he knew that he'd got it wrong, that someone would already be on their way to the hotel to check on them. He didn't have long. He went into the kitchen and looked through the knives, testing their blades for sharpness against his finger.

# CHAPTER SIXTEEN

Jonas didn't have much time. He tore down a curtain, overturned a chair, pulled the lampshade free from its stand. It took two blows with a heavy glass ashtray to shatter the television screen. He dragged Naseby's body into the centre of the mess he had created and pushed at his hips so that they were twisted and his legs splayed and placed one arm flung out to the side and the other palm outwards on his chest as though he had been attempting to defend himself. Naseby stirred and retreated into the foetal position; it took several minutes to get him back as Jonas wanted. He still wasn't satisfied. He had to avoid any hint of the neatness that had characterized Meredith's attempt at theatre. It was always the unexpected, hard-to-explain detail that made things look real; the corpse had been put to sea carrying an identification card that was deliberately out of date, since that was how life worked. Jonas found a half-eaten cheese sandwich in the fridge and added it to the scene. He removed one of Naseby's shoes, tore the bottom three buttons off his shirt and pulled down his trousers so that his pubic hair was exposed. Jonas stood at the entrance to the room and surveyed his work. It would do. He picked up the knife and took several deep breaths to steady himself.

The first sensation as the knife sliced deep into his palm was one of heat. The pain came soon afterwards. He would have to work quickly before he became dangerously light-headed and passed out. The blood poured from his hand on to Naseby's chest. He tried to divide it equally over the cuts in the material. It occurred to him too late that his blood might be either too bright or too dark to be consistent with multiple stab wounds to the chest. He tried to remain standing to maximize the flow to his hand and felt a tingling in his arm and a buzzing in his head that were almost pleasurable.

When the doorbell rang his head was between his knees and his hand was held aloft, wrapped in a towel.

"Hello? Mr Naseby? Hotel management, sir."

It was Harvey's voice, he was sure of it. After all, he had been in this position before, listening to Harvey speak from the other side of a door. On that occasion Jonas had been hiding from sight, and Tobias had been trying to keep him at bay, and there hadn't been a man covered with blood on the floor. He crossed the room as quietly as he could and looked through the peephole to confirm his suspicions.

"Is that you, sir? Hello? Please open the door or we're going to have to use our own key."

It was a bluff. He had a few minutes. Harvey was a military man, according to Raza: there was no way he would announce he was planning to walk through a door into a potentially unsafe environment. Jonas grabbed the phone and began to photograph Naseby's body from different distances and angles, focusing on those that took in the smashed television screen and upturned chair in the background, as though there had been a struggle. His audience had been raised on Hollywood films, the same as everyone else. They would want to see the action unfold in their minds, they would want to see a fight. The way he'd left those bloody palm prints on the wall, the way he'd pulled the curtain from its rail as he went down. He moved Naseby's hand to cover the notional entry wounds – and confuse the fact that no exposed bone or torn flesh was visible – as though he had died trying to staunch the flow of his own blood.

"Last chance, sir. We're coming in."

The door handle rattled and Harvey pushed at it twice with his shoulder. Jonas put the phone along with Naseby's passport in his rucksack. His head was spinning and he found himself sitting down abruptly in the spot where he had just been standing. The phone started vibrating in his rucksack. It was Harvey. He let it ring out.

"It's me," he heard Harvey say quietly in the corridor outside. Jonas crawled on his hands and knees to press his ear against the door. "Nothing. I heard someone moving around, though, and I think his phone's still…" – his voice faded as he walked off but then became audible again – "…problem, no problem. Leave it with me. I'll offer him twenty bucks or something. Call you back in ten." Then, "Hey, buddy. I'm up on the eleventh floor outside room 1129. Yes, that's right – Mr Naseby. British embassy, correct. Can you come up here with a key, please? Yes, a key. A key to his room. Yes, please. Well, he's a very heavy sleeper. I'm his doctor and I need to give him an injection. An injection. You know – a needle, a jab, pointy thing in his arm, for God's sake. Yes, I know it's four in the morning. Listen, make it quick and I'll give you fifty dollars. Yes, cash, what do you think this is? Of course you can come in with me. You want to go in first, that's fine too. Okay, okay, ten minutes." And then, after he had hung up, "No wonder they put you on nights, buddy."

Jonas knew not to assume he had ten minutes. Either the man from the front desk was coming up, in which case he'd be there to collect his fifty dollars in less than five minutes, or he wasn't, in which case it didn't matter. He grabbed his rucksack and was halfway to the bedroom when he realized he was leaving a trail of bloody footprints behind him on the carpet. There was a noise in the hallway outside. He took off his shoes. The towel was still wrapped around his hand. He switched off the bedside lights and drew the curtains so that it was dark and stood in the corner behind a tall lamp so that he could see down the length of the hallway. A closed door would look suspicious; he wanted Harvey to think that Naseby's attacker had left.

The front door began to open and then suddenly stopped as a hand came through the gap to take hold of the edge and stop it moving any further.

He heard Harvey's voice.

"I'll take it from here, buddy. No, that's very kind of you but it's better if you wait out here, doctor–patient confidentiality, you know how it is. Fifty dollars more, sure, why not? Now run along."

A short, athletic, crew-cut Chinese man in a black hooded sweatshirt and cargo trousers stepped into the hallway. He closed the door, pressed his back to it and looked around. If he took one step forward he would be able to see into the kitchen on his right and the living room on his left, where his friend's body lay sprawled on the carpet. But he just looked straight ahead down the long hallway, allowing time for his eyes to adjust to the darkness. It seemed to Jonas that he was staring right at him.

He took one step forward and looked at Naseby's body and then at the kitchen. And then back at the body, down the hallway and into the kitchen again, moving only his head. He repeated this several times. His hands were open and held loosely at his side. Jonas wondered why he didn't go to Naseby. It could be that he assumed Naseby was beyond the reach of first aid, or that his instincts told him not to do the one thing he would be expected to do, or that he had been trained to identify threats in the vicinity before attending to the wounded. Whatever the reason, he didn't approach Naseby's body. Instead he started walking down the hallway towards the bedroom.

Naseby broke wind noisily. Harvey stopped and stood still. He peered into the darkness of the bedroom. Jonas was fewer than ten paces from him. He looked back at the living-room door. This was getting annoying, Jonas thought: hurry up and do something. Harvey turned and walked back into the living room, leaving the hallway clear.

Jonas stepped out from behind the lamp, put his shoes back on, tightened the straps of his rucksack and approached the bedroom door. He had no more than a minute at most. It wouldn't take a person – even one without experience of combat in Iraq – very long to establish that Naseby was essentially fine. He took a step into the hallway.

"Desmond, Desmond, are you okay? Desmond? Desmond? Desmond?" Harvey's voice, the sound of slapping. "What's that sick fuck done to you, where does it hurt, where's the blood coming from, Jesus Christ, that's it, that's it, just breathe nice and easy, here, is your neck okay, good, let's put this under your head, that's it, let's get this off you and have a look, where did he cut you, Desmond, where's the blood coming from" – the sound of someone throwing up – "oh, oh, that's all right, get it out, what's that colour, man, what have you been drinking, Desmond, talk to me, where have you been cut, is it your arms, your hands, where did he cut you, Desmond, where's the fucking entry wound, where's the wound, Desmond, what the fuck's going on here?"

Jonas was at the front door.

He had to do this in one fluid motion. He turned the handle and pulled it and only then saw that Harvey must have thrown the latch to keep out the night porter. The door opened several inches and then stopped. He was amazed at how quickly Harvey turned, how quickly he moved. The front of his black sweatshirt had turned green with Naseby's vomit and Jonas could suddenly smell it and feel it on his own skin as Harvey collided into him, as they tumbled to the hallway floor. The pain in his hand was unbearable. Harvey swung a punch into him and grunted as it landed high on his forehead. Jonas tried to grab him by the hair but it was short and silky; his hand slid away. Then Harvey was on top of him with his head covered by his arms and it was impossible to find anything other than a hard edge until he opened up to throw a punch and Jonas got in there first with the heel of his hand under Harvey's jaw and his head snapped upwards. But he came back like one of those toys that rights itself when you knock it over. Jonas didn't know what was happening. Harvey was trying to turn his shoulder or reach for something but he didn't feel any discomfort. And then he felt a sharp pain in his neck and realized that Harvey knew what he was doing, that the small Chinese-looking kid who grew up to join the army had learned all sorts of things along the way, including pressure points and grappling manoeuvres, and then Harvey was scrambling for his hand, wrapped in the bloodstained towel, as though he was worried there was a weapon concealed in there, but as he worked the towel loose Jonas realized that it was worse than that, that he was going to put an end to any resistance by applying pressure to the wound, and he barely had time to prepare himself before Harvey made a claw with his fingers and tore at the cut across Jonas's palm.

He almost passed out from the pain. It was easy enough for Harvey to drag him into the kitchen and secure the door from the outside with a chair or a table. For a while it was quiet all across the eleventh floor, apart from the sounds of his own laboured breathing and an occasional car horn from the street far below. He found a tea towel in one of the drawers and wrapped it round his hand to stop the bleeding. He could hear Harvey talking with Naseby, making him more comfortable, bringing him a glass of water from the bathroom. It sounded as though Naseby was crying.

Someone knocked on the kitchen door.

"Hey. Talk to me. Say something so I know you're okay," said Harvey.

"I'm okay."

"Listen to me. If you go quiet in there I'm going to assume you're doing something you shouldn't be doing. If that happens then I'm going to have to come in there, and if I come in there I'm going to assume that you're armed with a kitchen knife, and that means I'm going to come in with a weapon of my own and this is going to a whole other level where you're going to end up being cut much worse than a scratch across your hand. Don't fuck with me, Jonas. Knives are my thing." He kicked at the door as though he was the one who had been locked up.

Jonas looked around the small kitchen. On the one side two white waist-high cabinets, on the other a small fridge, a hotplate and a microwave. A frying pan, a saucepan, a set of three plates, bowls, plastic cups, mugs. He tried to open drawers and cupboards without making a noise. Standard cutlery and a collection of utensils clearly bought by someone who didn't understand what a hotel kitchen was actually used for: a whisk, a cheese grater, two plastic ladles and a potato peeler. High up on the wall facing the door was a small window fitted with an extractor fan.

There was a noise in the living room and then Harvey's voice.

"Hi, it's me. Yeah, I know, more than ten minutes. So they're both still here. Looks like he drugged Desmond with something. No, no, he's okay. Thrown most of it up. He's sitting up and speaking, sort of. Not making much sense just yet. We'll take him to the hospital for a check-up. There was blood all over him but he's got no wounds. Trousers half-pulled down, shirt torn. Yeah, I know. No, doesn't look like he threw it up, it's not mixed with anything. Other guy's got a deep cut across his hand so it's probably his. I've locked him in the kitchen. Christ knows. Maybe he tried to drug Desmond, Desmond realizes what's happening and does something, they fight, the other guy gets cut with the knife and Desmond passes out. There's some blood on the wall, TV's smashed up. There's a cheese sandwich too. Don't know how that fits in anywhere. Yeah, good idea, didn't think of that. Poison in the sandwich. Desmond never turned down an offer of food, we both know that."

Jonas climbed on to the kitchen cabinet beneath the window. It creaked each time he shifted his weight. The glass around the extractor fan was covered with enough grease and dirt to delay sunrise by an hour at least. Another building was under construction in the plot next door. It was one floor lower than the hotel but still rising, its rooftop scattered with abandoned tools and wooden beams and concrete pillars with metal rods coming out of them. Two screws had been fitted to secure the window handle in place. Jonas bent down to select a knife from the kitchen drawer at his feet.

"Still there, Jonas?" shouted Harvey from the living room.

"Still here," he called back.

A portion of cool morning air slipped between the motionless blades of the fan. The screws weren't turning. He spat at the heads, scraped away at the dirt surrounding them with his thumb and tried again. Nothing. It was as though he was filing away at the bars of his cell with a smuggled nail file but instead of months and years of unsupervised nights he had at most twenty minutes. He selected another knife from the drawer. Someone flushed the toilet down the hall. He appreciated Harvey's hostility towards him – he respected it. Everyone else had gone out of their way to say that they understood how difficult it must be when a family member was involved. Everyone else had smiled sympathetically and suggested that Jonas should let the government do what it could while protecting its wider interests, as though they were the same as his. The woman in the embassy had even suggested that loyalty to family and loyalty to country were expressions of the same thing, just different in scale, like Russian dolls. Only Harvey understood the truth, which was that loyalty to one's family was not a distilled version of loyalty to one's country, it was a threat to it, in the same way that any kind of love is a threat to the state. The bottom screw moved.

Harvey was outside the door again.

"No, no entry wounds. I've checked all over. Plenty of blood but none of it his. Yeah, bright green. He's hallucinating, keeps calling me 'Daddy' and talking about some train that's due to leave in five minutes or something. He can stand but he's a bit shaky. Okay, okay. One minute."

He kicked at the door.

"Hey. What did you give him?"

Jonas squatted down on the kitchen counter so that his voice didn't sound as though it was coming from too high up.

"Methaqualone."

"How much?"

"Six tablets."

"Is the packet in there? Push it under the door."

The counter creaked as he stepped down to the floor. He had to take out the pills and flatten the box to fit it under the door. Harvey read out the details over the phone and hung up.

"Is he going to be okay?" Jonas asked.

"What do you care, you sick prick?"

He heard Harvey walk down the hallway and then come back to stand outside the kitchen door.

"I don't know how you ever got a job, you're such a fuck-up." He punched the door hard with his fist. "All your plans and you end up locked in the kitchen like a naughty dog that's taken a beating from its owner for shitting inside the house. Bad doggy, Jonas." He delivered a volley of punches to the door. "You don't get to do what you want, is that coming through loud and clear? You don't get to break the house rules." He hammered on the door with his fist between each word as he said, "Have you learned your lesson now? You're supposed to be house-trained. You sit when we tell you to sit, you fetch what we tell you to fetch, and if you bring back the wrong stick we snap your tail off and whip you with it. You're like a dog that's run full speed to the end of its chain and been yanked through the air to land on its back in the dirt. Now we're going to snip your balls to keep you quiet and fly you in the cargo hold somewhere in Eastern Europe and your boys will take it from there."

Harvey walked down the hallway to the bathroom and turned on the taps. Soon afterwards there were sounds of physical exertion from the living room. "Come on, Desmond, on your feet." Something fell over. "It'll wake you up," he heard. And a minute or two later, as Harvey shuffled Naseby down the hallway towards the bathroom, "Oh, Jonas? Your father's dead. It happened last night."

"Daddy?" asked Naseby. "Daddy's dead?"

"No, Desmond, your father's fine. I was talking to the doggy in the kitchen."

"Bertie?"

"Yes, Bertie. He's been a naughty boy."

"Bertie, Bertie!" called Naseby. He tried to whistle. "Come here, boy!" Then a shout and sounds of furious splashing as he was lowered into the cold bathwater.

Jonas would have a few uninterrupted minutes in which to work. It didn't take long to get the bottom screw out, and the top screw succumbed after several minutes to pressure from a blade he managed to remove from the potato peeler. The window, sealed shut by years of accreted cooking fat, opened with an audible pop, like the lid of a jar. A strong wind rushed about the kitchen. It seemed more likely that Harvey would feel the draught than hear any noise, especially with the sounds of splashing and shouting coming from the bathroom, and so Jonas jumped down to wedge tea towels into the gap beneath the door. He waited for a period of light-headedness to pass. He had to hold his rucksack in outstretched hands and send them out first, and it was only after some wriggling that he was able to fit his torso through the window. It was a sheer drop through the darkness to the road below. The wind was blowing fiercely, whipping at the edge of a tarpaulin on the roof of the building next door. Twisting at the waist so that he was sitting with his legs still inside, he threw the rucksack up and over the lip of the hotel roof and braced himself in case he had misjudged the distance and it came straight back down on top of him. The wind slowly unwrapped the tea towel from his hand and carried it away. He didn't know what to do next. He began to pull his left leg out to see whether he could stand on the ledge and reach up to the roof but then he slipped and it was only his right leg, still inside the kitchen, that hinged suddenly at the knee to find a grip against the wall and stop him from falling. He was tiring rapidly. His leg started to cramp.

Someone whistled. A solitary Syrian construction worker was smoking a cigarette and looking up at him from the roof of the neighbouring building, no more than twenty metres away. He smiled and waved. Jonas waved back and pointed to the top of the hotel, and the construction worker just nodded, as if that was an entirely natural place to want to be at this time of the morning, as though Jonas's was the most obvious way of getting there. He picked his way through the gloom between stacks of concrete blocks and disappeared from sight down a half-built stairwell. Jonas thought he might return with the foreman. But he emerged with a long wooden ladder that looked far too big for one person to lift, carried it effortlessly over to the edge of the roof, stood it upright and pushed it out into the void between the two buildings in full confidence that it was long enough to reach the opposite side. Only then did he pause to take the cigarette out of his mouth. A bundle of wires had been strung between the two buildings; Jonas wondered whether the ladder had been used for just this purpose before, whether the hotel was providing the Syrian labourers with their electricity and cable television. Suddenly the man's hand was dangling above him like a rope with a knot in the end. And once Jonas was safely on the roof the man gave him a cigarette and dressed his wound with a strip of cloth he tore from his shirt, and Jonas didn't even try to pretend that the tears of gratitude streaming down his face were anything to do with the pain in his hand or the bruises on his body or the cold wind that hurried down towards the sea.

# CHAPTER SEVENTEEN

The three black SUVs with diplomatic plates ignored the lukewarm protestations of the solitary security guard, roused abruptly from the comfort of his plastic chair, and parked directly outside the hotel entrance. Meredith climbed out of the first vehicle. In total seven people streamed into the lobby and across to the bank of lifts. Outside it was turning light and the wind had dropped. The building next to the hotel was open at its front to the elements like a doll's house, and from where he stood across the road Jonas was able to trace the route he had just taken past sleeping workers, around cement mixers and bags of concrete and down half-built stairwells to the street below. He had to get out of the area quickly. It would be unforgivable to have gone to such lengths to get off the eleventh floor only to stand around in plain sight as a series of American and British heads appeared at the kitchen window to see for themselves how he might have escaped, where he might be hiding, whether he was still in the area.

He checked again that he had switched Naseby's phone off and removed the battery. For what he had in mind he would need a certain kind of location – one with multiple exits, one that was somewhere along the route Meredith would expect him to be taking out of the city. He considered the airport road heading south out of Beirut and remembered signs for a 24-hour shopping mall and cinema complex. That might work. He pulled his cap down low, took a side street away from the hotel and caught the first taxi he saw.

The mall was open and he found five internet terminals in a cafe on the second floor. The manager was asleep on a dirty mattress at the back of the room. There was a payphone on the wall outside. Despite the early hour, Raza answered on the second ring.

"It's me," said Jonas.

"This number is strictly for emergencies only. Leave a written message in the other place."

"Wait, wait – this *is* an emergency. I wouldn't have called unless it was urgent."

Raza was quiet for a moment. "Where are you?" he asked.

Jonas told him the name of the mall.

"And this is one of the payphones on the second floor? Opposite the cigarette kiosk?"

"Yes."

"Hang up, walk around for five minutes and then go up to the third floor. There is a payphone at the furthest end next to a shop with video games in the window. Wait there."

"But this —"

The line went dead.

A huge banner advertising an action film was draped across the outside of the third-floor windows, cutting off what little daylight there was. Most of the shops were empty or boarded up. A warm breeze squeezed through smashed windowpanes and sifted through the rubbish – newspapers, food wrappers, cigarette stubs, dead leaves – that collected in corners and along edges. It was easy to find the phone because it was already ringing.

"Tell me what happened," said Raza. "Try to avoid names."

"Okay, okay," said Jonas. He took a deep breath. "I've found out what they're doing here, the people you told me about, the ones in the pictures. It's all to do with *tunnels*, Raza, it's going to happen *underground*, they've been *digging*. There's no time to waste – they're going to do it today. They've been working on this for months and months and after today they'll be gone and there'll be no trace of anything left behind —"

"Stop, please. Stop! You are not making any sense. Start again. This is the woman from your country and her colleague, correct?"

"And the man from the other country."

"Of Chinese appearance? All right. You said they are doing something underground. What do you mean?" asked Raza.

Jonas took another deep breath. "I've found out why they've come here, why there are so many of them. This secret project of theirs, it's something technical, they're running some kind of cables or wires – I don't know exactly – under the Iranian embassy. Sorry, I shouldn't have said that aloud. But I think they've found a way to tap into the electrical system or the communications exchange or the servers that will let them listen in to all the phone calls and read all the emails coming in and going out."

It had been known as Operation Gold. A joint CIA and SIS plan, conceived in 1951 and completed in 1955, to dig a tunnel that would allow them to tap into the secret communications of the Soviet military headquarters just outside Berlin. Jonas had decided to go with a plot that had some sort of historical precedent. He had considered saying something more futuristic, something about computer malware or nano-drones, safe in the knowledge that in the field of technology you could get away with almost anything, that even the wildest of claims would be difficult to dismiss out of hand. After all, Hezbollah and its Iranian backers must be in a permanent state of paranoia that someone on the other side was developing tools and techniques they hadn't even dreamed of yet – a tracking beacon the size of a mosquito, say, or a sensor capable of reading a person's mood from their eye movements at a distance of a hundred feet. But given Raza's age he would probably find it easier to grasp a threat he could understand, Jonas had decided, and so he went on talking breathlessly about tunnels and wires.

"It's taken them over a year to get to this point," he explained.

"Tell me how you learned this."

"It wasn't easy. But I pieced it together by —"

"Give me the individual pieces and I will assemble them —"

"I was drinking with the red-haired Englishman last night. At his hotel." Jonas didn't know whether their movements had been observed by Raza's men. "*Exactly* as you asked me to do. It didn't take much to get him talking about the woman. I *told* you that he was bitter about something, didn't I? Well, basically he's done all the work for this big project and now she's coming in at the eleventh hour to claim the credit. Apparently the only thing she's thinking of is her own career and how to get the top job. That's what he called it – the top job."

"Where were you before you went to his hotel?"

"At the embassy."

"His room number, what is it?" asked Raza.

"112 something. 1129, I think."

"What clothing was he wearing?"

"White shirt and chinos."

"What were you drinking?"

"Whisky."

"Which brand?"

"God, I don't know. Hang on, that's it – Tullamore Dew. I'd never heard of it before. Have you heard of it?"

"Continue."

"Right, okay, let me get this in the right order," said Jonas. "When he was telling me how much work he's done and how much credit he deserves, he says something like this, you won't be able to find many people who know as much as I do about *bricks*. Yes, *bricks*. I didn't know what he was talking about either. Then five minutes later he asks if I know what a clinker is, and of course I don't, and then he starts listing these other things – sand-lime bricks, engineering bricks, fired-clay bricks, dry-pressed bricks – and he says that *this* one is easier to drill through than *that* one, but that *other* one retains moisture which can damage wires or cables, and *this* one crumbles in very hot weather but – and this is the key bit – there's not much chance of the sun shining *thirty feet under the sodding ground*. You see? It's a tunnel! What do you think?"

"I am going to hang up. There is another telephone at the far end of the floor you are on. Do you have some money? Good. This time you will call me after two minutes. Write this number down."

The payphone was outside the toilets. On the wall someone had drawn a heart between two Arabic names. There was a smell of warm sewage and the sound of a broken cistern or a tap left running.

"You were in the middle of educating me about bricks." Raza sounded more amused than alarmed. "Please continue."

"Okay, so later on he's talking about the way that everyone in his office thought this project wouldn't work, and he said that he's been telling them for months now they'll need to hire seven or eight new linguists to deal with the amount of material they'll have coming in but personnel has been saying it's difficult to find them. And he says, how hard can it be, you can always retrain a couple of the Arabic-speakers, after all it's *practically the same alphabet*. That's Farsi, right? He's talking about Farsi!"

"Or Sorani or Urdu or Pashtu," said Raza. "There are probably fifty million people in the world who speak Pashtu. But go on."

"Whatever it is, it's happening today. He kept on saying he'd only have one more drink because today was match day. This is how he talks, Raza, it's like an Englishman's code. He can't step on to centre court with a foggy head, too much whisky will affect his service game, that sort of thing. He's being picked up at six by Harvey, the American. That's – goodness, that's right now. And he's flying back to London tomorrow, along with everyone else. He calls them his ballboys and ballgirls."

Raza was quiet. Jonas wondered whether he had hung up.

"So you are telling me that a senior officer," he finally said, "one whom they will no doubt assume is well known to us and our partners, is planning to visit the actual location of an underground tunnel they have constructed over many months and in complete secrecy to run underneath a heavily guarded embassy, this is what you are saying? Despite the strong possibility that this visit will be noticed and all their work will come to nothing? I want to understand you correctly, this is all."

Jonas heard the echo of footsteps and a squeaking noise. A man in grey overalls slowly came into view. He was using a mop handle to steer a shopping trolley loaded with cleaning materials across the floor.

"I'm just telling you what I know." Jonas's experience of Middle Eastern intelligence agencies was that there was little downward delegation of responsibilities, that any decision of even potential significance was pushed upwards to the man in charge. "Perhaps he has to approve everything before they flick the switch. As the boss, I mean."

"Their people have not come within a mile of the area you are describing and they have not made any serious attempt to remain hidden from us. Instead they have followed *you* around."

"I'm just telling you what I know," Jonas repeated. "Maybe everything else was a smokescreen. Maybe they've been pulling the wool over your eyes."

"You keep on saying you are telling me what you know, but you don't really *know* very much, do you?" said Raza. "Your friend didn't *actually* say anything about telephone calls or emails, this is correct?"

"Not in those exact —"

"He did not use those words."

"No, I suppose not."

"And he did not mention the embassy by name."

"Ah, I forgot this bit, when he had fallen asleep I looked round his rooms and found a map of Beirut that was folded so this part of the city was in the middle."

The cleaner steered the squeaking trolley past Jonas and into the toilets.

"Allow me to guess," said Raza. "Circles in red ink, arrows pointing to the embassy? X marks the spot? This is what you are going to tell me?"

Jonas ignored the sarcasm. "No, nothing like that. But I looked through his wallet and all the receipts were from places near the embassy: the Starbucks where he buys his morning coffee, a place called Al Balad on Nejmeh Square where he eats lunch, that kind of thing." Any details he could provide that matched what they might have seen for themselves would go a long way. "Except for two receipts from shops in this mall. It's so close to the Iranian embassy I thought it must mean something. Maybe they're using it as a base. Or maybe they've rented a shop here and that's where they're digging from, I don't know. Maybe I have got a bit carried away, you're right. I've never done anything like this before. But I thought if I came here I could keep a lookout and tell you if I see any of his team."

Raza was quiet. The cleaner emerged from the toilet and began mopping the floor just a few feet away. Jonas noticed that his overalls looked new, that the right buckle was twisted, that he hadn't done anything about the running tap. He wondered whether he had pitched the plot at the wrong level. There were so many elements in his story that might lead Raza to sense something was wrong. That a senior professional like Naseby was capable of such breathtaking indiscretion, that sophisticated agencies like SIS and the CIA would adopt such old-fashioned and high-risk methods.

"Are you still there?" Jonas asked.

Raza was saying something he didn't understand.

"What's that?" he asked. "I didn't —"

"Quiet." He spoke again in Arabic to someone with him. His voice sounded distant as though he had lowered the phone. "Listen carefully. You will leave the shopping centre immediately. If they see you there you will be compromised and no longer of any value to us. We will not be able to help you with your father. Is this clear? Go to the basement level, enter the cinema and use the fire exit inside screen 3. There will be no staff on duty at this time of the morning. This exit will take you into the parking area at the rear. The door is stiff and so you will need to push hard. Go now."

"Are you going to —"

There was a click and the line went dead.

Jonas went down to the internet cafe on the floor below. The first computer he tried wouldn't switch on, and as he worked his way down the line he realized that three of them didn't have any cables and the other two were just screens with no hard drives attached. The manager was curled up in a ball, his head resting on a pair of trainers. A closed laptop with a dongle attached was next to him on the floor. It was already online; three different pornography websites were open. Jonas logged into the email account he used to communicate with the kidnappers and typed, as softly as he could,

You told me to kill someone and send you the proof. Attached to this email are two photographs. The first one shows the diplomatic passport of a senior British spy and the second one shows his dead body. I have a video of his final few minutes. I will bring this with me and place it – and myself – in your hands along with the hundreds of intelligence documents I have stolen from the British government.

The manager turned over and settled into a new position with a grunt. Jonas paused to allow him time to fall back into a deep sleep. He took Naseby's phone out of his rucksack to check again that it was switched off. Meredith would have noticed right away that it was missing from the hotel and assumed Jonas had taken it, he had no doubt of that, or that a member of her team would have been instructed to stay on the line to Cheltenham and inform her the moment it reappeared on the mobile network. Once it was active it wouldn't be long before they identified his exact location, and if they had already deployed all possible British and American assets widely across the city to look for him it might only be a matter of minutes after he switched it on before the first team showed up. Pressing each key as quietly as possible, Jonas continued.

I have done everything possible to reassure you that my offer is genuine. But I understand that you will still have some doubts. It is in your own interests to put these to one side. As we both know, your new state is going to be put under huge pressure in the near future. This will come from the combined armed forces of America, Britain and their allies in the region, as well as from Iran and Russia. It will be unlike anything you have experienced so far. We both also know that this does not mean you cannot win. As the Prophet Muhammad defeated an army three times larger at the Battle of Badr, you can defeat your enemies too. But you will have to be wise and brave and seize the opportunities that are given to you, opportunities like this one.

Wise and brave? He thought about the teenager who had threatened to beat his father. Jonas had drafted and redrafted the message dozens of times in his head, but now that it was on the screen in front of him it looked insincere, the reference to Badr hopelessly clumsy. A pop-up ad with an image of two women kissing appeared.

In the battle that is coming, everything will depend upon intelligence – upon information collected in secret. Your enemies are already trying to discover everything they can about you: where your weapons are stored, who your leaders are and where they sleep at night, how your fighters are trained, who is plotting attacks in European cities. This is intelligence. Without it the West will not know who or what or when to attack. They will not know how to direct their proxy militias or where to drop their smart bombs. They will be powerless.

If you accept my offer, I will open up the intelligence world before you like a book so that you can see not only what your enemies already know but the ways that they operate and the techniques they use to steal your secrets and infiltrate your ranks.

This is my final message. I will not be able to check this email account again. In exactly two days from now I will be as close as I can get to the town of Arsal near the border with Syria. I know that you have fighters there and are able to move people in and out of the area. I will be using Lebanese mobile number +961 3 118883. I will have with me the hundreds of stolen intelligence documents concerning your state and a video showing the execution of the British official. I will hand myself over to you, along with these documents and the video, in return for the release of my father and the Swiss priest. They must be alive and unharmed. This is my final message and my final offer.

Jonas switched on Naseby's phone. It took several interminable minutes to come to life. Every second mattered. He connected the phone to the laptop, found the photograph of Naseby's passport and attached it to the email. Looking through the images of the body on the hotel carpet, he was struck by how unsuitable most of them were – in one Naseby was staring at the camera with open eyes, in another he seemed to be trying to lift himself on to an elbow. He settled on a picture that took in the torn curtain, the toppled chair, the smashed television screen and the bloody handprints across the wall. There wasn't any time to crop the edges or play with exposure levels or filters. He pressed Send.

Raza had mobilized his men quickly. From the window Jonas could see the same cream-coloured Mercedes that had once grabbed him off the street positioned directly outside the shopping-centre entrance. Seconds later the blue Ford Transit van from the underground car park pulled into place across the road. Everything looked quiet. He was wondering whether there had been any need to involve Raza after all, whether he would have been able to switch on Naseby's phone, send the email and leave without being intercepted, when he heard a squeal of tyres and saw one of the black SUVs arrive at speed. Harvey got out of the driver's seat and three men in dark jackets

273

spilled out of the other doors. The blue van pulled up immediately behind them to block their exit.

A car, one he hadn't seen before, drove slowly past, the back-seat passenger turning to consider the improbable crowd gathering outside an empty mall at such an early hour.

Jonas couldn't hear anything through the glass, but words must have been exchanged because Harvey was lifting his hands in the middle of the men gathered around him as though trying to calm everyone down. But when one of Raza's men tried to open the boot of the SUV to see what was inside everything started moving quickly and suddenly they were grappling and others tried to separate them and then punches were being thrown.

The passenger in the back of the slowly passing car made no move to stop or intervene in the fight. He simply adjusted the pink blanket that covered his knees and examined the windows of the shopping centre, floor by floor, as though he expected to catch sight of Jonas there, or find the answer to the profound mystery of why Harvey had come to visit a top-secret tunnel in an official US embassy vehicle, in a screech of tyres.

Jonas ran down the stairs to the basement and into screen 3. There was no one around. He threw himself against the fire exit and it clattered open. He had been running for several minutes before it occurred to him that he didn't know where he was going. To the border, yes, but how? There was only one main road over Mount Lebanon to the Beqaa Valley and Syria. He had little doubt that Meredith and Harvey would be mobilizing all available assets to look for him, and it wouldn't be long before Raza realized that Jonas had lied to him.

What would they be looking for? A British national of medium height, slim build, dark hair and a beard. He didn't have time to stop and change his clothes or his appearance – he had to leave Beirut while he still could. A man without luggage, a man in a hurry, a man on his own. That was the answer. He started looking for a payphone.

# CHAPTER EIGHTEEN

## 1

Jonas counted nine soldiers, seven handguns, four automatic rifles, two makeshift sentry boxes painted in the red and green of the Lebanese flag and one hundred and sixty-three sandbags. Three men in leather jackets sipped at small plastic cups in the back seat of a BMW parked beneath a tree. Something had happened to put the security forces on high alert. Something like an ISIS attack on Lebanese military positions along the border, perhaps, or an intelligence report of a vehicle carrying explosives. Or an urgent request from the British and American authorities for help detaining a fugitive. The text message from Harvey to Naseby might have clearly stated that London did not want the Lebanese authorities informed about Jonas, but there had to come a point when the risk of letting him run was greater than the embarrassment of announcing to the Lebanese – and therefore the world – that British intelligence had reverted to type and discovered a traitor in its midst. Ahead of him the soldiers waved through a red Toyota Land Cruiser and the queue rolled forward.

Maryam watched silently through the dirty car window. She had answered her mobile that morning on the second ring, despite the early hour, and listened quietly as Jonas explained what he was planning to do. He was surprised she hadn't put the phone down immediately. They met outside a church near the National Museum. He tried to prepare some kind of defence, to find a way to explain why he had lied to her, why he had lied to Tobias. It didn't matter. As soon as he saw her walking down the empty street towards him he knew that he was unimportant to her, that he was merely the latest in a long line of men who had lied to her, who had treated her cruelly – officials, militiamen, police, border guards. She wouldn't make a scene. Whatever the details, whatever Meredith had said about Jonas acting on his own, he was a government man. You only had yourself to blame if you believed men from the government.

They sat on the church steps and she made him tell her again, in detail this time, what he wanted to do. She looked thin and tired and fierce. Her dark hair was unwashed and there was dried blood on her hands where she had picked away the skin on her fingers. He told her about Meredith and her attempt to trick him into getting on a plane. He told her about Naseby and the smashed television and the bloody handprints on the wall, about Harvey and the ladder between the buildings. He told her about the 287 documents. He talked for a while about his father and how he wished things between them had been different. He described his original plan to get to the Beqaa Valley by taking a bus and pretending to be an archaeology student, and he unpacked his rucksack to show her a textbook on Greek and Roman temples and a biography of Howard Carter that he had found in a second-hand bookshop near the lighthouse. At some point she must have decided that she had nothing to lose by believing him, that going was marginally preferable to staying behind. She raised an eyebrow when he described his meetings with Raza.

"This is the most dangerous thing of all," she said. "You are sure he is Hezbollah?"

"Yes."

"Does he know about me?"

"I don't know."

"My name, how I look?"

"He may know everything."

She took a red and white keffiyeh from her bag and wrapped it round his shoulders. "Wait here," she said.

When Maryam returned less than ten minutes later she was seated in the back of a rust-coloured Volvo she had flagged down, its boot tied open to allow space for three wooden crates filled with chickens. She came close to Jonas and whispered, "Say nothing," before shouting at him in Arabic and roughly pushing him towards the car. The driver was an elderly Druze man, his black robe hiked up above his bare knees to allow him the freedom to operate the pedals. A small white knitted cap sat on top of his grey-bristled head. He looked back at Jonas and nodded sympathetically. His wife, sitting next to him, pulled her loose black headscarf across her face and muttered something under her breath.

They climbed out of Beirut without incident, through Hazmiyeh and Aley, past signs for Souq Al Gharb, Deir Al

Harf and Bsous, the road looping and winding through villages and towns. Jonas didn't see the SUVs or any other vehicles with diplomatic plates. The car had to be coaxed up the steepest stretches. In his search for the best line, for the most efficient route up the mountain, the old man would swing them out into the path of oncoming traffic, somehow managing to avoid the cars that hurtled down past them towards Beirut. Jonas felt like a flag in a slalom race. Maryam occasionally broke her silence to shout at Jonas in Arabic, and twice she tried to slap him around the head. When the driver intervened to say something – from his tone, Jonas thought, he was suggesting she calm down – she shouted at him as well, and his wife joined in, as though telling him to mind his own business, since that was the last time he had anything to say on the subject. He settled deeper into his seat, stroked his moustache and concentrated instead on his vigorous driving.

The checkpoint appeared before they had even begun their descent into the Beqaa Valley. Seven cars separated them from the soldiers. It seemed they were diverting one out of every three to four vehicles for further inspection. It made little sense to Jonas that they would be stopping traffic heading towards the Beqaa Valley and Syria, rather than traffic heading the other way. Was he right to assume the Lebanese authorities had not been told about him? He knew what factors Meredith would be considering. She would imagine the worst – that the news would leak immediately, to the Gulf States, to Yemen, to North Africa and down beyond the Sahel into Nigeria, Sudan, Kenya and all those countries with whom Britain had an important but fragile intelligence relationship. It could undo years of careful work, as those countries took a step back and stopped sharing their most valuable information with the British. Rumours of a leak could do almost as much damage as a leak itself.

They moved forward and Maryam hit him again, her hardest blow yet. His head bounced off the window. She started shouting and wagging a finger in his face, punctuating her words by jabbing him in the ribs, and when he tried to protect himself it only seemed to make her more angry. Then there were tears in her eyes and she started to sob, her shoulders shaking. None of the three cars in front of them had been stopped. They rolled forward and the elderly couple wound down their windows to show the soldiers they had nothing to hide. Maryam was crying and wailing and shouting all at the same time, and she took hold of Jonas and feebly shook him. He could hear the sound of laughter through the open window, and then the faces of two grinning soldiers appeared at the glass, curious to see who was on the receiving end of such a tirade. Maryam cried and cried and the old man pumped expertly at the pedals like an organist and they crawled forward, waved on by the laughing soldiers, who had taken one look at Maryam and decided it wasn't worth the bother. She cried for another minute or so, glanced out of the rear window to check that no one was coming after them, gave Jonas one last hard slap across his head and settled back into her seat. She was quiet for the rest of the journey.

## 2

The beard first. He needed to change his appearance. Within minutes of their arrival in Chtaura, Maryam had led him into the backstreets and begged a few items of clothing from a charity working with refugees. Now she had gone to get them food, leaving him in a petrol station toilet with a pair of scissors. He took hold of a clump of hair. It was like pulling at a handful of grass; he expected a sod of brown turf to come away with it. He cut close, leaving about a week's growth, like the old man who had driven them – any less than that would uncover the paler skin beneath his beard. He would leave a full moustache like the old man too. The dim yellow bathroom light flickered and the traffic on the road outside rattled at the thin door. Maryam was right. It was important that he look different from any pictures that had been circulated, but also that he look as Lebanese as possible, to put off any locals who might think to stop him heading in the direction of the border out of concern for his own safety. His hair sat over the plughole like a discarded toupee. Someone shouted through the door and pulled at the handle. As he cut his hair down he uncovered lumps and cuts and ridges that he had never seen before. He felt like an archaeologist, like Howard Carter, at work with his trowel and brush on the ruins of a face that had been taken by surprise, sacked and abandoned in a matter of months. New hollows, scars, grey hairs. Maybe Raza was on to something. Maybe it was possible to read a person's face in the same way that an expert could read the facade of a building. There were, after all, things that you might know about Jonas if you saw him. That he had been sad for a while, that he was lonely. That something had gone wrong. That he had discovered a wildness inside himself and it felt like home.

He undressed and put on the clothes Maryam had brought him: a dark grey sweater, a black jacket with a torn sleeve and a dirty pair of suit trousers that flapped around his ankles. He wrapped the keffiyeh around his neck and stepped outside.

# 3

TOP SECRET STRAP 2
1253 Zulu
Incoming call from 00961 3 118883 (rpt 00961 3 118883).
Caller identified as LEAKY PIPE, hereafter LP.

– LP greets unidentified female (UF). He comments on poor quality of telephone line. LP says maybe he should call later instead.
– UF is agitated and confused. She asks what is happening.
(Loud noises in background. Speech, music.)
– UF says wait a minute, she will turn the television off.
(Pause.)
– UF asks who is speaking. LP identifies himself by first name. UF expresses surprise. (Sound of crying.) She asks where LP is and why he hasn't called in such a

long time. She says whenever the phone rings she hopes it will be him. She says that she tries to call him every day but it never connects. She says that she doesn't know if she's dialling the number incorrectly. She says that she called the telephone company but the young man who answered just laughed at her and said there was nothing he could do. She says she is talking too much because she is happy.

– LP says that he is fine. He says he has been away with work but that everything is okay. He says he is sorry he hasn't been in contact sooner. He says he wishes he was with her now.

(Sounds of traffic, car horns. Foreign speech in background.)

– UF tells him that he doesn't need to pretend with her. She says that he shouldn't lie to her "of all people", she just wants to know that he is all right and on his way home. She says she doesn't care what has happened, it doesn't matter. She says she has made up a bed for him.

(Pause.)

– UF asks if he is still there. She says she misses him.

– LP states that he is fine. He says that he has lost a little weight but is in good health.

(Pause.)

– LP asks how the garden is.

– UF says why are you asking me about that. She says that a woman called something beginning with M came to see her a few weeks ago. From the Foreign and Commonwealth Office in Whitehall. It might have been Marjorie, she thinks, or possibly Mariella. An Edinburgh accent, dressed head to toe in black. UF says she (UF) burst into tears, it was very embarrassing, she thought the woman was in black because LP had died. She says she's losing her marbles. She says the woman was "of great comfort" to her. She says the woman talked about losing her son in a car accident.

– LP interrupts to say that he doesn't have much credit on his phone and can't talk for long. He doesn't want UF to get cut off mid-sentence.

– UF says that she can call him back. She asks for his number. She says that she doesn't know where she has put the notepad she always keeps by the telephone, she's forgetting all sorts of things these days. Like that woman's name. She says she left her shopping bags at the bus stop yesterday, when she went back for them someone had taken out all the eggs and smashed them on the floor. She says why am I wittering on like an old woman. Meredith, that was her name. She says she was called Meredith. She says she is ready to take down his number.

– LP says that it is a Lebanese mobile number. He says it is 00961 3 118883. He asks her to read it back to him. She says 00961 3 188833. He corrects her and gives the number again as 00961 3 118883. She reads it back to him correctly.

(Inaudible foreign speech. Sound of traffic.)

– UF says that there is one thing she wants to say now just in case the line is cut. She says she was looking through some old papers of LP's father the other day, sorting things out. She says LP wouldn't believe how complicated it is to get anything done when someone is in "that" position. She says the bank won't allow her access to any of his money and so she is behind on the mortgage. She says she saw an advertisement on television and was thinking of borrowing money from the internet but Aunt Rachel has been helpful and things are a little better now.

– UF asks if LP is still there. LP confirms.

– UF says she found an old letter from LP's father when she was sorting through his papers. She wants to read a line or two of it to LP. She says she has stuck it to the noticeboard by the telephone so she doesn't forget it. She says (pres. verbatim extract from letter): Interminable journey. I've never experienced such turbulence. Women were crying, children were screaming. Luggage was thrown from the overhead lockers. All I could think of was our little miracle. That I wouldn't see his first step, that I wouldn't be there on his first day at school, that I'd never get the chance to make him proud of his father. Landed just after midnight. In the bus on the way to the conference centre a woman sang a beautiful Nigerian hymn and I read aloud Psalm 121, I will lift up mine eyes unto the hills from whence cometh my help.

– UF says after that he just talks about his lecture the next day and how he ate something that disagreed with his stomach. She says she knows that you (pres. LP and father) didn't always see eye to eye but that this is the chance he (pres. LP's father) has always wanted. She says LP should just be proud of him. She says he (pres. LP's father) has more character and faith and heart than a hundred of those horrid extremists. She says she wouldn't be surprised if half of them were Anglicans by now. She repeats that LP should just be proud of him. She says just be proud of him and come home. She says that she has made a bed up for him. She says she will start baking a cake the minute she puts down the phone. She asks him what kind of cake he would like.

– LP says it's not that simple.

– UF says she found a very good recipe for cheesecake the other day.

(Sound of crying.)

– They exchange endearments.

(Call ends abruptly.)

Transcriber comment: According to call data UF makes fourteen attempts to call back subsequent to above but *883 switched off.

## 4

The first night Jonas and Maryam slept among the ruins of Baalbek, the second night they lay awake in the hills above Arsal. They were just nine miles from the Syrian border. Jonas waited until he thought she was asleep to cover her with his jacket, and over it he laid the blue plastic raincoat with tiny gold stars, in case water came through the roof of the cave. He was sure she wouldn't willingly accept anything from him, given the things he had done. In the weak flickering glow from his lighter he swept the earth around her head clear of ants and dust. She didn't stir, even though she was awake, but instead accepted his quiet industry for what it was: a gesture of regret, of affection, of solidarity.

It wasn't that either of them was trying to stay awake. But Maryam couldn't stop thinking about Tobias, and Jonas's mind was racing because of the noises made by the wind, because the conversation with his mother had upset him, because there was a reasonable chance he would die the next day and he didn't know what he thought about that.

They each came closest to falling asleep in the hour or so after midnight. But eight wild dogs turned up at the mouth of the cave, formed a semicircle around them and started barking, one by one and in no particular order, like bell-ringers. Jonas wondered if they usually slept in the cave and were asking them to leave. They looked starved and ragged, with torn ears and bleeding eyes and so many broken or missing teeth between them that when they snarled he couldn't help but feel sorry for them, as though they were showing him their guns weren't loaded, as though they were surrendering. It would have been unfair to throw stones at them. By sunrise they had all disappeared apart from the smallest one. Jonas tried to persuade it to join them in the cave, but it would only come near enough to accept its share of his bread and cheese before limping away to a safe distance.

Thinking about what lay ahead was not really what had kept him awake. After all, once he had run through the variables a few times, he understood it would be point- less to make too much of a plan. They might get lost in the hills. They might encounter Lebanese soldiers or Hezbollah fighters who turned them back. The kidnappers might decide the risks of an exchange were too great or be prevented from reaching Arsal by aerial bombardments and skirmishes with opposition groups inside Syria. They might not have read his email yet.

What had kept him awake more than any of that was the thought of Meredith making the journey to his parents' house for a second time and his mother's heart once again stumbling towards grief at the sight of someone approaching the front door dressed all in black. She would catch herself, though, and smile, shaking her head at the foolishness of an old woman who always thought the worst. She would open the door. And she would see the expression on Meredith's face and realize that this time the worst thing had happened. In one version she collapsed, in others she just cried and cried. The flower beds along the front of the house were tidy and the roses were red and pink and yellow. Jonas had never found the right moment to tell her that he would be doing the same thing if she had been the one taken hostage. He didn't know if she would have wanted to hear that.

It wasn't too late to turn back. He could have simply left Maryam in the cave and retraced his steps across the twenty-five miles of dust and rock and sharp brittle weeds, avoiding roads and dropping to the ground each time he heard the sound of a vehicle or an aeroplane, until he reached the outskirts of Baalbek. If anyone stopped him he would tell them he had gone for a walk and lost his bearings. He would happily submit to a search. At

some point there would be a group of tourists preparing for the return trip to Beirut, and for a few dollars
the driver would find an extra seat, and he would ask to
be dropped off near the airport. From then onwards it
would be a question of his word against the government's.
He would refuse to make any substantive comment on
what had happened. They would struggle to evidence his
theft of the documents, link him in a compelling way to
any cloud storage sites or produce physical proof of any
damage that would convince a jury something untoward
had occurred. There would be a long internal inquiry of
the sort governments can do in their sleep. He probably
wouldn't even lose his pension.

The easiest thing would be to move back into his parents'
house on a temporary basis and take the bed his mother
had prepared in the guest room. They would walk after
church on Sunday to a local hilltop his father had loved,
where they would sit on a bench and try to name the trees
and the birds and the flowers. He would consider a return
to academia and even go so far as to apply for a handful of
university research positions but decide in the end that they
were too far away from his mother. Instead he would get a
job teaching history in a local secondary school. He would
write occasional articles – on Middle Eastern politics, on
the role of the United Nations, on British counterterrorism
policy – and submit them to academic journals but grow
tired of the drive to the nearest university library and find
some pleasure instead in seeing his letters to the editors
of national newspapers appearing in print. He put back
on the weight he had lost overseas and a little bit extra.

No one called it the guest room any more. Once he imagined he was being followed home from the supermarket and he dived down an alleyway between the florist and the charity shop and doubled back through the pub car park to catch them out but there was no one there. He sometimes thought about Maryam and wondered if she had made it to England to join her parents, whether he should contact her to see how she was getting on. He took up gardening. It started with his mother asking for help with the weeding and mowing, since her back and hips made it difficult for her to bend, but quickly turned into a passion of his own. He tested his mind by taking part in a weekly pub quiz with their neighbours. Nothing wrong with this, he would think. Nothing wrong with any of this. Sometimes he would touch the scar on his forehead and think: I tried, I really tried. It's just so difficult for one person to swim against the current. He would think about tracking down Tobias's family and telling them what he had done, that it still kept him awake at night all these years later. He would think about his flat near the sea, the charts covering the walls, the endless hours of walking to evade surveillance, the late-night phone calls from that crazy CIA man, Naseby and his tennis whites. He would remember the cream-coloured Mercedes, the underground car park, the Syrian builder. He would remember the wild dogs.

When the sun came up Jonas packed everything into his rucksack. Maryam threw away the stiff bushes they had flattened into mattresses. He switched on the mobile phone. There were three text messages from his mother and one from the kidnappers. "Midday," it said. "Be ready."

# CHAPTER NINETEEN

"I already said it, bro, I ain't going to give you coordinates or nothing, I'm telling you in words clear as day where it is. If you're – where are you, to the what, to the south of Arsal? – Okay, if you're looking at where the border is nearest to you on the map, imagine there's a line from you in that direction. About, I don't know, it's about halfway. A little bit more maybe. Two stone buildings. Shepherd's hut, that kind of thing. Nothing else round for miles. One of them ain't got a roof. There's two of those oil drums outside. Painted orange. Got it? Right. Your father's in there. Been there since last night, the other bloke too. They haven't got any water so you better be quick."

A reedy voice, hard to place the age. No more than late twenties. Not the same man who had made the video recording of his father. A Londoner but echoes of a foreign parent. Definitely not Pakistani, probably not Somali, possibly Arab – based on his pronunciation of the name Arsal. Jonas adjusted the binoculars.

"How do I know they're in there?" he asked. "Anyone could be in there. You could be in there."

"I am in there, you idiot. Here, tell him."

"Hello?"

Jonas struggled to place the voice, it was so cracked, so faint. As though they were thousands and thousands of miles apart.

The kidnapper again but quieter, at a distance: "Just tell him who's in here with you."

"Hello? Hello?"

"Is that —"

"Jonas? What, what is this, what's happening?"

"Your old man just can't do what he's told, can he? We'll soon find out if you're a chip off the old block." Sounds of movement, a tearing noise. "Let's try the other one."

"So far as we can verify there is only one person in here with us."

Werify. Inwent, wery. That flat voice somehow expressing both sadness and anger.

"Tobias?"

"That's enough chatting."

"Send one of them outside."

"What?"

"So I know we're talking about the same building."

His father tottered about on newborn legs, lifting a hand to shield his eyes from the sun. They had dressed him in his own clothes, the clothes he had been wearing when they took him. Blue trousers, a crease neatly ironed into them, a clean white short-sleeved shirt. Someone had cut his hair and shaved him. The sun was so fierce that of his own accord he turned around and with outstretched hands groped for the darkness of the hut.

"Listen up, we're at the important bit. So you start walking, right? In case I don't see you, when you're about thirty, forty metres away, give me a bell. I'll send the two of them your way. You stay put. No one's going to do anything, you're useless to us dead. I bet you've put some bare encryption on that stick. Anyway, they come to you. Have a chat, hug it out, whatever. Then send the pair of them on their way. Now this is the bit you need to focus, right? I don't mind a couple minutes to see that nothing happens to them, that's human nature. They'll be moving slow, couple old fellas like that, just let them get on with it. They make it or they don't make it, that's up to Allah. The brothers ain't going to do nothing. But you've got to start walking towards me. Even if one of them falls over or something. If you head after them, if you walk away from me – I put a bullet in you and then I go and put a bullet in them. Easy. Wallahi you know I'll do it bro. I don't mind dying. But I'd rather keep everyone sweet and get you and those papers and we clear off the way we came. Happy days inshallah."

"That's too close," Jonas said. "I'm not standing thirty metres away in plain sight waiting for them to come out."

"What am I going to do? These hills are crawling with Lebanese soldiers and them rawafid. We've stuck our neck out coming here. Massively. Come on, let's do this, let's get on with it."

There was some truth to what he was saying. This was a difficult area for them: after staging a number of cross-border attacks in 2013 and 2014 with support from sympathetic locals, ISIS fought a five-day battle in Arsal with the Lebanese army in late 2014 and were pushed back into Syrian territory. They would have to move around covertly, in small numbers and on ancient smuggling routes, to avoid being engaged by Lebanese soldiers or Hezbollah fighters.

"We'll do it like this," Jonas said. "I'll get to about a hundred metres away, from whatever direction I choose. Enough so you can see me. Once they start walking I'll meet them halfway, at fifty metres, and then wait there till they are out of sight. Then I'll come to you. It'll only take a few minutes, no more. If you're not happy with something, well, from what I could see of my father he's not going to be able to outrun anyone."

"Whatever you say, bro, don't matter to me. End of the day neither of us is in charge. Start walking. Call me when you're close."

The line went dead.

He had been lying there for eighty minutes waiting for the call; he shifted to relieve the stiffness in his leg. Arsal was just over three miles to the north, according to the map. Trying to get closer to the town earlier that morning they had seen a tank, three armoured personnel carriers and over a dozen jeeps, some of them in the Lebanese colours of red and green, others flying the yellow flag of Hezbollah. So far as he could tell from a distance, Hezbollah fighters were the ones in desert fatigues, the ones with the newer-looking vehicles, including several Hummers. But the fortified lookout points on higher ground belonged to the Lebanese army, their heavy machine guns pointed east towards Syria and the Qalamoun Mountains.

Jonas and Maryam had tried to avoid being seen by moving quickly over open ground and keeping away from roads or tracks in favour of uneven terrain that involved scrambling on their hands and knees. Twice they were challenged by soldiers; Maryam told them they were returning to one of the dozen or so refugee camps that had sprung up around the edge of the town, and they were allowed to continue on their way. Jonas took one last look at the huts through the binoculars. If he moved off in a south-east direction before turning northwards at the last minute to approach them he would minimize his chances of being seen by soldiers on the lookout for people coming from Syria into Lebanon. He had to assume it was possible. The kidnappers knew the area well – they wouldn't have picked those buildings unless he stood a chance of reaching them. If he hadn't already been spotted, that is, lying there among the dusty weeds with the dog standing in plain sight several feet away just staring at him. He should never have given it any food. At least it wasn't barking.

Maryam was waiting for him in the bend of a dried-up riverbed. She was still wearing his blue raincoat, even though the sun was fierce above them. They had separated two hours earlier, wary of being seen together by the kidnappers. He recounted the conversation and for a while they discussed routes, distances and terrain. Then they were quiet. Jonas felt keenly aware of the difference between planning something on paper and planning something like this. Most of his life had been lived on paper, it seemed, with a title to keep him focused on the task at hand, a good clear margin along the edge, straight lines to maintain order. It was hard to be unruly on paper. There were so many things to say but he didn't know where to begin.

"I…" He faltered. "I want you to know that I'm sorry."

Where to start? He had so much to say sorry for. He remembered the gloomy hotel room, the way Tobias had sat on the bed with his head in his hands. It had been so easy to send him into Syria. It was only right that Jonas should learn what that felt like.

"If it goes badly, will you visit my mother?" he said. "She'll need some help. There's the garden, as well as just getting back to normal after everything that's happened, and there's a hill she likes to climb but I don't know if she'll be able to do it on her own any more. She can teach you the names of English trees."

"Your plan will work, Jones." Somewhere along the way she had dropped the Mr. "You will be there when I come to visit. We will take her and your father for a walk together."

He shook his head.

"I only know the apple tree," she said. "Will there be apple trees there?"

He covered his face with his hands.

"Jones?"

"There's a nice walk out beyond the church that passes through an orchard," he said softly. "It doesn't take more than twenty minutes, that's all my father will be able to manage, but there's a bench by the pond we can sit on while he catches his breath."

"One year from now. Give us time to make a home first. I will remember because it is my birthday today."

Something clicked into place.

"You can buy me some flowers. Properly, this time – not just one."

"Today is the fifteenth of May," he said.

*I walked into the room a priest and I walked out of the room a former priest, at least in their eyes.*

"Maybe your mother can prepare a cake for me," Maryam said. "An apple cake with apples from the orchard."

"You were born on the fifteenth of May."

*All because of that tiny little thing on 15 May 1985, or maybe it was August the year before that really upset them, it all depends on your point of view.*

"Tobias is your father," he said.

"Of course he is. Who did you think he was?"

They watched two helicopters pass high above them in the direction of the Syrian border.

"I... I didn't know —"

"We do not have time for this now." Maryam stood above him like his handler, her arms folded, waiting for him to keep his promise. "They will be waiting. You must go."

His route took him further along the dried-up river-bed. When he climbed its stony banks he dropped to his hands and knees to avoid being seen against the horizon. It was difficult to keep to a natural walking pace. As long as any soldier who spotted him was tired and bored and counting down the minutes to the end of his shift, he thought, he might just pass for a Syrian refugee, or a Bedouin farmer looking for his goats, except that no farmer would keep a dog that limped. He smoked a cigarette or two and found himself worrying that his father would be able to smell them on him. He struck out across a flat expanse dotted with bare, gnarled trees. For a brief moment, he caught sight of Maryam walking far behind him. Every few hundred metres he stopped to listen for the sound of vehicles or aircraft or voices. Four miles, he estimated. Eighty-three minutes. And then he was in sight of the two stone buildings. He dialled the number.

"Yeah, I already got you." That London voice again. As though they were arranging to meet in Ladbroke Grove or Whitechapel. "Stay put. Here they come, ready or not."

It was another few minutes before they appeared. From a door in the furthest of the two buildings, the newer one with the corrugated tin roof. Small, not more than a dozen feet across. Tobias first, his grey clerical shirt buttoned at the neck and spotted with sweat where it was tight across his belly but otherwise upright, his face unmarked. Then his father. Small shuffling steps but no limp, no visible bruises, no bandages, no blood. A couple of clergymen walking to church on an unexpectedly beautiful Sunday morning, their clothes clean and neat, leaning into each other to exchange reflections on a sermon or a prayer. In no particular hurry, certainly.

A cluster of old bullet holes had punched through the wall facing Jonas and he could see something moving inside.

With each step they took towards him he saw more clearly what had happened. The story of the last forty-eight hours patterned into waves of dried salty sweat on Tobias's shirt, on his father's trousers, like the scum left on a beach after the sea retreats. A sudden departure, long hours in the back of a truck. Their clothes were marked with oil and grease and blood. Tobias didn't have his glasses. Grey bandages covered the stubs of two fingers on his right hand. His father was shaking uncontrollably. The dog started barking.

Jonas took a bottle of water from his rucksack. Tobias held it to his father's lips and then had a drink himself. "Are they really letting us go?" he asked. He seemed doubtful.

"Yes. We haven't got much time." Jonas wrapped the keffiyeh around his father's head. "This'll keep the sun off." He took what food he had left and pushed it into Tobias's pockets. "You won't need this but just in case. It's important that you listen. You've got to keep walking that way." He pointed in the direction of a small hill less than seven hundred metres away where Maryam was waiting out of sight. "I know it's difficult but you mustn't stop. Keep going."

"Jonas?" said his father.

"Yes?"

"What are you doing here?"

"I've come to take you home."

"Home?"

"You've got to keep walking. Tobias will help you. There's no time to talk now, you've got to set off. Aim for that tree on its own over there, then fix that hilltop in your sights and walk as straight as the ground lets you until you get to a pile of large rocks and the ground starts to dip. There's someone waiting for you there – a woman called Maryam. She'll get you to safety."

"Maryam?" said Tobias. He blinked repeatedly. "You brought her *here*?" He sounded dismayed.

"Jonas?" his father asked.

"Yes?"

"You'll show us the way, won't you?"

"I'll catch you up in no time. I've just got a couple of things to do here first. I've got to give something to the man in that building. You mustn't wait for me, though. I may take a different route and meet you at the road. In case you don't see me. Just keep on walking."

"Jonas?"

"Yes?"

"Be careful. He's got a gun."

The dog followed them for the first twenty metres and then turned back to look at Jonas. They had shaved a patch at the back of Tobias's head and burned his skin with a hot instrument – it might have been a cross, it was hard to tell. He thought he saw his father try to turn around but Tobias kept him moving in a straight line. At the tree they didn't pause, just changed direction and headed towards the hill. At their pace it might take them fifteen minutes to reach Maryam. With his back still to the building, Jonas scrolled through the call log on his phone, pressed dial and put it back in his pocket. He walked towards the door and stepped inside.

A blinding light bulb, a dirt floor. The door swung shut behind him. Stepping to one side, shielding his eyes, he could just about see the outline of a person in the far corner. From the ground up: blue trainers, skinny jeans. A white T-shirt with a picture of a beach and the words "Surf Hawaii" in bright pink letters. He took another step to the side, his hands open to show he wasn't carrying anything. The bulb hanging low like a microphone into a boxing ring. Wispy beard, thin face. Long curly black hair, round wire-framed glasses. Mid-twenties at the most. He saw Jonas looking at his T-shirt.

"In case I get caught," he said in a reedy voice. "It might buy me a minute or two. Time to get this out." He pulled a large handgun from the back of his waistband. "Have you got the stuff?"

"It's in my rucksack. Can I...?"

He waved the gun indifferently. Jonas found the USB stick and threw it to him.

"Passwords, yeah? No problem. We'll get them off you later."

"You're very trusting."

"Yeah, well. None of this was my idea."

"We can call it a day if you want."

"Now that you're here. Sit down against that wall. Throw your bag into the middle."

The dark dead weight of the gun swung loosely from his left hand like a pendulum. He looked familiar, Jonas thought. Files held on British nationals in Syria would have crossed his desk at some point. Photographs, biographical data, source reports with gossip from people who had known him.

"I'm glad someone senior decided this was worth the effort."

"Oh man, did they love your email. Went down a storm." He tucked the gun into his waistband and knelt down to open Jonas's rucksack. "What was it, in the battle that is coming, everything will depend on intelligence, I will open the secret world before you like a book. They ate it up. But what's that book going to say at the end of the day, that's my question. This one's a rat, that one's a rat. Change up your emails. Don't trust the internet. None of that's going to make a real difference. We're not some little poxy group like them Irish fellas can be infiltrated and shut down. We're not hiding in the mountains like goat herders. We're a state. You know where we are. You want us, come and get us."

The light glinted off his round glasses. He took out the extra clothes Jonas had brought, shook them loose to check that nothing was hidden inside and threw them into a corner. It had been five or six minutes since Tobias and his father had set off. They would struggle to maintain that pace for long – at some point they would need to rest. Another fifteen minutes, no more than that, and they would be there.

"I suppose you're right," Jonas said. "The game has changed."

"Game's changed, your tactics haven't. That's what I'm saying." His voice was calm and unemotional. He looked through the textbook on Greek and Roman temples and the Howard Carter biography, wiped their covers clean with the edge of his T-shirt and placed them carefully behind him. "Nothing surprising in that. Fall of the USSR, 9/11, the Arab Spring. Behind the curve, that's where you lot are every single time. You talk about tactics as though they're some big secret. Harass Muslims, stop brothers and sisters when they travel, follow them round, stick bugs in their bedrooms, take pictures of them at juma'a prayers. Am I right? It's so low-level, it's just got nothing to do with us any more. You should be embarrassed. Like using blowdarts against an elephant. That stuff works against criminals, maybe, if they're dumb. It works against benefit cheats, people who put out their bins a day early. Yeah, that's it – *that's* your level. End of the day everyone should know their level. Fathers for Justice, people who wrap flags around chimneys. We're not some *group*. We're a nation."

He had almost finished searching the rucksack. Tobias and his father would be out of sight by now but still a few minutes from Maryam, unless she had come to meet them.

"Those blowdarts have stopped plenty of attacks," Jonas said.

"You're not getting me." He lifted out the binoculars and examined them from all sides. "It don't matter. One little thing here or there don't matter. You can kill me, you can kill everyone I know – it don't matter. I take the bigger picture, I take the *world-historical* perspective."

That's it, Jonas thought. University of London, 2008. International Studies. Parents from the Gulf, youngest of five, one arrest for bicycle theft, no convictions. He wondered why they were still talking, when they would leave for the border.

"Right, let's see what's in your pockets."

Jonas sat with his knees pulled up, the phone pressing into his stomach. He needed to keep it alive for as long as he could. "They taught you well at SOAS," he said.

"Eh?"

"That world-historical stuff."

"Yeah, whatever, nice one."

"Didn't they kick you out for something?" Jonas asked.

"We was obsessed with you guys them days." He stood up and brushed the dirt away from his knees. "Thought you were everywhere. No one would use their phone, everyone walking in circles on their way home, brothers passing round Sheikh Awlaqi talks like we was secret agents. Hiding them in the library behind the books, texting Dewey numbers to the other brothers. A cleaner found one of the hotter ones. We forgot about the cameras everywhere. Kicked out for, what was it, radicalization."

"You should write to them. An alumnus going on to bigger and better things."

"Man, we was so excitable them days. Like kids. First time you read about Sykes–Picot and then you see some politician talking about respecting international borders. There's no words for it. I've never been so excited in my life. Look, that man's lying on TV! He's actually being a real-life hypocrite! Get all the brothers here! In broad daylight! Oh my days! And he's wearing a suit! Someone arrest him!"

"Do you think you'll ever go back?"

"Come on, empty your pockets."

"What's that?"

"You heard me. Stop trying to buy time." He took a knife from a pouch on his belt and opened the blade. "If you want to play games I'll take a finger off right now for starters."

"Wasn't it drugs?"

"Eh?"

"The reason you were expelled."

"What are you talking about?"

"Maybe I've got it wrong. I'm sure I read something in a file about you getting caught trying to sell cannabis to freshers. Or was it that you were trying to pass off supermarket herbs as cannabis? Yes, that's it. What are we talking – April 2010, somewhere around there? Quite an achievement to get caught doing that in this day and age, and at SOAS of all places. It's clearly not for everyone – I'm not sure I could do it either. But I can definitely see how the whole radicalization story would go down better with your friends, given the strong position you take on hypocrisy, Hisham."

"Man's got a memory on him." He held out his hand and waggled his fingers. "Come on."

"Man's got a memory on him? You never used to talk like that. I remember listening to some of your calls. Mama this, Mama that. You were younger then but still. Home counties, grade-A school student, first member of your family to go to university – I bet Mama was thrilled. Child of —"

"Pockets."

"— a dentist and a teaching assistant but to hear you now you'd think you grew up on the roughest estate in the country."

"Stop talking and empty your pockets."

Jonas took out his passport.

"You came all the way to Raqqa but picked up a London accent, is that what happened, Hisham?"

"Give it here."

"You don't mind me calling you Hisham, do you? Some people want to leave all that stuff behind. You know: names, families. Who they used to be. Take on some kick-ass kunya. Abu Mujahid or Hamza al Britani or something like that." Jonas threw his passport on the floor. Let him bend down and pick it out of the dirt. "What was it the brothers used to call you back in the day? Specsavers? Have I got that right? Were you a bit of a geek? It might have been behind your back. I'm sure it was affectionate, though. That's how I recognized you, I think. All these years later and you're wearing the same glasses. No Specsavers in Raqqa, is that it?"

"You having fun? We'll have some fun later, don't you worry."

"Don't take it personally. My advice is to embrace that side of your character – put the gun away, smarten up your hair, take a desk job in a ministry. With your education you could go far. I'm not trying to wind you up. I've always been a bit of a geek too. At the end of the day, there's no point trying to get away from it, from who we are – it'll always be there, like a preference for tea or coffee, like a criminal record. This road to Damascus stuff is harder than it looks. Best case is you uncover something that had been kept hidden, but the idea that you can become a different person is pie in the sky. You know I'm right, don't you? I saw you put those books to one side so you can read them later. You were probably thinking, would that be 930 to 939, History of Ancient World, or 940 to 949, History of Europe? Whatever it is, once you've studied them you'll know exactly what Roman ruins you're blowing up if you ever get as far as the Beqaa Valley."

"That's enough chatting."

"It's a joke, Hisham. Lighten up. We both know you'll never get that far. In fact, you've probably got as much territory now as you'll ever have."

"We've only just got started."

"Yeah, but it gets complicated from here on in. You try running a country."

"We *are* running a country."

"You're running a patch of desert and a couple of towns. Don't get ahead of yourself. I can understand why people like you come out here, I really can. You get teased, people call you names, you feel like an outsider in your own country, you don't make enough money or get the job you want. Girls won't look at you. Truth is, though, that's how *everyone* feels. That's certainly how I feel most of the time. You just get on with it. It takes a special ego to turn some very ordinary feelings into a justification for raping slave girls and torturing old men. End of the day everyone should know their level, you said. If you were in America right now you'd be shooting up some school. That's *your* level. You'd be writing your manifesto on Facebook, having a final wank over some internet porn, putting on your black coat and the boots with the platform soles to give you a bit more height and heading off to take revenge on some science teacher who gave you a B or a girl —"

He swung the gun across Jonas's face.

"You can't imagine the things I've done." He walked over to the far corner. "Sit still and keep quiet."

Jonas turned to one side and threw up. Blood from his head dripped into the puddle of vomit. It was a new category of pain, he thought, being hit with the butt of a gun. He slumped against the wall, breathing heavily. The phone was warm in his pocket like something alive. There was a crackling noise and a burst of static followed by Arabic speech; Hisham reached behind him for a handheld radio. Jonas wondered what the hold-up was. He thought they'd be on their way to the border immediately but there seemed to be no rush, as though Hisham was waiting for something. Military vehicles in the area, possibly, or drones overhead. By now Maryam would be leading Tobias and his father to safety. He tried to stay calm, stay focused, he tried to control his breathing. Thirty-six bullet holes among all four walls. Target practice or gunfight. No pattern to the holes, no clusters around a single point. Beams of sunshine, like the world outside was a sieve leaking light. Strange that you can see light in a dark room but not the other way around. The light shines in the darkness and the darkness has not overcome it. He lifted his hand to his head and it came away covered in blood. He pressed his eye against one of the bullet holes. Sand, stones, weeds. He remembered his father teaching him to skim stones on a pond, the best ones the size and shape of a communion wafer. Some stones were big enough for a strongman competition, others were small and sharp like the head of an arrow whizzing through the air towards the sheriff's men, or like something a ninja would throw in the dead of night, landing in a squirt of blood.

He could hear a noise. On the other side of the room Hisham held the radio pressed to his ear. But Jonas could hear something else: a low hum, a crunching noise like tyres on a gravel driveway, voices. He rolled to the side and looked through a different bullet hole. Boots, the side of a jeep. The Lebanese flag. Hisham hadn't even looked up. It was three steps across to where he stood, but his balance might be off. Two steps to the door. The low-hanging light bulb would separate them, it would blind Hisham when he tried to aim. Better than waiting for the soldiers to walk in. They wouldn't know who to shoot. Hisham heard the noise and looked up.

Jonas lunged for the door, pulled it open and stumbled out into the daylight. Two soldiers were standing by the driver's door, a third at the back of the jeep. He put his hands up and ran towards them, shouting and pointing behind him to the hut so they would be ready with their guns when Hisham emerged. Jonas tripped and fell. When he looked up, the soldiers were laughing. Hisham, standing in the open doorway with the books in his hand, was laughing too.

"Calvary's arrived!" said one of the soldiers in a voice Jonas had last heard in the video footage of his father. "It's a bit crowded in the back but we'll find a place for you."

He sat next to his father and across from Tobias and Maryam. The two kidnappers he didn't recognize sat in the back by the tailgate, scanning the landscape behind them for other vehicles. Jonas's father was either sleeping or unconscious. He didn't want to disturb him if it was sleep, and if it was worse than that he didn't know what he could do to help. He took off his jacket, rolled it into a pillow and placed it behind his father's head. They picked up speed. It would be seven or eight miles to the border. Perhaps an hour's drive, given the hilly terrain ahead of them. They would have a vehicle hidden somewhere, a change of clothes, probably another truck filled with armed men to accompany them on the journey into Syria. Jonas could see the dog in the distance, limping after them.

Maryam had been beaten up. There were red marks on her face and some of her hair had been ripped out. Tobias tried to wipe away the blood coming from her nose but she caught his hand and touched the dirty bandages that covered the stumps where two of his fingers had been.

"Don't worry, everything will be all right," he whispered to her. He looked around the jeep, cleared his throat and blinked repeatedly, unsure without his glasses where precisely to address his comments. "Is there any way you can let her go?" he asked in a loud voice, anxious to be heard above the noise of the engine. His grey shirt was soaked with sweat. "You began with one foreign hostage and now you have three – three will be more than sufficient, three is a big success. You have won." His watery eyes settled briefly on Jonas. "She is just another Syrian refugee. You can't make any videos with her. Nobody cares about her enough to pay a ransom. I would appreciate it if you will let her go."

One of the guards had turned around to listen. His black hair was freshly cut and there were tiny shaving nicks along his jaw. "I've worked out who you remind me of," he said. "Remember those Robin Hood things on TV, Ahmed?" He nudged the guard opposite him. They might have been brothers, they looked so alike. "You know what I mean? Smelling of booze, cuddling up to the ladies? Not quite as fat as Friar Tuck, but we've had you on a diet, haven't we?" They laughed.

"Please," said Tobias. "She will just take up space in the truck. She is unimportant, she is not your enemy, she is just another victim in —"

"A wictim? She's a wictim? Are you joking me? She almost took Ahmed's nuts off back there." They laughed again. "She's not going anywhere. Truth is there'll be a long line of brothers wanting to marry her. Once those bruises go and she learns how to behave. And they'll all get a chance." He spat on to the desert floor. "Besides, she knows about the jeep and the uniforms."

They climbed a dirt track that twisted indecisively between fallen boulders, ravines and low, jagged cliff faces, the wheels slipping on the loose earth as the driver fought to maintain speed. There was no life to be seen anywhere, no plants or trees or birds, and no colour beyond the endless tones of brown and red like exposed muscle rippling beneath the pale blues of an empty sky. Jonas thought about what it would mean to cross a border in a place like this. The moment itself would pass unnoticed. He might have followed a trail laid down by others, but this time there would be no searchlights, no sirens, no soldiers in greatcoats. Philby had been disappointed by Moscow. Jonas suspected he would feel the same about Raqqa.

After a while Maryam fell asleep with her head against Tobias's shoulder. The tiny gold stars on her coat glittered weakly. Jonas held his father's hand.

"We talked about so many things," Tobias said, watching them, as though continuing a conversation that had begun in his head. "What it was like on the first day he met your mother, how nervous he was the first time he preached. Our best sermons, our worst sermons. What it is like being a father. He told me how proud he was of you so many times that I had to tell him some of the bad things you did, just to stop him talking. It didn't work. I told him what it was like to discover a daughter when she is already grown up, the heartbreak and the joy all at the same time. We found that we had a lot to be grateful for. On the days we believed were Sundays we would have a little service. Secretly, you understand. A hymn or two, as quietly as possible, and then prayers, and we would take it in turns to perform for each other the sacrament of communion with some water and a piece of bread we had hidden away. Yes, on Sundays we put our differences to one side. The rest of the week? You would not believe the arguments. Two old priests like us. One day the Pope, the next day the saints. One time the guards came running. Can you imagine explaining transubstantiation to those two? They didn't think it was funny."

Maryam stirred briefly. Blood from her nose had stained the front of her shirt. Tobias stroked her hair.

"I'm sorry," Jonas said.

"For what? For loving your father?"

"Shut up, you two," said one of the guards.

Tobias nodded at Jonas and smiled.

The guards grabbed each other and shook their weapons in the air as though in celebration. A pickup truck came into view thirty metres behind them, its cargo of fighters waving and cheering and shouting something Jonas couldn't hear. It must have happened, he thought. We must have crossed the border.

Suddenly there was colour everywhere. The ground was on fire around them and their jeep was on its side and everything was muffled, as though extremely loud noises were coming from a soundproofed room nearby. He tasted blood. Smoke was thick in the air and someone was coughing. One of the guards crawled on his hands and knees out on to the desert floor, blood trickling from his ears; he cocked his head to listen to the distant crackle of gunfire, twitched and lay down. They were all piled on top of each other as though trying to crowd through a small doorway at the same time. Maryam rolled to the side and pulled at Tobias's arm. She began to mouth words at him and slap him across his face. Through the smoke Jonas could see Hisham running in circles with his mouth open, the beach on his T-shirt speckled with blood, a gun in one hand and a book in the other. The truck behind them had driven into a gully and spilled five men on to the ground; three of them lay motionless while little explosions of red dust puffed at the air around them. Another two crouched behind the truck, pointing their guns into the sky and shaking them. Jonas couldn't hear anything; it was as though they were playing a game, as though they were playing at cowboys and Indians. One of them broke loose and came running towards the jeep and threw something that bounced twice on the ground, like he was skimming a stone on water, but he was never going to get more than two bounces with something as round and heavy as that. It came to a stop a few feet from the tailgate. As Jonas reached for it and drew back his arm he saw the pond and felt his father's hand on his shoulder, and he remembered a time when happiness was something that existed in the world regardless of him and would always be there, like God, or one of those balloons that could be twisted into different shapes but would never burst.

The grenade exploded before it hit the ground.

# CHAPTER TWENTY

When he woke up, men were running everywhere. Someone was leaning over him. He recognized the man who had knocked him down in the restaurant.

"Can you hear me?" he was saying. He had an English accent. "Can you hear me? Jonas? Jonas? We're going to get you out of here. Mate, pass me that tourniquet. Can you hear me? Jonas?"

So many questions. He was tired of questions, even though the answer was a simple one. In any case, he seemed to have forgotten how to speak. There would be time enough for that later. He could see well enough, though. He could see Tobias lying on the ground about a dozen feet away. He could see Maryam talking to him and stroking his hair while a medic bandaged his arm. He could see a helicopter. He could even see as high as the birds up in the sky, spinning in slow perfect circles like a mobile above a child's cot. He wanted to reach up to make them spin faster, but his arms felt so heavy.

"Is my father all right?"

"Did he say something?" the soldier asked. "Jonas, Jonas, can you hear me? Jonas?"

All right, too ambitious. It was like learning to speak again.

"My father?"

"Did you get any of that? We can't hear what you're saying, Jonas. Probably best take it easy, yeah?"

One last go. Can't get simpler than this.

"Dad?"

"What's that? Your dad? Your dad's all right. Don't you worry about your dad. We'll bring him over in a second, just get you patched up first. We need a lot more blood, get on the radio. Do you remember where the documents are, Jonas? Who did you give the documents to?"

How was he supposed to explain that? He tried to pick out Hisham's body with his eyes. Three of the soldiers were stripping the dead of their clothes and going through the pockets, running their hands along the seams and throwing them into a pile. He could make out the word Hawaii in pink lettering on a discarded T-shirt.

One of the soldiers came over with the USB stick.

"Jonas, is this it?"

He nodded.

"Are there any other copies?"

He tried to shake his head.

"Finish checking the bodies and search the vehicles. Get the lads to prep the explosives. We'll need the password, Jonas. Can you remember what it is? Jonas? What's the password?"

"Dad," he said.

"Your dad? What, his name? His date of birth? What is it, Jonas?"

"I want to see my dad," he said.

"I can't make any sense of this. Bring his father over here, maybe he'll be able to understand what he's saying."

With a soldier on either side his father was able to walk. They lowered him to the ground next to Jonas. He was thin and trembling and pale, as though milk was running through his veins, but he was alive; blood spotted the bandage wrapped around his head. He took hold of Jonas's hand and held it to his lips.

"Jonas, can you tell us the password?" the soldier asked.

The pile of clothing burst into flames. He glimpsed the wild dog watching him from the top of a nearby hilltop, clutching its mangled leg like a sceptre.

"The password, Jonas. What's the password?"

He tried to get the words out.

"What's that?" asked the soldier. "The law something he loves as a father. What does that mean?"

"The Lord disciplines those he loves, as a father the son he delights in," said his father.

"How can that be the password?"

"Try Proverbs 3:12. Please, can you stop asking him questions?"

Jonas could hear the tapping of a keyboard. Encouraged by his success, he tried to say something else. The helicopter came close and drowned him out but still his father smiled through his tears and nodded, as though what was important was that they were speaking to each other, as though the words themselves were a gift and what they contained didn't matter one little bit.

"There's nothing on here," one of the soldiers said.

"What do you mean? Maybe there's a second password."

"No, I mean there's nothing on here. I've got into it all right but it's empty. I don't understand. There are no documents."

It had taken seconds to delete the entire cache from its encrypted vault. Hisham would have understood, thought Jonas. He had promised something it turned out he was unable to deliver. Like Hisham with those students. Like Sykes and Picot, if you wanted to put it in those terms.

Looking up into the sky, he thought: helicopters make more sense than aeroplanes. There's a logic to a helicopter that even a child can understand. Its blades whirred above him like the spokes of a bicycle racing downhill. Why are there no wheels in nature? he wanted to ask his father. The robin redbreast on the edge of the birdbath, the woodpecker who lives at the bottom of the garden. Why didn't God give them wheels instead of wings? Jonas needed answers more than ever. He was glad he had his father with him. He wasn't brave enough for this.

"Daddy," he said. His mouth filled with blood. "Daddy."